Timothy —
The heart
be control

ROYAL
CREED

USA TODAY BESTSELLING AUTHOR
T.K. LEIGH

ROYAL CREED

Published by Carpe Per Diem, Inc

Cover Design: Cat Head Media, Inc.

Cover assets:

© 2023 Tony Maturano

Used under license from iStock Photo.

BOOKS BY T.K. LEIGH

For more information on any of these titles and upcoming releases, please visit T.K.'s website:

www.tkleighauthor.com

PART I

Duty

Duty is what one expects from others,
it is not what one does oneself.

~ Oscar Wilde

CHAPTER ONE

Esme

Home.
    It's a word that usually conjures fond memories of love. Laughter. Belonging.

Coming home after a long time away is often an occasion to celebrate. Moms hug their daughters, telling them how much they missed them. Fathers embrace their sons, asking how they're getting on in the world. Siblings make jabs, sometimes teasing each other about a new love interest. But through it all, one thing is constant.

Their love for each other.

Unfortunately, that's not what it's like for me.

There are no warm greetings.

No hugs from family members.

No love.

There hasn't been for years now.

After all, there's no room for love in a monarchy.

Or so I've been told my whole life.

Instead, the second I step out of the SUV driven by my chief protection officer and stare up at the imposing brick walls of Lamberside Palace in the Nation of Belmont, I'm met with formality. Custom. Tradition.

"Your Highness," a man in a dark suit greets me with a bow, as is expected.

I offer one of the palace butlers a cordial smile. "Good afternoon, Oliver."

"How were your travels?"

"Uneventful. It's a short flight from Paris."

"Lovely to hear. The Queen Mother has requested to see you upon your arrival." He does a once-over of my attire. "Would you like a moment to…freshen up?"

I've been around this life long enough to know this is his polite way of suggesting I change into something more in line with the unspoken dress code.

The jeans, white, off-the-shoulder top, and wedge sandals revealing my bright pink toenail polish certainly aren't appropriate attire.

Especially the wedge sandals.

I give him a knowing smile. "That's not necessary. My grandmother's time is valuable. We can go there directly. It's why Adam drove me here instead of my apartment at Gladwell."

Oliver arches a brow, silently questioning if I'm certain. When I don't respond, only holding my head higher, he nods, extending his arm toward the entrance.

As I cross the threshold into the lobby of the residential wing, a weight settles on my chest.

Or perhaps a noose wraps around my neck.

To the outside world, I live a fairytale. I have the best clothes. Designer handbags. Expensive shoes. A vault containing priceless jewels.

But it's all a façade. A show we put on to keep the public entertained. To stay relevant in a world that finds the concept of royalty less and less relevant with each passing day.

Nothing about this is real.

It makes me long to feel something that *is* real, even if it's fleeting.

"Is my father in residence?" I ask as Oliver leads me through the familiar corridors, everything maintained with the precision and care of a museum. Crystal chandeliers float overhead. Portraits of past members of the royal family hang on the walls, reminding me of my place in a life I'd give anything to escape.

"He's in London through the end of the week. If you'd like, I can reach out to his private secretary to schedule a meeting upon his return."

I force a smile, acting as if going through my father's private secretary in order to see him isn't a big deal. Considering he's been king for over fifteen years, I should be used to it.

But I miss when he was simply my dad with no ambition of ever ascending to the throne.

It's amazing how quickly your life can change.

One minute, we were living a relatively normal life, my father's only claim to fame being that his father happened to be king.

The next, his older brother, the heir apparent, perished along with his wife and all their children in an avalanche during a skiing holiday. My uncle, aunt, and cousins may have died on that mountain. But a part of me died there, too.

My childhood.

My freedom.

My independence.

"That won't be necessary. I'll see him at some point."

"Of course, ma'am."

Nearing my grandmother's study, Oliver slows to a stop and gently knocks, the door immediately swinging open. My grandmother's private secretary, Lieutenant Colonel Williams, receives me with the same stoicism I've come to expect from all members of the palace staff.

Particularly from our private secretaries, who are all former military.

"Your Highness," he says, bowing. "This way, please." Spinning, he leads me across the sitting room, pausing outside a pair of ornate double doors.

I smooth a hand down my hair, taming my long, blonde waves as best I can. At least I didn't put on too much makeup this morning. I've never been one to wear an inordinate amount, preferring a touch of liner around my green eyes and gloss on my lips.

After knocking, Lieutenant Colonel Williams opens the doors and steps into my grandmother's study.

"Her Highness Princess Esme," he announces, then moves to the side.

As he does, my grandmother turns her cold stare on me from behind an oversized desk, no hint of technology to be found. Her silver hair is styled in a pixie cut, petite body clad in a navy blue dress, lips downturned in obvious displeasure of my appearance.

"Your Majesty," I greet with a curtsey, even though it's not required. The obligation to do so ended when my grand-father passed away. Now it's merely a gesture of respect for her years of service to the monarchy. Service she continues to this day as one of my father's top advisors.

"Take a seat, Esme." She gestures to the chair opposite

the desk once her private secretary leaves, closing the door behind him.

I do as I'm told, crossing my feet at the ankles, angling my legs down. It's about as comfortable as sitting with a stick shoved up my ass, but it's protocol.

"How are you settling back in?" she inquires.

"I've only just arrived. Haven't even been to Gladwell yet. But it appears everything around here is exactly as it's always been."

"Do I sense a hint of annoyance?"

"Merely an observation."

"You may find it dull that nothing's changed much over the years. Our customs and traditions are important. They're what make us...*us*. Without them, our monarchy would be nothing. Do you understand?"

"Yes, ma'am."

"Good."

Her voice brightening, she attempts something resembling a smile, but it looks foreign on her face.

"Now that you're finished with your studies—"

"Actually, there's something I'd like to discuss with you," I interject. "I'd hoped to—"

"It's time to start thinking of your duty to the crown," she continues, as if anything I say is of little consequence.

"I've been fulfilling my duty to the crown, even when out of the country. I've continued supporting various charities, regardless of the time constraint on my studies. The reason I'd like to talk to you and my father face-to-face is—"

"And that means getting married."

Her statement steals my breath, and I snap my mouth shut, swallowing hard.

"E... Excuse me?"

"It's *pardon*, Esme. How many bad habits have you picked

up while away? Have those French friends of yours undone all of your etiquette training? You don't *excuse* yourself. You *pardon* yourself."

"Okay. Then *pardon* me," I say somewhat dramatically, "but it sounded like you mentioned me getting married."

"I did."

I blink, lips parting, but no words come.

"I'd prefer to announce an engagement by the end of the summer. Then a wedding in late spring. I do think that's the best time of year for a wedding, don't you? All the flowers in full bloom."

She doesn't look up from her notepad, prattling on as if discussing which place settings to use at the next state dinner. Not the fact she wants me to get married. And who does she think I should marry? I'm not even dating anyone.

Then again, I fear she has an answer to that, as well.

She always does.

"I've had our public relations team do some polling of possible matches. We believe the best match for you is Jameson Gates. He's purported to be named one of the world's most eligible bachelors, if you believe some of those publications. His father is Henry Gates, head of Gates Enterprises, the largest private military company in all of Europe and arguably the world. In addition to that, they've spearheaded several non-profit organizations to help combat human rights violations they've witnessed in war-torn countries. Extremely charitable and successful family. Plus, the public recalls seeing photos of you and Jameson dancing together at a gala last year and thought you made a great couple. I've set up—"

"I'm sorry, but what fresh hell have I walked into?" I blurt out, finally finding my voice after listening to her drone on about Jameson Gates' finer qualities.

Or, more accurately, the finer qualities of his bank account.

"Have I just stepped onto the set of some regency romance where females have lost all say over their own future? You do realize how absurd this sounds, right? Tell me you haven't lost your goddamn mind."

Pinning me with a glare that would make most people run for cover, she forms her lips into a tight line and squares her shoulders.

"I'll ignore your rather...colorful language for the time being, as it appears some etiquette refreshers are in order. But I assure you, this is no 'fresh hell,'" she responds, using air quotes. "This is your reality, Esme. You're the Princess Royal. Second in line to the crown. As such, you have a duty to marry, and marry well. Lord forbid anything happens to your brother. In that case, you'd be heir apparent, which is why it's so important you have a...masculine presence supporting you."

Every feminist bone in my body is on the verge of rioting, ready to burn bras and dismantle the patriarchal system that's still alive and well, even in the twenty-first century.

Especially in a monarchy.

"Now, I trust you haven't been sexually active?" She lowers her glasses over her eyes, pen in hand, ready to jot down my response.

"Excuse me?"

She scowls, but doesn't correct me.

For once.

"It's important to know, Esme."

"I..." I shake my head, still in disbelief. Then I avert my gaze. "No."

I don't know what's worse. Her question about my sexual

history, or my admission that, at nearly twenty-five years old, I don't *have* a sexual history.

When you're a royal, it's not as easy. Especially when you're female. The last thing I need is for the tabloids to report on my sexual escapades, painting me as a slut, all while my brother is cheered for sticking his dick into anything with a pulse.

The double standards are exhausting, especially in upper-class society.

"And your monthly cycle… It's regular? No issues?"

"Why does that matter? Is there an application I don't know about?"

She heaves a frustrated sigh, removing her glasses. "It's imperative we're aware of any potential reproductive problems beforehand. Regardless, I'll schedule an appointment with the palace physician so he can do a thorough check. Make sure everything's in working order."

"Working order?" With every word she speaks, I feel less like a person and more like a piece of property. "Are you shitting me right now?"

"Esme! This behavior is incredibly unbecoming of a woman with your breeding and status. I'd caution against using language like that in front of Jameson and his father. Otherwise, I'm not sure how you'll be received."

Unable to tolerate another word of this discussion, I jump to my feet. "I'm not one of your goddamn horses that you parade around and put out to stud. I'm a bloody human being. And I'd appreciate it if I'm treated as such."

I storm out of her study, needing to get as far away from her and her ridiculous plan as possible. My blood boils, anger blinding me to my surroundings. I've been in this place for less than an hour and I wish I'd never come back.

Wish I'd escaped when I still had the chance.

Wrapping my arms around my stomach, I keep my head lowered, not looking where I'm going until I run into something incredibly hard and firm, the force of the impact causing me to lose my balance.

I teeter on my feet, but before I fall, firm hands clutch my hips, keeping me upright. I dart my head up, inhaling a sharp breath when I meet a pair of familiar, dark eyes.

CHAPTER TWO

Creed

Deep pools of green meet my stare, the surprise of running into Esme turning me into a statue. But it's not simply her presence that's left me frozen in place. This *is* Lamberside Palace after all. Before she and her brother moved to the apartments at Gladwell, she lived here. Her father and grandmother *still* live here.

Instead, my inability to conjure a single thought has more to do with the fact that the Esme I remember is nowhere to be found in the person standing before me. The girl I once knew is all woman, the way she carries herself full of sophistication and grace. There's no longer a hint of awkwardness or uncertainty about her.

Then again, there wasn't much awkwardness or uncertainty about her the last time I saw her, either.

Eight years ago.

The morning I left for basic training.

Despite the passing of time, I recall that day with striking clarity. How she wrapped her arms around me and ordered me not to do anything stupid. To make sure I came home in one piece before pressing her lips to mine.

It was probably just a friendly gesture. We practically grew up together, our mums having been close before multiple sclerosis took hers from her.

But not a single day in the past eight years has gone by that I haven't thought about that kiss, even when another woman's mouth covered mine.

And now that I'm mere inches from Esme, her lips parting as she stares into my gaze, I'm reminded of that kiss once more.

Something I shouldn't be thinking of, considering she's my best mate's little sister, not to mention the Princess Royal. And in a few months, I'll be sworn into the royal guard, one of the elite few tasked with protecting the lives of the royal family.

An honor to many.

A legacy for me.

After all, a member of the Lawson family has been a part of the royal guard from the inception of this monarchy over five hundred years ago.

My family's legacy to protect is as steeped in tradition as her family's legacy to rule. To govern.

Once I swear that oath to protect her family above all else, any romantic notions I've foolishly held onto will go up in flames. It will no longer merely be a bad idea because of my close relationship with her older brother.

It will be forbidden.

Remembering my place, I quickly drop my hold on her, increasing the space between us and bowing.

"Your Highness."

She rolls her eyes, crossing her arms over her chest. "Stop

with that rubbish, Creed. We used to have spitting contests when we were kids."

A small smile forms on my lips as I recall our younger years. Before everything became much more complicated. Back when my best friend and his sister were so far down the line of succession that most people didn't even recognize them, especially outside of our small country.

In the blink of an eye, that all changed.

"That may be true, but we're past those days. Wouldn't you agree?"

"You're just saying that because you lost miserably last time."

"Maybe." I smirk, gaze roaming her tall, slender body.

Long, golden strands of hair fall delicately around her shoulders, the billowy top she wears allowing a peek of her tanned skin. Her jeans hug her curves, making her long legs seem even longer.

Making me imagine what it would feel like to have those legs wrapped around me.

I do my best to suppress the twitching in my pants at the thought, clearing my throat and bringing my eyes back to hers.

"When did you get in?" I ask, even though I know the answer. After all, my older brother, Adam, is her chief protection officer. But I need to distract myself from my growing inappropriate thoughts.

Thoughts that can never come to fruition.

"About thirty minutes ago."

"Glad to be home?"

Heaving out a long sigh, her expression falls, frustration mixed with irritation covering her face.

She looks around the high-ceilinged hallway, framed

portraits hanging every few feet on the textured walls, ghosts of her ancestors watching her every move.

"Not sure I'd really call this place home."

I nod in understanding. After eight years in the military, the last four working special ops and traveling all over the world, I have trouble thinking of Belmont as my home, too.

"And you? What brings you to the palace?" she asks.

"Adam called and said he was back, so I thought I'd stop by. It's been a while." I shove my hands into my pockets. "With him splitting his time between Paris and here as part of your security detail, and my deployment with special teams, our schedules never seemed to line up."

"Are you on leave? Or do you have another deployment coming up?"

"No more deployments. My latest one was my last."

She tilts her head. "You're leaving the military?"

"Not leaving. Transferring. I'll be inducted into the royal guard at the end of the summer. I was originally supposed to be sworn in next week, but considering I haven't had any time off since I enlisted, I figured I'd take the summer. Plus, with Adam's girlfriend having a baby in a few months, I thought I'd hang around here to lend them a hand before I'm sworn in."

"Right. Of course." Her shoulders fall as she briefly averts her gaze. "Family legacy and all."

"Exactly."

An awkward silence settles between us as we simply stare at each other for several long moments. Then she steps back, eyes bright once more.

"Well, I should get to Gladwell and unpack. Although I'm sure it's already been done for me, like everything else in my life."

The annoyance in her tone is clear, but I don't press the topic. It's not my place.

"Don't worry," she adds quickly. "I'll have one of the other guys on my protection team drive me so you can visit with your brother."

"I appreciate that."

She nods, a thin smile pulling on her mouth. "It was good seeing you, Creed." Her expression softens. "Really good."

I bow slightly. "Your Highness."

Her lips part as if she's about to berate me once more for the way I address her. Instead, she pushes out a resigned sigh. "Lieutenant Lawson."

She spins, her steps full of purpose and frustration as she walks away. I debate going after her, asking if she wants to ride horses or take a walk along the canals, just for old time's sake.

But those days are gone.

They ended the second I joined the military and took my rightful place in this world.

And my place is to serve the royal family. Serve Esme. Not be her friend.

Or *more* than her friend.

CHAPTER THREE

Esme

"They want you to get engaged by the end of the summer?" Harriet whisper-shouts.

"Shh," I hiss, glancing around to make sure no one's eavesdropping as I sit with Marius and Harriet at a table outside one of my favorite cafés by the famous canals that line Belmont's capital city of Montrose.

But no one's sitting close enough to overhear our conversation. Captain Adam Lawson made sure of that after I informed him I wanted to stop for tea with my friends, something I haven't been able to do for too long now.

"That appears to be the plan." I grit out a smile as I sip on my tea. "And I don't even get a say in the matter. The palace PR team has already decided who I should marry."

"And that is?" Marius inquires.

"Jameson Gates."

My friends pause to consider my future husband.

After a beat, Harriet gives a small shrug. "Could have

been worse. He's not too harsh on the eyes. Plus, he does quite a bit of charity work. Like you."

"He's certainly much more genuine than most people in upper-class society. Especially someone with his family's vast wealth. But… I don't know…" I slouch in the chair, throat tightening in irritation.

"It doesn't matter that Jameson is a decent bloke." Marius covers my hand with his, expression sincere. "It should be your choice who you spend the rest of your life with."

"Exactly." I return his smile, then pull my hand from his, bringing my tea to my lips. "And who gets to be my first."

"What do you mean, Ezzy?" Brows furrowed, he leans closer. When he speaks again, his voice is no louder than a whisper. "You haven't had sex yet?"

Placing my teacup on its saucer, I worry my bottom lip, remaining silent. But I don't need to say anything.

"Seriously?" Harriet shoots back, eyes wide.

"It's kind of hard to lose your v-card when you're sleeping in tents on a humanitarian mission," I remind them of how I spent my first three years following graduation from secondary school.

"But you spent the past *four* years at university in Paris," Marius states.

"You can't tell me the opportunity didn't present itself there." Harriet grabs a *petit fours* off the plate on the center of the table, taking a bite. "The French invented casual sex. And, in my experience, multiple orgasms."

"It's not that easy for me. People know who I am. If I were to get involved with anyone, even casually, it has the potential to make headlines. Because of that, I never saw the urgency."

"That settles it then."

"What?" I ask.

"It's time you got laid," she declares as she lifts her teacup to her mouth, her movements exhibiting all the etiquette she grew up with, considering her family also has noble blood.

"So... What? Am I just supposed to go up to someone and ask them to fuck me?"

My grandmother would have a heart attack if she found out I was sitting at a sidewalk café, openly discussing the idea of having sex before marriage. To say she holds somewhat outdated views on female sexuality and empowerment would be putting it mildly.

"Your Highness!" Marius brings his hand to his chest, feigning shock. "Such language!"

"I hear much worse coming out of that mouth on a regular basis, Mari."

"True." He winks. "And I don't think you can go up to just anyone. It needs to be someone you trust. Someone who won't go to the bloody pappos with the story."

I scan Marius' frame, everything about his physique impressive, thanks to his Norwegian roots. His polo shirt hugs his chest and biceps, giving way to muscled forearms. His blond hair is disheveled in a sexy way, blue eyes glimmering in the sun. With a tanned complexion and square jawline, he's quite handsome, even more so now that he's in his mid-twenties. I imagine he's broken his fair share of hearts since I've been away.

"How about you?" I ask nonchalantly. "I trust you."

He chokes on his tea, eyes wide. After a moment, he sputters, "Me?"

"Why not?"

He clears his throat several times before continuing. "Don't get me wrong. I'm bloody flattered. Any other time,

I'd haul your beautiful arse into the nearest dark corner to have my way with you." He grins lasciviously, waggling his brows. "But I'm not meant to be your first. That's too important to waste on someone you're not attracted to. At least not like that."

"Then who do you suggest? Hate to break it to you, but the list of people I trust is quite short. Apart from my brother, you're the only member of the opposite sex on it."

"There's got to be someone else out there." Harriet scans the sidewalk teeming with people enjoying the beautiful summer weather along the picturesque canals. The aroma of flowers, mixed with delicious smells from the nearby cafés fills the air. "Maybe a tourist who doesn't realize there are countries other than England that have royalty."

"But what if he eventually does? It'll be this huge scandal. Not to mention, the entire world would find out I was still a virgin at almost twenty-five. No thank you. It's embarrassing enough to admit it to you two, and you know how much I adore you both."

"I can't argue with that," Marius replies as he stares into the distance, deep in thought.

I do the same, watching all the passersby, when a familiar figure comes into focus, causing my cheeks to heat. Not because of the way his shirt clings to his chest and arms. Or the definition in his legs as his feet hit the pavement, one after another in quick succession. Or the intense concentration on his chiseled face as he runs along the canals, making it look so effortless.

No. It's the memory of Creed's body pressed against mine after I ran into him mere days ago. The way his hands clutched my hips. The way my heart felt like it was about to burst through my chest, my body reacting in a way it never had before.

I knew enlisting in the military would change his physique, just as it had my brother. Hell, just as it had Creed's own brother, who's been my chief protection officer these past few years.

I hadn't expected Creed to look *that* good, though.

I've always found him attractive. I'd have to be blind not to.

Tall stature that even towers over my own five-nine frame. Dark hair. Even darker eyes. Square jaw. Full lips. Angled cheekbones. And a smile that's equal parts sexy and mysterious.

But this more mature version of Creed is something else altogether.

My *reaction* to him is something else altogether.

Even with several yards separating us, I can't control the heat prickling my skin, my pulse increasing, breathing growing ragged.

"What is it?" Marius follows my line of sight to see what's stolen my attention. It's silent for a moment before he slams his hand on the table. "That's bloody perfect!"

"What is?" I rip my eyes back to my friend.

"Creed Lawson," he mumbles, trying not to move his mouth too much.

"I don't follow."

"You can ask him to take care of your little…problem."

"That's crazy! He's Anderson's best mate. We grew up together. He was always around."

"So was Marius," Harriet reminds me. "That didn't stop you from propositioning him mere seconds ago."

"You little hussy." Marius winks.

"You know what I mean." I steal a glance over my shoulder at my constant shadow before facing my friends again. "His older brother is also my chief protection officer."

"All the more reason he's perfect," Harriet encourages. "The elder Lawson would never suspect anything."

"But—"

"You're not asking him to marry you," she interjects. "Hell, you're not even asking him to date you. Just to screw your brains out before you're married off to someone the establishment chose for you."

"So… What?" I laugh nervously. "I'm just supposed to walk up to him and ask him to sleep with me so I'm no longer a virgin? There's no way he'll go for that. He's too…noble."

"If that's the case, it's not because he hasn't thought about it," Marius states very matter-of-factly. "If I were a betting man, which I am, I'd go all in and wager he's thought about it. A lot. Probably jerked off a time or two moaning your name."

"*Marius!*" I chastise, playfully swatting him.

I have to admit, the idea of Creed thinking of me while pleasuring himself certainly turns me on. I could just picture his taut muscles, face strained as he chases his release, my name on his tongue as he comes undone.

"But in the event he *is* too noble…" Marius' voice pulls me back to the present, "I'm chuffed to be your plan B. It's an honor I take quite seriously," he says with mock solemnity. "And should I be called upon to serve, I will deflower the fuck out of you."

I can't help but bark out a laugh at how ridiculous this situation is. I don't know many normal people who would discuss propositioning someone to take their virginity.

But, as I learned years ago, I'm not a normal person.

Not anymore.

"Can we please talk about something else?" I beg, hoping

to steer the conversation away from the topic of having sex… especially with Creed Lawson.

The longer we discuss it, the more I won't be able to stop thinking about what it would be like to have his body move in time with mine. I may not have had many sexual experiences, but I know Creed. He approaches everything in life with focus and determination. I can only imagine how mind-blowing sex with him would be.

But even when Marius shifts the conversation to the breaking news story about some race car driver claiming one of the female members of his pit crew has been missing for several months and the police refuse to look into it, I barely hear a word he says.

Instead, every single thought is consumed by one man.

And it's not the man the royal household wants me to marry.

CHAPTER FOUR

Esme

I make my way along the corridors of the palace toward my father's office, the staff I encounter bowing as I pass. Now that my father's home from his travels, I'm eager to speak with him, hopeful that once he learns of my grandmother's intention for me to marry, he'll put an end to it.

My relationship with him isn't one I'd consider close or loving, but surely he won't force me to get married before I'm ready. I'm not even thirty. Haven't even begun to experience life yet.

Upon finishing secondary school, I spent the next three years traveling the world as part of the Humanitarian Corps, my country's version of the Peace Corps. While it wasn't originally by choice, I enjoyed the relative freedom I found.

And it taught me about the world. The struggles most people face daily. It made me want to do more for those with less. Bring attention to their plight, whether it be clean water, reproductive rights, or gender equality.

All causes I continued to champion once I went to Paris for university.

Again, I didn't get to choose where I was to study. Or what, for that matter.

Like the trained puppet I am, I went along with it.

But I can't go along with this.

I'm well aware I'll eventually have to marry in order to provide the required "heir and a spare". I'd hoped to figure out who I am as a person first.

My father's receptionist, Lila, jumps to her feet and curt-seys as I enter the waiting area of his office. "Your Highness."

"Good morning, Lila. I'm here to see His Majesty."

"I'll let them know you're here."

I arch a brow. "Them?"

"Of course." She smiles, spinning from me and scurrying into the conference room.

I curse under my breath. I should have known my grand-mother would find a way to weasel into my meeting with my father. I thought by scheduling time with him, I'd be able to discuss this in private. Instead, it gave my grandmother an opportunity to insist on attending, as well, considering she's a senior member of his privy council.

When Lila returns, my father's private secretary, Lieu-tenant Colonel Winters, is with her.

"Your Highness." He bows. "This way please. They're ready for you."

As I follow him toward the conference room, I push down the nerves swimming in my stomach. Remind myself this is merely an informal discussion between family.

But as he announces me and I step over the threshold, any lingering hope I had that my father would put a stop to this plan is dashed when I see he's surrounded by my grandmother, a few other members of the privy council, as well as the head of palace public relations.

And that's not all.

Also rising to their feet to greet me are none other than Jameson Gates and his father, Henry.

I was apprehensive about speaking with my father, so maybe this is just an anxiety-fueled hallucination. I'd only just scheduled this meeting yesterday. There's no way they would have been able to arrange for all these people to be here on such short notice.

Unless it was scheduled earlier without my knowledge and *I'm* the late-minute addition.

I didn't pick the time or date. My father's private secretary chose it for me. It didn't seem odd at first. My father *is* a busy man. Now, though, I feel like I'm getting played. Pushed around a chess board like the pawn these people want me to be.

At the sound of a loud throat clearing, I snap out of my increasingly irritated thoughts, my grandmother's glare reminding me of the required protocol.

Turning toward my father, I do a small curtsey, briefly lowering my eyes. "Your Majesty."

He stands, he and my grandmother the only ones not obligated to stand when I entered. His dark hair has more flecks of gray than the last time I saw him, his face sporting a few more wrinkles now that he's in his fifties. But he's still quite handsome.

Approaching me, he wraps me in a hug that feels more for show than affectionate. "Esme, darling." He kisses my cheek before dropping his hold on me. "Welcome home."

"Thank you."

As he returns to his place at the head of the table, I look

at my grandmother, greeting her with a curtsey. "Your Majesty."

"Have a seat, Esme," she instructs, gesturing to a chair between Jameson Gates and my father.

I walk toward it, everyone at the table muttering "Your Highness" as I pass.

"Esme, you remember Henry Gates, don't you?" my grandmother offers as I approach the empty chair, a hint of superiority in her smile. "He's been a frequent guest of mine at the palace."

"Of course." I smile at the older gentleman, doing my best to remain courteous.

I've known the Gates family almost my entire life. My grandfather's former private secretary, Silas Archer, is a long-time friend of Henry Gates. Even though my grandfather passed over fifteen years ago, Silas still holds a prominent position in the royal family as a member of my father's privy council. And because he was my grandfather's right-hand man for many years, he's quite close to my grandmother. I get the feeling he had a hand in concocting this arrangement.

"Mr. Gates. It's nice to see you again."

"Likewise, Your Highness." He bows toward me, then straightens, placing his hand on the shoulder of the man at his side. He's practically a carbon copy of the older gentleman. Blond hair. Blue eyes. Dazzling smile. And dressed in a suit that would have most women drooling at how well he fills it out.

But not me.

"And you remember my son, Jameson."

All eyes are on me as I turn my attention to Jameson, pretending as if this entire scenario doesn't make my skin crawl. The anticipation in their gazes reminds me of the way my grandmother looks at the horses she hopes will act as a stud.

Jameson bows slightly. "Pleasure to see you again, Your Highness."

"Mr. Gates."

My grandmother glares at me from just over Jameson's shoulder, warning me to play nice. I offer him my hand. When he takes it in his, I feel absolutely nothing.

"Please, call me Jameson."

I nod, forcing a smile. "Jameson."

"You look lovely today," he states. "Congratulations on completing your studies. And in Paris, no less. Did you enjoy your time there?"

"Very much so. I'd love to go back."

To anyone else, my statement implies I'd like to return at some point in the future. In reality, I'd give anything to leave this place right now and go back to the simplicity of my life in Paris. When I was no one special. When the only reminder of who I am were the undercover bodyguards who accompanied me wherever I went.

I came home to spend the summer with my brother before he leaves on one final deployment. A deployment he volunteered for, probably to avoid this exact situation. Once the summer ended, I'd hoped to return to Paris.

With every second I sit in this room, I feel those plans slip further and further away.

"Shall we get started?" my grandmother suggests, taking charge, as she's prone to do.

My father may be king, may be the one who makes the important decisions about how this country is run, but when it comes to matters of the royal family, my grandmother is the driving force. The venerated matriarch. And all members of the royal household, the people who make decisions for the monarchy and royal family, look to her for guidance.

As everyone lowers themselves into their assigned seats, I remain standing. I don't want to admit defeat just yet. Taking my seat will send a message that I'm okay with this when nothing about it is okay.

My grandmother meets my eyes, her gaze floating to the empty chair beside Jameson, a silent admonition to sit there.

"Allow me." Jameson pulls out my chair for me.

My grandmother passes me a warning look, the severity in her expression reprimanding me not to make a scene. Truthfully, I have no desire to make a scene. But I absolutely plan to speak my mind.

"Thank you." I make a concerted effort to ensure my response lacks any warmth. I don't want anyone to think I'm on board with this asinine plan because Jameson Gates acts like a gentleman around me.

Once I'm situated in my chair, I open my mouth to voice my opposition. Before I can utter a single syllable, my grandmother directs her attention to Gianna, the head of palace public relations.

At least, that's her technical title.

In reality, she's more like a fixer.

Whenever someone associated with the royal family finds themselves in trouble, Gianna cranks up the "spin machine", as I call it.

Her straight blonde hair and blue doe eyes may make her look sweet and innocent, but I know from experience she's a wolf in sheep's clothing. Her connections and ability to help the royal family whenever we're in trouble make her a powerful force to be reckoned with. Not to mention the secrets she keeps on our behalf.

"What have you come up with?" my grandmother asks.

"As I mentioned, we'd like to use the summer season to our advantage."

I fight to keep myself from rolling my eyes. I've stayed away from this world for so long, I'd forgotten about some of the antiquated traditions that are still alive and thriving.

While it's not as "do or die" as was the case back in the nineteenth century — when young women used the summer party season to find a suitable match, suitors pursuing barely legal girls based on their assets, both monetary and bodily — there's still an unspoken "season" here. The summer is a constant revolving door of events — art auctions, polo matches, regattas, galas. Each event becomes fodder, not just for the tabloids, but also the more reputable news outlets, everyone speculating about who's dating whom.

I have no doubt my grandmother hopes to put Jameson and me front and center.

Gianna will ensure that happens. After all, she has the tabloids in her back pocket. Most of the more reputable newspapers, too. They all eat out of the palm of her hand in the race to be the first to get the scoop on some breaking royal family news.

"Our hope is to make these two the top story across Europe," my grandmother continues. "Possibly even the world."

"And we plan to do just that," Gianna assures her. "We believe—"

"Before you go into details…," a voice interrupts. I look toward the man at my grandmother's right, Silas Archer.

He glowers at me with his dark eyes, contempt in the thin line of his lips. In all the years I've known him, I don't think I've ever seen him smile.

"It should go without saying that nothing we discuss at any of these…meetings is to leave this room."

Everyone nods their acceptance.

Except for me.

My grandmother joins Silas in his stare, waiting for me to acquiesce. After several seconds, I give them a small nod. I have no intention of following through with my promise, though. I've already told my most trusted friends. If these people expect me to go through with this ridiculous charade, I need *someone* I can talk to. Someone who understands it's nothing but smoke and mirrors.

Just like this entire world we've built around ourselves.

"Thank you, Esme," my grandmother says, then looks at Gianna. "You may proceed."

"As I was saying, our plan is to make Princess Esme and Jameson Gates' relationship the top headline everywhere. But first, we need to build a...history between these two. Give them a love story for the ages."

Gianna pushes two binders across the table toward Jameson and me. "These notebooks contain everything you both need to learn about each other if we're to convince the public this isn't a new relationship."

"But it is," I argue, not bringing up the fact it's not a real relationship to begin with.

"We believe it's best to tell people you've been dating in secret since last summer. Immediately after the photos of you two dancing at the King's Day gala were published." Gianna gestures to the binders. "It's all in there. Everything you both must know."

I stare at the binder, not wanting to give them the satisfaction of opening it. At the same time, I can't help but be intrigued about its contents. I glance at Jameson, curious as to where his head is. He simply shrugs, his expression a mask of indifference.

Facing forward, I open the binder, bile rising in my throat.

I sensed it would contain more information than either one of us could want or need. But this is sickening. A gross invasion of privacy.

Not only does it include a fabricated love story detailing every day of our months-long secret courtship, it also contains background information about our lives since birth.

Including sexual history.

While I find some solace in the fact that Jameson has only slept with six women in his thirty-three years, having expected someone with his wealth and privilege to have quite a few notches on his bedpost, it's still disconcerting to see this information available for all to see.

Especially my lack of sexual history.

Not caring about the break in decorum, I shoot to my feet, eyes focused on my father. "I need to speak with you in private."

"Now isn't a good time, Esme," he says evenly. "There's still much to discuss. I—"

"No." I slam my fist against the table, the sound echoing in the vast space.

My grandmother focuses her fiery stare on me, her displeasure heavy in the room. I don't care. I learned long ago if I don't stand up for myself, no one else will. That's what I plan to do, regardless of how futile it may be.

At least I'll know I tried. That I didn't willingly allow them to string me up and turn me into a puppet so they could do what they wish.

"I believe now is the perfect time." I clench my jaw. "Your Majesty," I add for effect.

Then I spin, striding purposefully toward my father's private office.

CHAPTER FIVE

Esme

I pace in front of the built-in bookshelves for several long seconds, listening intently to any conversation filtering in from the conference room. Gauging everyone's reaction to my little outburst.

But it's silent, not even a hint of a rustle.

When a figure finally appears in the doorway, I expect it to be my grandmother to berate me for acting in such a "displeasing" manner.

Thankfully, it's my father.

He closes the door before crossing the room toward the mahogany desk. Unbuttoning his suit jacket as he sits, his disinterested eyes meet mine.

"You wanted to talk to me." His voice is even, calm. "This is your chance. Talk."

"You can't seriously be okay with this."

He stares at me for several long moments, uncertainty flickering in his expression.

This is a man who's led our country through quite a few crises in the past fifteen years. When it comes to matters of state, something he does have a great deal of control over, he *is* a good leader.

In his time as king, he's garnered much love and support, being nicknamed "The People's King" for encouraging all elected officials to reach across the aisle as much as possible in order to enact meaningful legislation for the benefit of the people.

But when it comes to personal matters, to his own daughter, he seems completely ill-equipped.

Like he doesn't know how to talk to me.

Like I'm no more familiar to him than a stranger on the street.

Finally, he pushes out a sigh, relaxing into the chair, but still maintaining an air of authority about him.

"As I'm sure your grandmother informed you, this is expected of you. You have a duty to provide heirs in order to continue the bloodline in the event that, God forbid, something horrible happens to your brother. As you're aware, he's being deployed for six months beginning in September."

"I know."

"Then you're also aware you can only provide legitimate heirs if you're married."

Placing my hands on the smooth surface of the desk, I lean toward him. "I'm not even twenty-five yet."

"I was around your age when I married your mother."

"And I'd argue that *you* were too young. Why can't I wait a few years like everyone else my age? Enjoy the rest of my twenties. In fact, I was thinking—"

"You're not like everyone else your age, Esme," he interrupts. "You have obligations. Expectations. Duty."

I fight the urge to groan. If I had a dollar for every time

someone's reminded me of my duty, I could run away from this life and be able to live rather comfortably.

"Jameson Gates is a good man," he continues. "A good match for you. He's a natural leader, which can only work to your advantage, should the unspeakable happen to your brother."

"Why should that matter? He won't be expected to lead. I will."

He tents his fingers in front of him. "That's true. Our country's made great strides toward gender equality. But—"

"Some people don't like the idea of a woman being in charge."

"They'd feel better if there were a strong male presence. Mr. Gates can be that for you. He's well-liked by many. Charismatic. Has a natural draw. His charitable contributions, not only here in Europe but also around the globe, are remarkable."

"I know all about his philanthropic endeavors," I tell my father, not wanting to admit it puts my own charity work to shame, something I've always prided myself on.

"Then you see why he's a good fit for you. And from a good family."

"You mean a *wealthy* family."

I doubt they'd be so quick to marry me off to some of the people I volunteered with through the Humanitarian Corps. They're just as giving as Jameson. Possibly more so. But they're lacking something needed to get your foot in the door in my world. A large bank account.

"I understand your frustration, Esme. I *anticipated* it. But the wheels are already in motion. Trust me when I say there's nothing anyone can do to stop them now. If the royal household wants you to be married, you *will* be married. Jameson is a good man," he repeats, as if the more he reminds me, the more accepting I'll be.

"You expect me to be okay marrying someone I don't love? *You* got to marry for love."

"That was a different set of circumstances. By the time I met your mother, your uncle, Prince Nicholas, was already married with four children, bumping me down to sixth in line. No one could have anticipated what happened to them. Which is why it wasn't of great concern who I married. To be fair, I still married someone my parents approved of. Just like you will."

"But what if I want to experience the kind of love you and Mum once had?"

He floats his gaze to a frame on the corner of his desk. One containing a photo of my mother and father on their wedding day.

"This life and love can't co-exist."

Even though my parents had grown distant in the last few years of my mother's life, which my brother and I blamed on the royal household seeing her MS diagnosis as a sign of weakness, her death still hit my father hard. Hell, it hit all of us hard.

"If anyone should understand that..." There's a slight tremble in his voice as he lifts his eyes to mine. Sorrow flickers on his face before he schools his expression, pushing down any sign of emotion. "You should. Especially after witnessing it tear your mother and me apart once I became king."

"But—"

He holds up a hand, silencing me. "It's your duty to marry and provide the requisite heirs," he states, any hint of emotion gone from his voice. "I know it's not what you want to hear, but I'm confident you and Mr. Gates will make it work. You may never love him. In my experience, it's better if you don't. Regardless, I'm certain you'll find a way to develop a...mutual respect."

He stands, re-securing the button on his suit jacket.

"Take a minute to collect yourself. When you join us, I expect your full compliance." He narrows his steely gaze in warning. Then he strides past me, leaving me alone in his private office.

I pinch my eyes shut, jaw clenched, head throbbing. I thought by appealing to my father's love for my mother, he'd want the same for me, even if I've never had much desire to find some once-in-a-lifetime love.

From the day my father was coronated as king, I knew I'd have to marry.

I just wanted it to be my choice.

I guess I should be relieved they chose Jameson. They could have paired me with any number of stuck-up members of society, many of whom make my skin crawl. Instead, they selected someone who routinely uses his wealth for good. I don't know many other people with the same upbringing who would do the same.

He may not be my choice.

But at least he's not a *horrible* choice.

Reminding myself that Jameson's a handsome, charitable man most woman would love to be with, I take a fortifying breath. Then I return to the conference room.

"Your Highness." Jameson jumps to his feet upon noticing me, interrupting Gianna as she discusses her comprehensive plan for the proposal.

It shouldn't surprise me that every last detail about my so-called relationship with Jameson has already been planned and decided, probably based on market research and polling. But it does. Any reassurances I'd tried to convince myself of moments ago instantly disappear. I'm frozen in place, unable to put one foot in front of the other, even when Jameson pulls my chair out for me

"Esme," my grandmother says when several protracted seconds pass, her voice low and even. "Please, have a seat."

Everyone looks my way, waiting for me to join them.

I thought I was ready to join the conversation. Thought I'd be okay with this.

But as I look around the room, everyone planning my life for me, it's all too much.

"I…" I begin, but can't squeak out another word. My throat closes up, the noose around my neck suffocating me the longer I stand here.

My eyes lock with Jameson's, searching them. For what? I'm not sure. Then my gaze falls on the binder in front of him, which is open to a list of potential wedding dates, all of them in less than a year.

My grandmother had mentioned a spring wedding, but seeing it in black and white makes it real.

Too real.

Panic races through me, and I finally summon the strength to move.

But it's not toward an expectant Jameson Gates.

Instead, I whirl around, darting out of the room as fast as I can.

CHAPTER SIX

Esme

Sunlight warms my face as I walk past the famous Lamberside Palace gardens and toward the back of the property where the stables are located. When we first moved here following my uncle's death, my grandfather having died shortly thereafter and making my father the new king, my mother brought me out here practically every day. Wanted to give me something that reminded me of my old life.

My horse, Lightning, did just that. During that difficult time, she became like a therapy animal to me. Gave me a taste of something normal in a world that was anything but.

I hope she still holds the same soothing magic she did when I was a little girl.

As I follow the line of perfectly manicured trees, the weight suffocating me grows lighter, becoming almost nonexistent when I slip through the open barn door of the stables. I don't even care my heels are covered in dust. All that matters is the peace surrounding me.

Inhaling the comforting scent of earth, grass, and manure, I make my way down the line of stalls, taking time to visit with each of the horses for a few moments. Some of them I've known most of my life. Others are relatively new additions. While I appreciate each of these animals, there's one in particular that will always hold a special place in my heart.

As I reach the last stall, I smile when I see the chocolate Arabian with a streak of lightning between her eyes.

"Hey girl." I run my hand down her forehead and to the bridge of her nose.

Her excitement at seeing me is obvious, a whinny escaping her throat. I bring my head to hers, breathing in her scent that reminds me of simpler times. This horse has been one of the few constants in my ever-changing life. Which is why the palace stable head knows not to even think about selling her and replacing her with one he can train to race.

Lightning may be slowing down for an Arabian, especially now that she's nearing twenty, but I don't care. She's one of the last reminders I have of my mother. Because of that, she's irreplaceable.

I duck into her pen, taking a few minutes to brush her coat, the repeated movements calming me. I understand why people suffering from PTSD or anxiety find success with equine therapy. Just being in the presence of this magnificent creature settles my nerves. Something I didn't think possible minutes ago when I stormed out of that kangaroo court of a meeting.

"Rough day?"

Spine stiffening, I immediately look toward my right, worried my father sent someone to drag me back to his office. When my eyes fall on Creed, I exhale a relieved breath.

His imposing frame is clad in a pair of camouflage pants and a tight-fitting, olive green t-shirt, his chest and arm muscles on full display. It should be a crime for someone to look that good in just a t-shirt.

Then again, Creed Lawson would probably make a paper sack look sexy.

"You could say that." I slip out of Lightning's pen, but still make a conscious effort to maintain a respectful distance between us. "What are you doing out here?" I cross my arms in front of my chest.

"I'm meeting your brother at the armory so we can do manly things and shoot guns." He makes a show of scowling and widening his stance, flexing his arms slightly.

Which only causes my mouth to water even more than before, but I attempt to mask the heat crossing my face with a subtle laugh.

"Then I saw you walking out this way and sensed something was wrong, especially since a dress and three-inch heels aren't typical riding attire."

"They're not," I agree.

"I followed you to make sure you're okay. So…" He steps toward me, eyes awash with concern. "Are you okay?"

"I…," I begin, but struggle to find the words I need to explain how not okay I am. Especially when I peer into his dark gaze, the breeze kicking up his addictive scent of citrus and leather.

Now that I'm in his presence again, I'm reminded of my conversation with Marius and Harriet. About how I should ask Creed to take my virginity.

Days ago, I had no intention of ever propositioning him.

Or anyone, for that matter.

That was before I learned my father, my last line of defense, is actually on board with this arrangement.

Before I realized there's nothing I can do to stop this out-of-control freight train.

"I'm a virgin," I blurt out.

"Umm…" He runs his fingers through his hair.

"And I don't want to be anymore." I keep my head held high, despite the nerves wracking me. "This is probably going to come off as a…strange request. You'll think I'm crazy for even asking this of you. And maybe I am. But I was hoping you'd…" I wave my hand around, avoiding his stare, "help me take care of that."

"I'm sorry." He coughs. "Are you asking me to…sleep with you?" His voice is barely louder than the gentle wind blowing through the stables.

"I know how it must sound." I laugh under my breath. "Now that I hear it out loud, it sounds absurd. But the royal household is determined to announce an engagement by the end of the summer. For me," I clarify.

"To Jameson Gates?" His jaw ticks as he clenches and unclenches his fists.

I look at him quizzically. "How do you know?"

He shrugs. "I saw him roaming around. Thought it unusual, but now it makes sense."

"I don't get a say about much that goes on in my life. I've made my peace with that. I can try to resist all I want, but experience has taught me that if the royal household wants to announce an engagement by the end of the summer, that's exactly what they'll do. I don't want to give them this, too," I manage to say through the heaviness in my throat. "I want to decide who gets to be my first."

"And you're choosing me?"

I swallow hard. "I am."

He stares at me for a protracted beat, rubbing the back

of his neck. Then he expels a long breath, arm falling to his side.

"You're my best mate's little sister. And the Princess Royal." He leans closer, his proximity causing a shiver to roll through me. "I'm to be royal guard in a few months. And not just one of the ceremonial guards on display in front of the palace for the tourists. But part of the elite protection squad. I could be assigned to *your* protection team."

I erase the last remaining space between us and tilt my head back, meeting his eyes. "But you're not yet."

He hesitates, neither pushing forward nor retreating. His gaze fixates on my mouth, pupils dilating, breaths coming quicker.

I wonder if he's recalling that kiss I gave him all those years ago right before he left for basic training. I didn't know what came over me back then. I just hated the idea of something horrible happening to him before I could have a taste of what I'd fantasized about since I discovered boys weren't as gross as I'd originally believed.

"Esme…" His Adam's apple bobs up and down in a hard swallow, every muscle in his body growing taut with indecision. He flexes his hands, like he's desperate to yank me against him and kiss me in a way that would leave me utterly breathless. At the same time, he knows he should walk away. That this will only end in disaster.

But that doesn't stop the anticipation from coiling within me, his need for me palpable in the lust that consumes his dark eyes. I may not be overly experienced when it comes to sex, but I know what hunger looks like.

And right now, Creed peers at me as if he's been starved for days, *months*, and he's finally stumbled across the one thing that will satisfy him.

"Please, Creed," I breathe, inching closing still. "Kiss me. There's nothing saying we can't. Not right now."

He doesn't move for several long moments, seemingly consumed by indecision. Finally, he groans, dipping his head toward me, lips so near I can taste them.

I close my eyes, bracing myself for his kiss, his touch, his anything.

"Except my conscience." He abruptly pulls back.

I snap my stare to his. "But your conscience will allow some guy I have no history with to sleep with me after my grandmother and Silas Archer all but whore me out to him."

He winces, my words like knives against his flesh. "Don't put it that way. Please."

"It's the truth. You weren't in that meeting." I point in the general direction of the palace. "I have no doubt there's money changing hands here. Not to mention, you should have seen the dossiers the PR team put together that we're to study and memorize in order to sell our relationship to the public."

"Jameson Gates is a good man."

"I don't give a fuck about that!" I throw my hands up in frustration, my irate tone unsettling a few of the horses.

Squeezing my eyes shut, I inhale a deep breath. When I open them again, I lean toward Creed, keeping my voice as even as possible.

"When I look at him, all I see is a man who was *chosen* for me. Don't you see how messed up this is? That I don't get to choose who I marry? I understand things are different for me, but at least give me a goddamn option, instead of ordering me around like a puppet. Nearly every decision has always been made for me. I don't get to decide what to wear. What to drink. And now, who I spend the rest of my life with. I don't want them to control this, too. I want this choice to be mine."

"Esme…" He shakes his head, pinching the bridge of his nose. Then he brings his gaze back to mine. "I… I can't."

I suck in a quivering breath, swallowing the tears wanting to fall. I refuse to cry. Not over this.

I didn't cry when I was told I had to leave the only home I knew to live in this damn prison.

I didn't cry when I learned my mother was sick and may soon lose control of her limbs.

I didn't cry when I walked into her bedroom and discovered her unconscious body.

This life has dealt me harsh blow after harsh blow, and I've taken them all in stride.

I'm not going to let it break me over this.

"I'm sorry," he offers.

"Don't, Creed," I bark out. "I don't need your pity. Don't need your apologies. I don't… I don't need you. If you're not interested, I'll find someone else."

"Esme," he sighs, stepping toward me.

Something in the way he peers at me makes me think he's about to reveal some earth-shattering truth.

That he's about to wrap me in his arms, forbid me from asking someone else, then press his lips against mine, treating me to a spine-tingling kiss.

But before he can utter another syllable, footsteps grow near, and he jumps as far away as possible.

I whirl around, momentarily disoriented, before I focus on the doorway and see Jameson Gates standing there.

CHAPTER SEVEN

Esme

"Your Highness." Jameson bows in my direction.

"Mr. Gates," I greet formally.

I don't bother telling him it's not necessary to bow. Or address me as "Your Highness" past the first one of the day. He'll figure that out soon enough once he starts learning all the rules and traditions that accompany being part of the royal family.

"I told you." He steps closer. "Call me Jameson."

"Of course. Jameson." I pinch my lips into a tight smile. "What are you doing out here?"

"Looking for you," he declares, everything about his demeanor put-together and confident. "I figured you might have come out here for some…clarity. What, with your love of horses."

"Did you read about that in the binder?" I snip out.

"No," he chuckles, his blue eyes shining in amusement. "Although I'm certain it's covered quite extensively in that dossier. Truth be told, I've learned a few things about myself I didn't know, thanks to their disconcerting invasion of privacy."

My lips part, his response surprising me. I'd assumed he was on board with this asinine plan, but his snide remarks make me question his motives. Perhaps he's as much a victim of circumstance as I am.

He may not be royalty, but his family is one of the wealthiest in all of Europe. It's possible he's being pressured to marry in order to increase his family's social standing even more. And there's no higher to go than the royal family.

It's not the first time this kind of arrangement has been made.

And it won't be the last.

"If you didn't read about it, how did you—"

"You'd mentioned it at the King's Day gala last year. Sure, you spoke about a lot of things, but when someone brought up horses, your eyes lit up. Like the mere idea of your horses breathed life into you. With the way that meeting was going, I took a chance you might be out here."

How do I even respond to this? I can't remember a single conversation I had at that gala, let alone a brief one about my love of horses.

But Jameson does.

I'm about to respond when I sense a motion behind me. A reminder we're not alone.

Turning, I meet Creed's eyes, his jaw ticking as he stares at Jameson. Although I'm not sure stare is the correct word. It's more akin to a glower. But he has no reason to glower. After all, *he* turned *me* down.

"Creed Lawson." Squaring my shoulders, I address him as if he's just another acquaintance. No one special. "May I introduce you to Mr. Jameson Gates." I move closer to Jameson. "Jameson, this is Lieutenant Creed Lawson. He's a friend of my brother's."

Jameson smiles that same charismatic smile I've seen plastered all over magazines and gossip websites, teeth white against his tanned skin. "Pleasure to meet you." He extends his hand.

Creed glares at it, several tense seconds passing before he finally takes it. "Likewise," he growls.

My gaze ping-pongs between the two men, both seeming to size up one another.

While Jameson is tall and fit, maybe only three inches shorter than Creed's six-five stature, he's no match for his muscular physique. And the longer Creed shakes Jameson's hand, the firmer his grip becomes, to the point Jameson winces.

"Well, then…" I jump between them before Creed rips off Jameson's balls with his bare hands.

A few minutes ago, he insisted Jameson was a great guy. But now, he's on the verge of breaking every bone in his hand. His behavior gives me whiplash.

"I'm sure my brother's waiting for you," I direct at Creed. "Aren't you supposed to meet him at the range?"

"The range?" Jameson repeats, interest piqued.

"Gun range," Creed explains curtly.

"That sounds like fun. Perhaps one of these days, I can join you. I'd like to get to know Esme's friends. And family." He wraps an arm around my shoulders.

If looks could kill, the venomous stare Creed gives Jameson's hand on my body would incinerate him.

"That's a fantastic idea," I say brightly, wide grin trained on Creed. "I'm sure Lieutenant Lawson would be quite agreeable. As would my brother. Fair warning, though. They both can be quite competitive."

"I'm always game for a little friendly competition."

"I'll be sure to bring it up with my brother," I tell Jameson before turning my gaze back to Creed. "Good day, Lieutenant Lawson."

He hesitates, glancing between me and Jameson. The romantic in me wants him to refuse. To fight for me. To draw me into his arms and tell me he can't stand the idea of another man touching a single hair on my body.

Instead, he does what he's been trained to do. He follows orders.

Stepping back, he bows, expression stoic and unwavering. "Ma'am." Then he spins, strides purposeful, as if marching in formation.

"He's...intense," Jameson remarks after several long moments of stiff silence.

On a long sigh, I face him. "He's spent the past eight years in the military. The last four on special teams. Creed Lawson only knows one level. And that's intense."

"Have you known him long?"

I shrug dismissively. "Most of my life."

"He's like a brother to you then."

"Yes." I give him a reassuring smile. "That's exactly what Creed Lawson is. A brother."

A brother I just propositioned to take my virginity.

So, no. He's not like a brother at all. But I'm not about to tell Jameson that.

"Right then." He clears his throat. "Can I interest you in a walk?"

"Shouldn't we get back to the meeting?"

"Why bother? It's not like they'll listen to us. A walk might do us both some good. Plus, it'll give us a chance to talk freely, if you know what I mean."

"Probably more than you can ever imagine," I mutter under my breath.

As Jameson and I stroll along the path leading from the stables and back toward the gardens, he maintains a respectful distance. Birds chirp overhead, some of them swooping down and cleaning themselves in one of the marble baths strategically placed throughout the well-maintained rows of flowers. The bright sun causes some of the dew-stained petals to sparkle and gleam, everything about the grounds pristine and perfect, the palace backdrop making it look like a scene ripped from a fairy tale.

But it's all a façade. A show to make those who tour the palace think we lead a charmed life.

In reality, this place is nothing more than a prison. The surroundings may be posh, the food prepared by a Michelin-starred chef, but I'm still trapped here. Still serving a life sentence for committing the crime of being born.

"Can I tell you something?" he asks after several minutes.

"Isn't that why we're here?"

A smile teases his mouth. "Too right." He looks forward again. "When my father told me about this plan, I had the same reaction as you."

"Really?" I tilt my head, partly surprised. Partly relieved.

"You think because you come with all of this…" He waves his hand at our surroundings, "that I wouldn't put up a fight?"

"It felt like the playing field was a bit uneven during that meeting. Like I was in one of those dreams where you're shouting to be heard, yet everyone's carrying on as if you're not even there."

"Believe me, Esme…" He narrows his gaze on me. "You're not alone. I'm on your side, too."

I pause in my tracks, studying his expression. He *seems*

sincere. But is he? Or is it just some ploy to get me to agree to my grandmother's plan?

Or have I been around this world so long that I've become cynical whenever someone offers me a moment of honesty?

"Then why did you agree to this?" I ask as we continue walking. "You're an attractive guy." I gesture down his frame, taking the time to fully appreciate him now that we're not on display for the royal household.

Dusty blond hair. Crystal blue eyes. Angled jaw. It's no surprise he's been named one of the most eligible bachelors these past few years, especially with the way he fills out his suit.

And he's not wearing a regular suit. Oh, no. Jameson Gates has to go above and beyond, donning a perfectly tailored three-piece suit. I'm a complete sucker for a man in a vest. It's better than porn.

Then again, I'm also a sucker for a man in camouflage, fitted t-shirts, and work boots.

"Based on some of the comments I've encountered on social media, there's no shortage of women who would happily marry you."

"You're correct." A nervous laugh falls from his throat as he fights a blush.

I've been around privileged and powerful men like Jameson all my life. Not much gets to them. It can't, not if you're to be successful, like Jameson's family is. Like *Jameson* is.

It's refreshing to know some things *do* embarrass him. That he *is* human.

"There have been plenty of women."

"Then why agree to this?"

"Probably the same reason you're talking to me right now."

When I pass him a questioning look, he flashes a sad smile.

"Because we're powerless to fight this. When those photos of us dancing together were published and all of Europe salivated over what an amazing couple we made, this was bound to happen. My father would never allow me to turn down this kind of opportunity, not when marrying you would raise our family's social standing higher than it already is.

"So, he gave me an ultimatum. Agree to this arrangement or he cuts me off financially. And before you accuse me of needing Daddy's money, I don't. I can support myself. Perhaps not at the level I've grown accustomed to, but I'd be fine. Unfortunately, all the charities I've spearheaded would suffer, and I couldn't stomach that.

"Plus, we both know how things really are for people like us. So many people think you can do anything you want when you're born into a wealthy family. In reality, there are certain expectations placed on your shoulders. Marriages are essentially business transactions entered into in order to increase power or further concentrate wealth. It may be the twenty-first century, but some vestiges of the past remain, including parents arranging marriages."

"But what about love? Don't you want to marry for love?"

I glance his way as his expression falters, emotion sneaking through the cracks. And not just any emotion. Heartache. Sorrow. Despair.

"Let's just say love isn't in the cards for me." His Adam's apple bobs up and down in a pained swallow. "Lightning rarely strikes the same place twice. I'm not holding out for another strike of lightning."

"I'm sorry." I want to press for more information but sense it's not something he's ready to share.

"And you?" he asks after a brief pause. "Don't *you* want to marry for love?"

I push out an annoyed laugh. "When you grow up being told there's no place for love in a monarchy, you give up any adolescent notion of a fairytale ending."

He nods, processing my response. Then he comes to an abrupt stop, grabbing my hand and forcing me to face him.

"Listen, I'm not a bad person. I'm just as much a pawn as you are. Maybe not to the same extent, but that doesn't mean we have to torture ourselves for the rest of our lives. I'd like to think I have some rather endearing qualities. I don't slurp my soup. I don't ask a thousand questions during a movie, all of which would be answered if I'd shut up and watch."

My mouth relaxes into a natural smile, the noose wrapped around my neck loosening.

"And I promise our dinner conversations will never be boring. I tend to be a sieve of useless information."

"Is that right?"

He nods. "Did you know that you're fourteen times more likely to die on your birthday than any other day of the year?"

I tilt my head, biting my lower lip. "Really?"

"It's true. They did a study in Switzerland."

"Leave it to the Swiss to research what day of the year you're more likely to die. What other tidbits of information do you have stored?"

"Dragonflies have six legs but can't walk. They can stand,

but their legs are too weak to support their bodies to walk any distance."

"Interesting."

"And did you know when the telephone was first invented, most people answered with 'ahoy' instead of 'hello'? Personally, my inner pirate thinks we should go back to that. In fact, I may start just to hear everyone's reactions." He winks. "Perhaps throw in a few scallywags and mateys for good measure."

I struggle to stifle my laugh. "People will think they reached the wrong number."

"All the more reason to bring it back. The world would be a better place if everyone was forced to speak like a pirate."

"I can't disagree with that."

He treats me to another smile, the sun reflecting off his brilliant white teeth. Then his expression sobers. He inches closer, his gaze narrowing on me.

"In all seriousness, I *am* a good person. I won't stand here and tell you I'm perfect. That the sun shines out of my arse, pardon my language. Based on the things said earlier, that's what everyone wants you to believe. Like everyone else, like *you*, I have my faults. I know we won't always see eye to eye. But I'd like it if you'd allow me to show you who I am before rushing to judgment. Can you do that?"

I bite my lower lip, searching his eyes. When I walked into that meeting and saw him there, it never crossed my mind he could merely be a pawn, too.

But as my grandmother taught me all those years ago, two pawns in the center of a chess board are strongest when standing side by side. Advancing one may leave the other weak.

We may both be pawns, but if we're to survive, I need to stand by Jameson's side, regardless of the personal sacrifice.

"I can do that."

"Thank you." He squeezes my hand, briefly floating his eyes to my mouth. "Do you…" He expels an anxious laugh. "Would you object if I kissed you?"

On a sharp inhale, I stiffen. My lips part, but no response is forthcoming.

"If we're to sell this relationship to the masses," he continues when I remain mute, "at some point, we'll have to kiss. It might be better if our first kiss didn't occur under the scrutiny of the palace PR team or the media. Or worse yet, the powers that be in the royal household." He rolls his eyes. "I'd rather not receive kissing pointers from that sniveling troll, Silas Archer."

"You have a point." I laugh at his rather astute assessment of my grandmother's most trusted advisor.

"So, what do you say? Can I kiss you?"

I swallow hard, wracked with indecision.

It's only a kiss, not a life or death situation.

I can't help but feel that if I allow Jameson to kiss me, my fate will be sealed.

But isn't it sealed anyway?

I can fight this all the way to the bitter end, but it won't change anything. I may as well make the most out of the situation. May as well take the small victories where I can find them. And that includes doing as much as we can on *our* terms. Like our first kiss.

"I'd like that."

He swipes his tongue along his lips, moistening them as his expression changes from playful to more serious. More sensual.

Stepping toward me, he drops his hold on my hand,

bringing it to my cheek. His grip is resolute, determined. It reminds me of the way Creed's hands felt on my skin.

He's the last person I should be thinking about right now, but I can't stop myself from wishing it were his hand cupping my face. His dark gaze I were staring into. His lips descending toward mine.

I close my eyes, trying to forget how Creed's mere proximity brought me to life. But when Jameson's mouth brushes mine in my first taste of him, all I can do is long for Creed's kiss.

Maybe then I'd feel something.

Because right now, even as Jameson coaxes my lips to part in a deep yet respectful kiss, I feel absolutely nothing.

CHAPTER EIGHT

Creed

I shouldn't have followed them. Should have found Anderson and forgotten all about what just transpired.

But I can't.

Esme asked me to sleep with her.

And not just sleep with her, but take her virginity.

I tell myself I did the right thing. She's the bloody Princess Royal. Anderson would murder me. He's always been protective of his sister, even from miles away. Not to mention, my brother's her goddamn chief protection officer. He knows everything she does.

But all these reasons don't make my decision any easier to swallow.

I've spent the better part of the past decade serving my country. Passed special teams training at the top of my class. Was airdropped into some of the most dangerous places in the world and managed to make it out with my life.

But turning down Princess Esme Louisa Victoria Grace

Wellingston of Belmont's proposal is the hardest thing I've ever done.

And when I watch Jameson lean in and press his lips to hers, all I see is red, teeth clenched, hands fisted. The idea that he gets to touch her, *kiss* her, makes me wild with jealousy.

Makes me wish things were different.

As I've learned time and again, I can wish all I want. Nothing will change who we are to each other.

"Looks like they're hitting it off."

When I hear Anderson's voice, I take a minute to school my expression and pretend I'm not planning a certain billionaire's murder, even if it's simply a fantasy.

"What's that?" I glance at my best mate.

His features are similar to his sister's, albeit much more masculine. His hair is the same shade of blond, transitioning into various hues of copper and brown toward the ends. He has the same charming smile. Same tanned complexion. Same tall stature. But where Esme's sleek and slender, Anderson's more built. Not as muscular as me, but his dedication to working out hasn't gone unnoticed, especially from the girls he meets at bars.

It irritates me that he's allowed to go to bars, clubs, parties, and the royal household doesn't bat an eye. If Esme were to do the same thing, they'd lose their minds.

The double standards must be exhausting.

Especially for her.

"Jameson Gates and Ezzy." Anderson nods toward them as they meander through the gardens, hand-in-hand.

At least they're no longer kissing.

"You're okay with this?" I arch a brow.

He adjusts the duffle bag slung over his shoulder, starting in the opposite direction from where Esme and Jameson are walking. At least we won't risk running into them. I doubt I'd be able to watch them kiss so close to me. I better wrap my head around it, though. I have a feeling I'll have no choice but to witness that quite a bit this summer. Hell, the rest of my life.

"It could have been much worse. Jameson's a good guy. He has many of the same interests as Esme. Have you seen all the charities he's involved with? Compared to the two of us, he's a bloody saint."

"But does *she* want to be with him?" I ask, not sure how much he knows. Or how much I'm supposed to know. Then again, we've both been around this life long enough to understand how these things work.

"It doesn't matter what she wants. Only what the royal household wants. She's almost twenty-five. I'm twenty-six. In their minds, these are prime breeding years. We need to work on the next generation of prisoners- I mean, royals."

In typical Anderson fashion, he flashes a sarcastic smile, making light of the situation. In reality, he's as frustrated as Esme about their lack of choice. He just masks his contempt with sarcasm and humor where Esme... I guess Esme takes matters into her own hands. Attempts to exercise free will whenever possible.

"If I weren't about to get shipped off for one last deployment—"

"Which you volunteered for," I remind him.

He hushes me, glancing around to make sure no one overheard. If it were up to him, he'd probably stay in the Royal Air Force as long as possible. I've never seen anyone love flying as much as he does.

In another life, maybe he would have been a pilot.

But he doesn't get to follow his dreams. Instead, he's forced to live a life that's been planned for him.

"Regardless, if I weren't currently doing my four years of service, I'd be the one on the proverbial chopping block. Hell, once my deployment is up, I most likely will be. I can only hope the royal household chooses someone halfway decent for me."

"What about someone *you* choose? I understand the requirement for you both to marry in order to continue the family line, but why the rush? Why not wait until you fall in love?"

"Love?" Anderson comes to an abrupt stop outside of the military operations building on the palace grounds.

"This may be a difficult concept for you to grasp, but most normal people marry for love."

"Therein lies your problem, Creed. Esme and I aren't normal. And don't you know?" He stands tall, his expression stiff, making it appear as if he has a stick shoved up his ass. "There's no place for love in a monarchy."

I don't have to question who he's mocking. From the proper tone, it's apparent it's his grandmother, Queen Veronica. The Queen Mother.

She may be royal through marriage, but she was essentially bred to be queen. She's always put the monarchy first.

Even above her own family.

"You care about her."

"What?" I tear my gaze to him, suddenly feeling defensive.

And guilty, even though I didn't do anything wrong.

I wanted to, though.

My god, I *still* want to.

"Esme. You care about her. I do, too. But you don't need to worry about her. We may not have much say about the bigger things in life. Like I had no choice about what I was to study at university. Or about serving our country in the military. Just like Esme had no choice about serving her country in the Humanitarian Corps. It's all part of our duty to the crown. We can complain about it all we want, but it's out of our control. You should know as well as I do there are certain traditions that simply can't be changed." He gives me a knowing look.

Lately, I've become painfully aware of that fact. Hell, in the past hour, I have.

"Instead of bitching and moaning about the things you can't change, you learn to take advantage of the things you *can* control. You celebrate the small victories. The small 'fuck yous', so to speak. That makes all of this suck a little less."

"And Esme being forced to marry a man she didn't choose? What's going to make that suck a little less?"

"Esme's always been an extremely resourceful woman." He winks. "I'm sure she'll figure out something."

"I'm sure she will," I mutter as I follow him inside the building, desperate to take out some of this aggression with a bit of target practice.

All the while, imagining Jameson Gates' face on one of the targets.

Is it immature?

Most definitely.

But right now, it's the only thing that will make this suck a little less for me.

CHAPTER NINE

Esme

W hy am I this nervous?

I go to black-tie charity events all the time, especially ones benefiting causes I promote, like mental health awareness, prevention of domestic violence, and multiple sclerosis research. Tonight's gala in support of eliminating human trafficking, particularly in Europe, which has a tendency to be a hotspot, is yet another cause I champion.

But tonight isn't a typical black-tie charity event I'm invited to in order to give a speech encouraging people to open their wallets and donate even more money than the exorbitant plate fee.

Instead, I'll be attending with billionaire bachelor and philanthropist Jameson Gates, confirming the rumors that we're an item.

To most, it wouldn't be a big deal. Couples go out in public all the time.

For a royal, being seen in public with a member of the

opposite sex, particularly at a formal event, sends a message. And that message is to prepare for wedding bells.

Once I step out of the limo and take Jameson Gates' arm, the photographers the palace paid to be there feverishly snapping photos, there will be no turning back. We'll be committed.

When I hear a knock, I tear my gaze from the windows where I've been admiring the city lights, wishing I were just another nobody living on the other side of these walls.

"Come in," I call out.

The door opens and one of my butlers steps into my private suite. "Mr. Jameson Gates for you, ma'am."

I make my way across the room, meeting Jameson as he enters. Wearing a dashing tuxedo that hugs his body in all the right places, he's the picture of sophistication.

"Your Highness," he greets with a slight bow as the butler retreats. Once we're alone, he presses a soft kiss to my cheek. "You look absolutely stunning." His voice is a seductive murmur, eyes flaming with appreciation as he takes in my fitted black gown that leaves my back exposed. "Then again, I always find you stunning."

I want to tell him he doesn't have to say things like this when we're in private. Maybe it's a good thing, though. Maybe it'll make this feel less forced. More real.

"Thank you, Jameson."

"Are you nervous about tonight?"

"It's going to change a lot. Maybe not for you. You seem to welcome the spotlight. You're a natural in front of reporters and photographers."

"And you're not?" he shoots back. "I've seen how comfortable you are with the public, especially children. And what of the modeling you've done? If anyone's a natural in front of the camera, it's you."

"I know. I just—"

"I understand everything's about to change." He pinches my chin, tilting my head back, our eyes locking.

A week ago, the idea of sharing a personal moment like this with Jameson Gates made my skin crawl.

Now that I've gotten to know him on a deeper level, I actually like spending time with him. He may never make my stomach flutter or my heart skip a beat, but I respect and appreciate him, including all the good he's done, most notably in helping refugees from war-torn countries rebuild their lives. Maybe that's enough for me.

"We may both be used to the spotlight, but going public with our relationship will make us a perpetual target," he continues. "Every single reporter, photographer, paparazzi will want to be the first to break the news about each tiny development in our relationship for months and years to come. Just promise me one thing."

"What's that?"

"That you won't shut me out. We're both in this together. And the only way we'll get through it is if we have an open line of communication. Not only are we navigating a new relationship—"

"It's not a new relationship. According to the dossier, we've been dating in secret for several months," I retort sarcastically.

"Of course. My mistake." He rolls his eyes. "Still. The next few months may be…trying." He moves his hands to my face, his touch gentle and reassuring. "I just want you to know that you can always talk to me. And I hope I can talk to you. Especially when it comes to the table setting at the state dinner I'm supposed to attend with you in a few weeks."

He drops his hold on me, running his long fingers through his blond hair. A shy smile tugs on his lips. "I've been studying the diagram. The amount of silverware boggles my mind. I grew up attending formal dinners, but we didn't have *that* many forks, even during the fanciest of affairs."

"To be honest, I don't even know what all those forks are for."

"Then I guess we'll figure it out together. Much like we'll figure this out." He gestures between our two bodies.

"I guess we will."

His light expression sobers, his gaze floating to my lips. He touches a hand to my lower back, pulling me against him as he curves toward me. I close my eyes, Jameson's breath heating my skin.

Until a knock echoes, forcing him to increase his distance.

"Come in," I instruct, somewhat relieved our kiss was interrupted.

"Ma'am," my butler greets as he enters my suite once more. "Captain Lawson is ready to drive you and Mr. Gates to the hotel."

"Tell him we'll be right out."

"Of course." He spins on his heels, leaving me alone with Jameson.

"Shall we?" he asks, holding out his elbow for me.

"Thank you." I loop my arm through his, allowing him to escort me through my apartment.

As we step into the foyer my apartment shares with the one across from it, which happens to be Anderson's, I glance at the door, wondering if Creed's inside. If he's standing by the window, about to watch me leave with Jameson. I don't have long to ruminate on that, Jameson steering me outside, where a man dressed in a dark suit waits for us beside an idling limo.

"Your Highness," Adam greets with a bow.

The sight of him catches me off guard.

Sure, I knew my chief protection officer would be accompanying us to this evening's event. But it's the first time I've seen him since I propositioned his younger brother to take my virginity.

The more I think about it, the more I realize it wasn't one of my finer moments. Even so, it doesn't stop my heart from wishing Creed had said yes.

"Good evening, Adam," I say with a smile. "This is Jameson Gates. My boyfriend." I wince slightly, the term sounding foreign and wrong. But I need to get used to referring to him as such. "Jameson, this is Captain Adam Lawson of the elite protection squad. He's my CPO. Chief protection officer."

"Pleasure to meet you, Mr. Gates," Adam says evenly.

If he finds it suspicious that I suddenly have a boyfriend when he never saw me spend much time with another man the past three years he's been on my protection team, he doesn't say anything.

"Didn't we meet the other day?" Jameson glances my way. "In the stables."

"That was Creed." I force a smile. "Adam's younger brother."

"Oh." He blinks rapidly. "My apologies."

"It's a common mistake," I assure him. "They do bear a strong resemblance."

Once Jameson and I are situated in the back of the limo, Adam jumps into the driver's seat.

As he navigates away from the Gladwell Penal Colony, as I refer to the compound of apartments and cottages where various other members of the royal family live, Adam finds my eyes through the rearview mirror, a question within.

Then his gaze moves to Jameson, studying him with suspicion.

I'm pretty sure Jameson senses it, too, reaching across the seat and grabbing my hand. When I bring my gaze to his, he treats me to an endearing smile. But there's a reminder there, too. After all, everyone's supposed to think this is a real relationship. Including my chief protection officer.

Instead of pulling my hand away after a gentle squeeze, I keep it there, enjoying the warmth as Jameson brushes his thumb along my knuckles, his touch settling my nerves.

Until we near the Monarch Hotel and I see the crowds of reporters, photographers, and other royal watchers swarming the sidewalk, all of them here after receiving an anonymous tip that they'd catch some big scoop.

An anonymous tip called in from Gianna herself.

Once the limo comes to a stop, I draw in a calming breath, the camera flashes blinding even against the darkened windows. Neither one of us says anything right away, enjoying these last few moments of silence.

Of freedom.

But it's fleeting, Adam soon jumping out of the limo, opening my door, and extending his hand toward me.

In an instant, I transition from the woman I've been the past several years into the woman I now have to be as the Princess Royal.

Plastering a smile on my face, I accept Adam's hand and stand, waving to the assembled crowd as they shout my name. Then Jameson steps out behind me, the flashes becoming even more incessant, photographers fighting to snap our photo.

He places a hand on my lower back, and I lift my eyes to his, looking upon him as if he invades my every waking thought. I thought it would be harder to pretend like this, but it's not. How could it be when every part of my life has been a lie? An elaborate display the royal family puts on to keep the masses entertained.

At one point, I thought I'd be able to use my position to do good in the world. Fight gender inequality. Eliminate child hunger. Provide resources for victims of domestic violence.

As I grew older, I learned the harsh reality that my duty to the crown doesn't include making a difference. Instead, my main role is to put on a show. To give the impression I live a fairytale life. Any good we do is second to that. The illusion always comes first.

And now, that illusion includes pretending I'm madly in love with Jameson Gates so the royal household can chain us to each other, all because he possesses the star quality the establishment deems desirable.

"Should we give them something to talk about?" Jameson leans toward me, his breath hot on my neck. "Play hard and fast with the royal household's plan for tonight?"

I pinch my lips together in a small smirk. "And what did you have in mind?"

"This." He brings his hand to my face, his lips covering mine before I have a chance to stop him. I stiffen, not immediately responding to his mouth attempting to coax mine open.

This certainly wasn't part of the plan. As Jameson's learned over the past week, the royal household doesn't take too kindly to overt displays of affection. A touch here and there is allowed, but that's it. I can only imagine how Silas Archer and my grandmother will react when they see the videos and photos of this kiss.

Which is why I wrap my arm around Jameson's neck,

curving into him and parting my lips, tongue swiping with his.

Like we promised when we played hooky from that first meeting. We may be pawns in the royal household's game.

But we don't have to play by all their rules.

CHAPTER TEN

Creed

"She was cute. Don't you think?" Anderson slurs from beside me in the back of the SUV, his chief protection officer, Captain Xavier Green, navigating the mostly vacant streets after three in the morning.

To say it's been quite a day would be putting it mildly. I'd spent the afternoon with Anderson at the football stadium, watching our hometown team beat one of the top teams in the division in an incredible fourth quarter comeback. Riding the high from the win, he wanted to celebrate with the rest of the city. So we went to a local pub, which I'm sure Xavier hated. But part of being a royal guard means catering to the last-minute whims of the royal family, most notably Anderson's reputation for wanting to party at every possible opportunity.

And that's precisely what Xavier did, securing an area in a local pub, then a nightclub when Anderson decided he wanted to go dancing.

Most people would love being friends with someone with these connections. Not me.

Don't get me wrong. I love Anderson like I do my own brother.

But now that we're adults, things are different.

It's awkward to have the men who will be my colleagues in a few weeks offer me the same protection services I'll soon be providing.

Like I don't belong on this side of things.

Which is what I've reminded myself of since Esme's proposition. That I don't belong in her world.

But when footage of some black-tie charity event flashed on the TVs, Jameson and Esme displayed in a passionate locking of lips, I would have given anything *to* belong in her world.

Seeing them kiss on national TV, then listening to so many people in the bar comment about what a beautiful couple they make, irritated me. Made me want to order an entire bottle of scotch so I could drown the animosity raging inside of me.

It won't change anything, though.

Not now that Esme and Jameson have confirmed the rumors that they're together.

Even if I weren't about to be sworn into the guard, I never had a chance with her. Not when she needs to be with someone like Jameson Gates.

When she *deserves* to be with someone like Jameson Gates.

"Which one is that?" I ask Anderson.

"The one with the long legs."

I give him a sardonic look. "They *all* had long legs. Pretty sure that's one of your most stringent requirements. 'Must have long legs. Brains optional,'" I say, as if reciting a personal ad.

"No, it's not." He playfully punches my arm. "I'm more an ass man than anything. But I'm talking about the one in red. What was her name?" He leans his head back against the headrest, closing his eyes, concentrating as hard as he can in his inebriated state. "Carlie? Cammie? Cathy?"

I blow out a breath. "It was Alyse. Her name was Alyse."

"Alyse. That's it. I knew I was close."

I roll my eyes. "Sure you were. Alyse and Carley, Cammie, and Cathy sound *so* much alike."

"In my defense, I wasn't really paying all that much attention to *what* she was saying. But *how* her lips moved. If you know what I mean." He waggles his brows, but his slow reflexes make it look like he's getting ready to nod off.

He probably is.

"So, what do you think? Should I call her?"

"They'll want to do a background check first," I tell him, needing to be the voice of reason. "And make sure she signs an NDA."

"That's bloody bullshite," Anderson declares loudly.

I glance at Xavier, noticing him shake his head.

While it's considered a privilege to serve as chief protection officer to the future king, it's obvious Xavier is over it. Anderson may be heir apparent, but he's also a twenty-six-year-old soldier about to leave on deployment in a few months. Who will most likely be forced to get married the second his military service is over. I don't condone him sleeping around. But I can appreciate his frustration with all the hoops he has to jump through to bring a girl home. All things normal people would never have to worry about.

All things *I've* never had to worry about.

"We'll talk about it tomorrow, Anders. When you're thinking a bit more clearly. And with your head instead of your dick."

"But my dick wants her," he whines.

I pat his shoulder. "And if your dick still wants her tomorrow, we'll figure it out."

He groans. "Just once I'd like to meet a hot girl at a bar and be able to bring her home. Not have to get her full name so my security team can run a background check. Sometimes…" He sighs. "Sometimes this life sucks. I mean, look at Esme."

I whip my eyes toward him. "What do you mean?"

"Oh, come off it, Creed. You know what I'm talking about. You don't actually think she *likes* that guy. Do you?"

"They make a beautiful couple." I maintain an even expression. "I have no doubt they'll be quite happy."

While I may be aware of the circumstances surrounding her relationship with Jameson, they do seem content. At least they did in the clip I couldn't stop watching earlier.

Do I think there's a connection there?

I don't want there to be. Don't want anyone else to possess her heart, even though I'll never be allowed to possess it, either.

"Happy," he scoffs. "Happiness in this life is an illusion. Something we make the masses believe so they don't see the truth."

His candor surprises me. He's typically a happy drunk.

Perhaps he's held it in for long enough and is done masking his frustration with humor.

"What truth is that?"

He brings his gaze to mine just as Xavier pulls up to the security gate outside Gladwell Palace.

"That we'd do anything to be able to make one decision of our own." He holds my gaze for a beat. "I'd love to go home with a pretty girl without needing permission to fuck her. Just like Esme…" He trails off. "Well, I'm not sure what

Esme would like, but she wouldn't willingly choose to be with Jameson."

Approaching the building where both Esme's and Anderson's individual apartments are housed, Xavier pulls the SUV to a stop and jumps out, rushing to Anderson's door. I do the same, helping him upright, a feat after all the alcohol he drank in the past twelve hours. If it weren't for Esme and Jameson's relationship going viral on social media, I'd be concerned that news of the playboy prince, as Anderson's been called, partying it up in the city would be headline news.

"I'll take him in," I tell Xavier.

"You sure?"

"Yeah. I got this."

I give Xavier a thankful smile, draping Anderson's arm over my shoulder as I drag him up the short flight of stairs and press his code into the door. When I hear it click, I open it, helping him into the shared foyer, Esme's apartment to the right, Anderson's to the left.

"God, I bloody hate this place," Anderson groans as I carry him toward his apartment. "It's a prison. You know that, right? And you... In a few months, you'll be nothing more than a glorified prison guard."

I try not to take his comment to heart. I've had a front-row seat to how difficult life can be for Anderson and Esme. In twenty-six years, Anderson's rarely been in a place where someone doesn't watch his every move.

It's no wonder he volunteered for another deployment.

At least overseas he can enjoy the freedom he can't here.

It's sad he has to go to a war zone to get that.

"Don't forget. One day, you'll be in charge and can change how things are."

He barks out a laugh, the sound reverberating against the

high ceilings and marble tile floor that probably cost more than I make in the entirety of my military career. "That's rich, Creed. Do you really think anything here will ever change?"

"I—"

"It won't. Nothing's changed in the past hundred years. And nothing will change in the next hundred. It's such bullshite."

I hush him, but it's useless, especially when he's drunk. I'd like to say this is the first time he's done something like this.

It's not.

I'd like to say it'll be the last time I'll have to carry him into his apartment after he went on a bender.

It won't be.

Humor may be one of his coping mechanisms. Alcohol is the other. It helps him not to feel like himself. If there's one thing I know about Prince Gabriel Anderson Joseph Xavier Wellingston — Anderson for short — it's that he often hates being who he is.

I drag him into his apartment, hesitating as my eyes fall on Esme's door. I try not to think of the woman who lives within those four walls. Try not to imagine her sleeping peacefully in her bed.

Try not to wish I could be in that bed with her.

But it's a lost cause.

I've always thought about Esme. Always longed to be in her bed.

Suddenly, her door flies open, and my gaze falls on Esme in a tank top and boy shorts, face devoid of makeup, hair piled on top of her head in a messy bun. It makes her look... normal. And so damn beautiful my heart aches.

Makes me want to crush my lips to hers, erasing every last trace of Jameson from her body.

And her mind.

"What's happened?" She storms across the large space, looking from me to Anderson then back to me.

"Ezzy!" Anderson exclaims, a lazy smile crawling on his lips. "I was just telling Creed how bullshite this life is. He had the audacity to think that, when I'm king, I can actually change anything. That's like suggesting inmates can change how they're treated. Except most prisoners know why they're locked up. Us…" He trails off. "We did nothing to deserve this except be born. And it's fucked."

"You're drunk." She approaches, lightly patting his cheek. "Let's get you inside so you can sleep it off." She pushes her way into his apartment, heading in the general direction of the bedroom. As she does, I catch a whiff of her fragrant scent, the lavender aroma like a natural aphrodisiac.

"I'm not drunk," Anderson argues as I follow her down the hallway. "I'm telling the truth. This life sucks. I can't even bring a girl home, Ezzy. Not without the powers that be wanting to run a full background check and have her sign an NDA so I can shag her. Do you understand how fucked that is?"

Reaching his bedroom, I carefully lower him onto his bed.

"That was a stupid question," Anderson continues as Esme helps him out of his shoes and I grab a trash bin from the bathroom in case he needs to vomit. "Of course you know how fucked it is. They're planning to marry you off to a man you don't love."

"Jameson isn't that bad," she protests, keeping her gaze averted. "He does a lot of volunteer work."

"But do you actually *want* to be with him?"

Esme nervously glances at me before looking back at Anderson. "It doesn't matter what I want." Grabbing a blanket, she drapes it over his body.

"See. Fucked. We're both bloody fucked." He pulls the blanket up to his chin, curling onto his side, eyes closing. "Sometimes I wish I was never born."

On a long sigh, she leans down to kiss his forehead. "But I'm glad you were. I don't know what I'd do without you in my life. Just sleep it off, Anders. I'm sure you'll feel better in the morning."

"Not likely."

She stares at him for a beat, pulling her lips between her teeth. When she briefly looks to the ceiling, I catch a glint of moisture in her eyes. But she schools her frustration quickly, tousling Anderson's hair.

"I love you."

Leaving another kiss on his forehead, she turns, briefly catching my eyes before heading out of his bedroom.

I follow her through the living room, and into the foyer, quietly closing his apartment door behind me.

"Thanks for taking care of him tonight," she offers evenly. "I know my brother can be a bit much, especially when he drinks. So, thank you."

"I'll always be here for him, no matter what." I pause. "Just like I'll always be here for you. No matter what."

She lifts her gaze, lips parting, unease stifling the air between us.

This is the first time I've been this close to her since that day in the stables. Since I turned her down out of duty and obligation, essentially pushing her into Jameson's arms.

What choice did I have? Did either of us have? There are much bigger forces at play here, something I've reminded myself of every time I saw footage of them kissing, pretending to be madly in love.

Every time I found myself wishing I could kiss Esme whenever I want.

"Listen, Creed…"

At the sound of my name on her lips, I snap out of my thoughts.

"I'd like to apologize for my behavior the other day." She holds her head high but doesn't look at me. More like just past me. "I was caught off guard by how fast everything was progressing with Jameson. I said things I shouldn't have, put you in an uncomfortable position, and regret it." She finally floats her eyes to mine.

"You're Anders' best friend. He's being deployed soon, and I won't see him for six months. Since I'd like to spend as much time with him as possible before then, it follows that the two of us will also be spending a great deal of time together." She gestures between our bodies. "I'd like it if things can go back to the way they were. If we can both forget what I asked of you. It was inappropriate, and you have my sincere apologies."

Her words linger in the air for several long moments, neither one of us moving.

What do I even say to that?

Maybe if I were thinking clearly, I'd reply with something meaningful. The only response my brain manages to come up with is that she shouldn't be sorry.

That I wanted to accept her proposition.

That I still do.

But I can't tell her that.

Can I?

"Well…" She clears her throat when I remain mute. "I'm sure you want to get home. I'll check on Anders every so often." She crosses the foyer toward her apartment, stepping inside. "Good evening, Lieutenant Lawson." With a final cordial smile, she closes the door, leaving me alone.

I don't move for several moments, torn between what I want and what's expected of me.

All my life, I've chosen the latter. Enlisted in the military at eighteen. Trained for special teams and made it through without quitting, something not many people do. Became one of the few selected for the elite protection squad when I'm sworn into the royal guard. This is the path that's been charted for me since birth.

Just like Esme's path has been charted for her.

Am I really okay always wondering what if? With depriving myself of what I want simply out of duty or obligation?

I thought I was. Thought I was content with my place in this world.

Not anymore. Not when it means sacrificing my own happiness, even if that happiness only lasts a few hours.

So instead of doing what's expected of me, I step toward Esme's apartment and gently knock on her door, praying this doesn't turn out to be a colossal mistake.

CHAPTER ELEVEN

Esme

Why was that so damn difficult?

It shouldn't have been.

I should have been able to apologize to Creed, then walk away, my conscience clear, my indecent proposal no longer hanging over us like a cloud.

But that's not what happened at all. If anything, the way he simply stared at me with those soulful eyes only made things worse.

Made me want him more.

Made the ache even worse.

Pushing out a long sigh, I lean against the door, needing to feel grounded when my unease threatens to overwhelm me, making it difficult to breathe. But instead of giving in to my anxiety, I run through the coping mechanisms my therapist taught me years ago, starting with listing five things I see around me.

The moon shining through the large windows overlooking the courtyard. A bookcase holding all my favorite books. A photo of my mother and me riding horses on the table beside the couch. A half-drunk glass of wine I'd consumed before this evening's gala abandoned on the coffee table. And the ridiculously expensive shoes I'd kicked off the second I arrived home.

Four things I can touch. The cotton material of my tank top. A few strands of blonde hair that had escaped my messy bun. The wood grain of the door at my back. The smoothness of the wallpaper beside it.

Three things I can hear. My steady breathing. The whirring of the air conditioning. And a subtle knock on my door.

I stiffen, whirling around to stare at it. I don't even have to look through the peephole to know who stands on the other side. I feel his presence.

I always can.

Bringing my hand up to the doorknob, I slowly turn, words escaping when I'm met with Creed's intense stare.

Before I can form a single thought, he advances on me, pushing me into my apartment and kicking the door closed behind him. Rough hands cup my cheeks, my breath catching, heat prickling my skin as his eyes search mine for what feels like an eternity.

Then he presses his lips to mine, soft and invigorating.

I still, unsure how I'm supposed to react, especially after everything I just said to him. I didn't expect him to knock on my door and kiss me like this. But I can't ignore the fact that the warmth of his mouth on mine jumpstarts my heart, making me feel alive for the first time in years.

Probably since the last time his mouth was pressed so tenderly against mine.

Despite knowing how wrong this is, I part my lips,

moaning when he slides his tongue against mine, kissing me with more fever. More passion. More need. The raw need pouring from his kiss is enough to light me on fire.

To set me ablaze and incinerate every last part of me.

He moves a hand from my face, gripping my hip as he walks me backward until I hit the wall. When he presses his body against mine, I whimper at the feel of his hard length.

He tears his lips from mine, both of us panting as we stare at each other. I half expect him to snap out of whatever trance led him to knock on my door. Instead, his eyes remain locked on me, powerful and desperate.

"I fucked up," he declares, voice unwavering.

"About?"

"That day in the stables. I gave you the response I felt obligated to give. Not the one I *wanted* to give."

"Okay." I swallow hard, butterflies flapping their relentless wings in my stomach.

"I thought I was doing the right thing. But there's nothing right about you being forced to marry that guy. About the royal household essentially deciding who gets to be your first." He brings his hand back to my cheek, his touch gentle. "I want that to be me," he whispers, lips slowly descending toward mine.

But before I allow myself to fall victim to his kiss yet again, I place a finger over his mouth, stopping him. "I'm not looking for a pity fuck, Creed. If I wanted to have sex with someone who only wants to because they feel bad, I would have just let Jameson sleep with me."

His spine stiffens, jaw ticking, eyes flaming. "Has he tried anything with you? Has he done anything you didn't want?"

The anger in his voice sends a thrill through me. It shouldn't. I'm a strong, independent woman.

At least I try to be as independent as possible. As independent as the royal household will allow me to be.

But the protectiveness in his words, in his need to make sure Jameson hasn't harmed me, causes my pulse to increase even more, a need I didn't realize I had being satisfied.

"Jameson hasn't done anything wrong. While it's obvious he *wants* to sleep together, and I know I'll eventually have to, that's not at issue. What *is* at issue is that I want you to sleep with me because you want to. Not because you feel bad for me. If that's the only reason you're here, you—"

He yanks my body toward his, my protest lost in his touch, especially when he pulses his hard erection against me.

"Does this feel like someone who doesn't want you? Like someone who only wants to sleep with you because they feel bad for you?" He lowers his mouth toward mine, but changes direction at the last second, lips skimming against my neck. "Because I've wanted you for years, Esme. Thought of that kiss for years."

His teeth nip at my skin, the combination of pleasure and pain causing my core to clench, moisture pooling between my legs.

"Do you have any idea how many times I've jerked off thinking of it? Of you."

I moan, the sensual tone of his words making me feel things I've never experienced before, everything new and electrifying. One thing is certain. Creed Lawson has a great bedroom voice.

But is that reason enough to take this leap when I thought I'd made peace with my arrangement with Jameson?

"Yes, I initially turned you down because of our circumstances." He holds my face in his hands, forcing me to see the truth in his words. "But also because I knew I had no chance with you. Knew if I had you one time, I'd want you *all* the time. Knew I wouldn't be able to walk away."

"You'll have to, Creed. If that's a deal-breaker, I apologize, but nothing more can ever come of this. If we do this, it can only be once. Tonight. And when tonight's over, you need to walk away and pretend it never happened. Just like I will."

He stares at me for a beat, chewing on his bottom lip, brows pulled in. Finally, he nods his agreement. "I understand."

"Are you sure about that? You just said—"

He grabs my cheeks, mouth hovering over mine. "Having you for one night is better than not having you at all." His lips curve into a playful smirk as he waggles his brows. "I just need to make it sure it's a night you never forget."

CHAPTER TWELVE

Creed

I slam my lips against Esme's, tongue tangling with hers, sealing my agreement with a kiss. I didn't come over here with any misplaced expectations of her promising me more than tonight. Granted, it'll be torture to watch Jameson touch her, kiss her…marry her.

But I'll have something Jameson Gates never will. The privilege of being her first. Of showing her what intimacy should be like. What pleasure should feel like.

And that's exactly what I plan to do.

Tonight, I'll show her how incredible sex can be. Give her all the pleasure she deserves but has been sheltered from experiencing. Help her feel things she never thought possible.

Help *me* feel things I never thought possible.

Desperate to catch my breath, I tear away, gaze fixated on her kiss-swollen lips.

Swollen from *my* kiss.

It shouldn't turn me on this much, but god, I love seeing the evidence of my touch on her.

Want to see more of it on her body.

A craving more intense than I thought possible consumes me and I cover her mouth once more as I wrap her in my embrace. I was to feel her on every inch of me. But even with her frame molded perfectly to mine, it's not enough. Does nothing to satisfy the hunger that's increasing with every addictive swipe of her tongue.

I've thought about kissing Esme again for years, that tease of a kiss permanently etched in my mind. But this isn't the kiss of a shy seventeen-year-old girl. This is the kiss of a woman who knows what she's doing.

Jealousy bubbles at the idea that I'm not the first person she's kissed like this. That after tonight, she'll most likely never kiss me like this again. I can't think about that right now. Not if we only have one night.

Sliding a hand under her tank top, I graze the skin near her hipbone, savoring in how soft it is.

How *responsive* she is.

"Creed," she mewls, shuddering from my touch.

"Holy shit." I pepper hungry kisses down her jawline before locking my eyes with hers. "Make that sound again."

I crush my lips back to hers, hand on her hip as I lead her through her living room and down the hallway, easily finding her bedroom, since her apartment is the exact mirror to Anderson's. When the back of her legs hit her four-post bed, I reluctantly pull my mouth from hers.

I don't take time to appreciate my surroundings, even though this is the first time I've been in her bedroom. The opulent furnishings and expensive décor will only serve a reminder that we shouldn't do this. That I don't belong in her world.

Tuning it all out, I lay her down and crawl on top of her, focusing on her and only her. Which isn't too difficult to do, especially when she hooks a leg around my waist. The heat between her legs makes me want to rip off our clothes and sink deep inside her, to hell with foreplay.

But I need to be patient. Need to take my time worshiping her. Make sure tonight is one she'll never forget.

Because I sure as hell won't.

Snaking down her body, I leave a trail of kisses along her neck and collarbone before stopping at her chest, her nipples visible through her thin tank top. I smooth a hand over a breast, my touch barely there. But that doesn't matter. She still squirms, panting in anticipation.

As I lower my mouth to her and take her covered nipple between my teeth, she releases the same whimper that drove me wild mere moments ago.

One I'll probably hear in my dreams from now on.

"Creed," she exhales, my name more of a plea than a moan.

"What do you need, princess?" I briefly meet her eyes before returning my attention to her chest, about to give her other breast the same treatment.

She clutches my cheeks, forcing my gaze back to hers, nothing but raw determination and desire within.

"You. Inside me. Now."

Her words cause me to harden, my pulse kicking up, especially when she drags my mouth to within a whisper of hers, her breath kissing my lips.

"I need you to fuck me, Creed. Right. Fucking. Now."

I swallow hard, my dick straining against my pants, begging to come out and play. I'm not sure what I expected from Esme. Her inexperience doesn't seem to affect her, not like I thought it would. Then again, I should have known better. Esme isn't the type of woman to stay quiet. When she knows what she wants, she goes after it.

Like she did with me.

"Who knew the princess had such a dirty mouth?" I muse, bringing my fingers to her nipple and squeezing. She yelps at the initial contact, then moans, succumbing to the pleasure.

"This is what you do to me, Creed. You make me forget everything. Everything other than feeling good. And I've never felt so goddamn good."

"Good." I press another kiss to her mouth. "But as tempting as fucking you sounds, I have other plans."

With a smirk, I push off her.

"Other plans?" Her lips part, brows scrunched in confusion. "But we agreed. We're doing this. Tonight. I told you that—"

I silence her with a kiss. "I need to taste you first," I murmur against her mouth. "Need to make you come with my tongue. Need to lick your pussy. Need to bury my face between your legs and give you an orgasm so intense you go fucking blind."

"Holy shit," she whimpers as I thrust my tongue into her mouth, giving her a taste of what she can expect when I put my lips on other parts of her body.

"Can I do that, Esme? Can I fuck your pussy with my tongue?"

"God, yes." She revels in my touch as I move back down her body, lifting her tank over her head and tossing it onto the floor.

When my gaze falls on her breasts, my jaw tenses, need coursing through me.

"Goddamn, baby." Cupping them in my hands, I lower myself back to her, taking a nipple in my mouth, flicking my tongue against the pert bud. "You are so fucking perfect." I run a hand along her torso as she digs her fingers into my hair, her body quivering, desire consuming her.

When I push her shorts aside, she holds her breath.

So do I.

Until I run a finger through her slickness and both of us sigh simultaneously. I bring my mouth to her other breast, thumb pressing against her clit as I slowly ease a finger inside her.

She gasps, lips parting, chest heaving.

"You're so wet. Say it's for me."

Tongue circling her nipple, I massage her insides, loving how she pulses beneath me.

"It's for you, Creed. I need you. Please."

"I've needed you for years. Thought of this moment for years."

She moans as I move from her breast, dragging my tongue down her stomach, dipping it into her belly button. All while she moves against my fingers, chasing her orgasm.

"Do you like fucking my hand, you greedy girl?"

"God yes." She closes her eyes, circling her hips in time with the motion I set. Her body grows taut, her release imminent.

"Good to know."

Abruptly, I remove my hand from her shorts. It takes every ounce of willpower I have not to bring it up to my lips. But I want my first taste to be all her, not from my fingers.

"Are you fucking kidding?" she pants, stomach rolling through her labored breaths, eyes wide in frustration and disbelief. "Why did you stop? I was about to... You know."

"Say it," I demand. "Say what you were about to do."

She swallows hard. "Come. I was about to come."

"Is that how you want to come? On my hand? Wouldn't you rather come on my tongue?"

She pinches her lips into a playful smile that makes my chest fill with warmth and affection. "Who knew the body-guard had such a dirty mouth?"

"This is what you do to me, Esme," I murmur seductively, repeating her words from mere moments ago as I tease her with my erection. "You make me forget everything." I capture her lips in mine. "Everything other than making you feel good. And I plan on making you feel so fucking good."

"Then what are you waiting for?" Our gazes lock as she lifts her hips.

I hook my fingers into her shorts and slide them down her legs, tossing them onto the floor with the rest of her clothes. Then I push her thighs open, settling between them. As I run a light finger along her slit, she whimpers.

"More?" I ask, glancing up at her.

She nods quickly. "More."

I return my attention to her, my touch more decisive this time as I press my thumb to her clit.

"More?"

She fists her hands, breathing labored. "More," is her gritted response.

I move closer, blowing on her as I tease her entrance with a finger, not slipping it all the way in.

"More?" I ask yet again.

"Yes. Goddammit. Give me more," she heaves out. "Give me all of it."

Grinning at how vocal she is, I sweep my tongue against her. She releases something between a scream and a moan, her body arching into me before falling back onto the mattress, the tension rolling off her in waves.

"So fucking sweet," I murmur between licks.

I've fantasized about doing this an unhealthy number of times, especially considering she's the Princess Royal and my best friend's sister. Two big reasons I *shouldn't* be doing this. But I can't walk away now even if a bomb were about to drop on the city.

Which makes me wonder if I'll be okay walking away when our one night together is over.

But I'm not going to think about that now. I'm going to do something I've never done. I'm going to live in the moment.

Because this moment, my tongue teasing Esme's clit, is fucking hot.

Hotter than I ever could have imagined, especially when she moves against me, fucking my face, encouraging me to lick her faster, deeper, harder.

"I don't think I'll ever get enough of this pussy."

"More." She bucks against me, running her fingers through my hair, nails scratching my scalp. When I look up, I'm surprised to see her watching me.

And it makes my dick even harder.

"I need more."

"I'll give you everything," I respond, circling my tongue around her clit as I press a finger inside her. When I add another one, stretching her as much as possible, she gasps, body momentarily stilling.

"You okay?" I meet her eyes, sliding my fingers out of her.

She nods quickly, chest heaving.

"Words, Esme. I need your words. Need to know this is okay."

She takes several more breaths. When she returns her gaze to mine, it's full of hunger and potent lust.

"I'm far better than okay, Creed." She places her hands

on my shoulders, gently nudging me back between her legs. "Keep doing what you were just doing, and don't you dare stop until you make me come."

"I love that dirty mouth, princess," I remark, her words causing a renewed fire to course through my veins, an ache settling low in my belly. "I've been wanting to do this for years." I move my tongue along her clit once more, pushing a finger inside before adding another. "Been wanting to watch your body shake. Drink every drop as you come on my face."

"Creed," she moans, throwing an arm over her head as she pulses with the rhythm I set.

I try to take my time and enjoy the way she moves. The way she moans my name. The way she fucking tastes.

But with each flick of my tongue, each circle of my fingers, each declaration of how much I want her, she becomes putty in my hands, her body climbing higher and higher until she's nothing more than a bundle of sensation.

"Oh, fuck! Creed!" she screams, her cries echoing against the walls. Her body quivers and shakes, but I don't stop licking her, massaging her, pushing her. I need every ounce of pleasure I can possibly get out of her. Want to remember them all. Want to savor them all.

Want to own them all.

When she has nothing left, she falls slack against the mattress. Then she clutches my face, pulling me toward her lips.

"Lieutenant Lawson," she pants, struggling to catch her breath. "I do believe that tongue should be categorized as a deadly weapon."

"And why's that?"

She threads her fingers through my hair, tugging at it,

and I arch into her touch. I'll never tire of feeling her nails dig into my scalp.

"Because I'm pretty sure it just killed me. This *is* heaven, right? I've died and gone to orgasm heaven. That's the only possible explanation for such a mind-blowing experience."

A throaty chuckle tumbles from me as I wrap her in my arms, never wanting to let her go. I bury my head in the crook of her neck, inhaling her delicious scent.

"I take it you enjoyed that?" I meet her eyes.

"I'm not quite sure there's a word in the English language to properly convey just how *much* I enjoyed that." Her lips seek out mine, our kiss tender at first. "How much I needed that."

She draws me closer, tongue swiping against the seam of my lips, coaxing mine to part. When she wraps a leg around my waist and pulses, I release a needy growl.

"Don't make me wait any longer to have you." I move my mouth to her neck, teeth grazing her skin. "To feel you."

"I'm yours."

"Mine," I repeat, as if my confirmation would make it a possibility.

We both know she's not mine. That she never *can* be mine. But right now, in this space, that doesn't matter. We can live in the fantasy. Even if it's fleeting.

"Yours." She grabs the back of my neck, urging my lips toward hers. "Take me, Creed."

CHAPTER THIRTEEN

Esme

C Creed's fiery eyes remain glued to mine as he climbs off me, fingers going to the top button of his shirt. As much as I'd love to watch him strip for me, if this is our only night together, and it is, I want to experience everything Creed Lawson has to offer.

And that includes helping him undress.

When I stand from the bed, Creed stops, surveying me with worry.

Until I bring my fingers to where he left off and lean toward him, lips skimming the scruff of his unshaven jawline. "Please, allow me."

With a subtle bob of his head, he drops his hands to his side, watching me with hunger as I leisurely unbutton his shirt. It's a test in patience. Not just for him, but me, too.

I've often imagined how Creed would look shirtless, especially over the past few days. The way he fills out his clothes makes it clear he has an amazing body. But when I unfasten the final button and push his shirt down his arms, every inch of him defined muscles and hard edges, I realize my fantasies were woefully inadequate.

The man is a walking Adonis.

And for tonight, he's all mine.

Just for tonight.

Smoothing a hand down his chest, I meet his stare, relishing in the unwavering greed filling his dark eyes. His jaw ticks, muscles taut, chest heaving. All because of my touch. It makes me feel incredibly…powerful. When I palm his crotch, he releases a hiss, lust consuming him.

"Let's lose these, too," I murmur in a sultry voice as I run a lithe finger along the waist of his pants. "What do you think about that?"

He brings his hand to my face, long fingers cupping my cheek as his thumb brushes that spot right below my earlobe. It's an innocent touch, but the way he holds me, so resolute and assured, sets my insides ablaze.

"I think that's a bloody brilliant idea."

Lips finding mine, he coaxes my mouth open, his tongue enticing me as I fumble with the button on his jeans. When I lower the zipper, unable to avoid brushing my hand against his erection, my pulse kicks up even more. I tease my fingers along the waistband of his briefs and he pulls out of our kiss, his eyes more dangerous than I've ever seen.

Slowly, I push his jeans and boxer briefs down his muscular legs, swallowing hard at his impressive size. Once he steps out of his shoes and discards the rest of his clothes, he returns to me.

If you'd told me that before the night ended, Creed Lawson would be standing naked in my bedroom about to take my virginity, I would have laughed. He seemed so resolute in his reasons why this couldn't happen.

I did, too.

At least, I thought I did.

Maybe, deep down, a part of me knew we'd always end up here.

Maybe, deep down, a part of Creed knew that, too.

My heart hammering, I run my hand across his chest, along the ridges of his abs, and down that delicious little V before wrapping my fingers around his erection, stroking him.

"Jesus," he exhales, closing his eyes, face tight, breathing uneven.

Encouraged by his response, I increase my motions, thumb spreading the bit of pre-cum that escaped his tip. I edge toward him, peppering kisses to his chest before dragging my tongue along his warm skin.

As I start to lower myself to my knees, he grips my wrist and growls, "Stop."

Dropping my hold on him, I dart my confused eyes toward his, cheeks heating. "Was I doing it wrong?" I lower my head. "I don't have a lot of experience with this kind of thing. I just thought—"

"Look at me, Esme."

Unable to deny him, I slowly lift my gaze. He releases my wrist to cup my face, his eyes filled with admiration.

"You weren't doing it wrong." A smile teases his lips as he adjusts his stance, his erection brushing against my stomach. "In fact, you were doing it *too* well." He lowers his mouth to mine. "So well that if I let you keep going, I would have come in your hand. And I can't have that. Not when I'm so desperate to bury my cock deep inside you."

My god, the things that come out of this man's mouth. I doubt I'll ever get enough of it. Will think back to all the wanton and needy words he growled for the rest of my life.

He crushes his lips against mine, and I moan, overcome with the combination of his words and the feel of his body surrounding mine.

"There it is," he croons as he walks me backward a few steps toward the bed. "The sound that drives me fucking crazy."

His hand on my back, he lowers me onto the mattress before settling between my legs. When he does, I whimper, his erection pressed against my heat making me pant with need. He buries his head in the crook of my neck, the scratching of his jawline against me driving me wild. Then he pulls back.

"Are you sure about this?" The sincerity in his voice is a complete change from his lust-filled declarations mere moments ago.

"Creed, we're both naked and your dick is less than a breath away from thrusting into me." I laugh nervously. "I think it's too late to ask if I'm sure about this. Changing my mind now would just be cruel."

"I don't care about that." He brushes a rogue tendril of hair behind my ear, his touch achingly tender. "I won't do anything you don't want me to. That you're not ready for. It's not too late to change your mind, Esme. Even if I'm inside you and it's too much, you can still change your mind."

"Do you *want* me to change my mind?"

"Fuck no," he replies without a moment's hesitation. "Don't you feel how desperate I am for you?" He teases me with his erection, the feel of him on my clit causing a jolt of electricity to zap my core, my skin on fire.

I grab the back of his head, forcing his lips to mine. "Then stop procrastinating and fuck me, Creed. This is my choice. I can't remember ever wanting anything as much as I want this." I wrap my legs around him, slowly circling my hips. "I can't remember ever wanting anyone as much as I want you."

With a groan, he deepens the kiss, but keeps it short, pulling back to stand. He picks up his jeans and fishes a condom out of his wallet.

"Was this your plan all along, Lieutenant Lawson?" I prop myself up on my elbows, half joking, half serious.

"Sorry to say it wasn't. I usually keep a few condoms on me in case Anders—"

"Say no more," I interject, not wanting to bring my brother into this. Not wanting a reminder of one of the reasons we shouldn't do this.

He's about to rip open the packet, but pauses, arching a single brow, silently asking me one more time if I'm sure. I don't even hesitate in nodding. His eyes locked with mine, he tears the packet and rolls on the condom. Then he returns to me, expression calm as he brings his erection to my entrance, easing his tip just inside.

At that first hint of pressure, I inhale sharply, a flash of trepidation overcoming me.

"You okay?" Creed asks.

I close my eyes and nod, reminding myself I want this. That I need this. That I deserve this. Deserve to make one decision for myself, despite any apprehension about how much it will hurt. And that's all this is. I *want* to do this with Creed. I just know it will be painful. But if there's anyone who will do everything to make sure it's not, it's this man.

"Words, Esme." He feathers his mouth against mine. "I need to know you're okay. No closing your eyes or giving me the silent treatment. Like I told you. I refuse to do anything you don't want me to."

I draw in a deep breath, returning my gaze to his. "I'm okay. Just... Do it."

He straightens. "You sure?"

"Stop asking me if I'm sure and just fuck me, for crying out loud."

"Gladly." He pushes inside a little more, pressure mounting with every second.

Leaning toward me, he touches his lips to mine and murmurs, "I'm sorry."

I don't have a chance to ask what he's apologizing for before he drives forward in a single harsh thrust.

I scream, but he swallows my cries, kissing me sweetly through the pinching and burning. He doesn't move yet. Instead, he stays here, giving me time to work through the pain.

"I'm so sorry," he comforts again. But he still doesn't move. Just kisses my cheeks. My lips. My neck.

As he works his way to my breast, circling my nipple with his tongue, I moan, any momentary discomfort waning, replaced with increased pleasure.

I close my eyes, wrapping my legs around his waist as I run my fingers through his hair. Instinct takes over and I slowly pulse against him.

He cups my face, mouth a breath from mine.

"You feel so damn good. So soft. So warm." His grip on me tightens as he finally moves inside of me, each retreat and thrust gentle at first. "So mine."

I tighten the grip my legs have on him, pulling him closer, needing to feel him everywhere all at once.

"Yours," I promise as I lose myself in him, not caring about the impossibility of ever being his.

In this space, the real world doesn't exist. All that does is this incredible sensation of bliss I never knew existed. If I did, maybe I would have shunned the royal household's rules years ago and had sex. I'm glad I didn't, though. Glad I waited for Creed. Something about this just feels…right, regardless of how wrong it probably is.

But I'm not going to worry about that now. Not going to allow the little time I have with Creed to be riddled with guilt or regret. Instead, I'm going to bask in the moment and pretend we're two normal people finally succumbing to our desires after years of pent-up want.

It's not that far from the truth.

"Mine," he repeats, this time more forceful, his motions mirroring his tone.

I relax my legs, scratching my fingers up and down his back, relishing in the groves of his muscles. "Yours."

"Mine," he says once more, thrusting into me at the same time.

"Yours," I whimper again, grabbing his face in my hands. "Don't hold back, Creed. If we only have tonight, I want to feel you everywhere. Want to know how wild it can be."

A roar rips from his throat as he slams his lips to mine, his kiss needy and desperate. A delicious shiver of ecstasy ripples through me when he increases his motions, each drive harder and deeper.

"Oh, god," I exhale.

"God's not fucking you, princess. I am." He covers my nipple with his mouth and my core clenches, body careening toward that peak once more.

I've heard my friends talk about multiple orgasms like it's the Holy Grail of sex. Something so many people seek but never find. I didn't think it was possible for me.

Then again, I didn't think sex with Creed was possible, either.

"Don't fight it, Esme." Creed forces my eyes to his, raw and steadfast as he drives into me. "Just let go. Let me make you feel good." He straightens, pressing his thumb to my clit.

I move against him, a myriad of sensations filling me. My chest heaves. Pulse races. Muscles clench. Fire scalds my veins, everything so intense and pronounced I'm convinced I'm on the brink of shattering into a thousand pieces.

If I am, I could think of far worse ways to die than death by orgasm.

"That's it. Just let yourself feel. Let yourself feel me."

"I feel you. I feel you everywhere." I swallow hard, gripping the sheets below me. I need something to keep me grounded when I'm about to catapult into the atmosphere, never to return to earth.

He leans down, lips brushing mine as he rubs my clit with even more intensity. "Come for me," he demands, breathing ragged. "Let me feel your pussy clench around my cock. Let me hear you scream for me, princess."

Powerless to fight it any longer, I detonate, my cries of ecstasy echoing against the high ceilings. He quickly covers my mouth with his, swallowing my screams as he completely unravels me.

"Good girl," he grunts, increasing his motions. "You're such a good fucking girl."

I didn't think it possible to come from words alone, but Creed's praise does it for me, prolonging my ecstasy. Or it could be from his frantic rhythm as he pushes into me, a man obsessed.

I close my eyes, reveling in the sensation, knowing he's on the brink of losing what little control he managed to hold onto.

"Look at me, Esme."

I snap my gaze to his.

"I want to look into your eyes while I fuck you."

Holy shit.

This man and his mouth. It's going to be my undoing.

Then again, I'm pretty sure it's already completely destroyed me.

He straightens to kneel, eyes boring into mine. He grabs a leg, hooking it over his shoulder, driving into me with even more force, each thrust more punishing than the last.

Taking a page from his own playbook, I pull him toward me and nibble on his earlobe as I murmur, "Come for me."

"Fuck," he exhales, pistoning into me several more times before he jerks, a growl thundering from his throat.

Finally, his muscles give out and he falls on top of me, the only sound that of our ragged breathing. He drags me into his arms, peppering soft kisses along my collarbone.

"Jesus, Esme. That was…" He shivers, meeting my eyes. "I have no words."

I run a hand through his hair, relishing in the warmth of his sweat-dotted skin against mine. "So I'm guessing it didn't suck."

"Not even close. It was…" He shakes his head, as if searching for a word that simply doesn't exist. "Incredible." He smooths a finger along my torso. "You're incredible."

"You're not so bad yourself," I retort in a light voice, pushing down the ball of emotion that unexpectedly forms in my throat over the idea of never experiencing anything remotely close to this again. "And we should definitely add your dick to the list of dangerous weapons. In fact, I think it should be at the top, right above your tongue."

He throws his head back and laughs, a moment of levity before he schools his expression. "How do you feel?"

"A little sore." When I see the concern in his gaze, I touch my lips to his. "But it's a good sore."

"Good." He briefly deepens the exchange, then rolls off me to stand. "Just give me one second." Leaving a kiss on my temple, he strides toward the bathroom.

When he returns, the condom is gone and he holds a wet washcloth, bringing it between my legs as he lowers himself back to the bed.

"I can do that." I sit up and reach for the cloth, feeling somewhat embarrassed when I notice the tinge of blood on the material.

"Let me take care of you."

I meet his pleading gaze and nod.

This is a man I just slept with. Who I allowed to take my virginity. Yet this gesture feels much more intimate than anything we just did.

When he's done, he stands and disappears into the bathroom once more. I take the opportunity to slip out of bed and tug my tank top and shorts back on. As I fix my just-fucked hair back into its bun, Creed reappears, pausing awkwardly when he sees I'm dressed.

"I um... I guess I should go." He glances toward the window, the first light of day filtering through. "I probably shouldn't be here when the staff starts to arrive."

A part of me wants him to stay. Wants to know what it feels like to fall asleep in his arms. But this was never about that. It couldn't be. This was just sex. Just once.

Nothing more.

"That's probably for the best," I agree, eyes purposefully avoiding his naked frame.

He hesitates, as if waiting for me to change my mind.

But I can't.

It would only end in disaster for both of us. Him more so than me.

Finally, he walks to his pile of clothes and pulls on his briefs, turning away as he dresses. This feels so wrong. But what choice do we have?

We don't, both of us victims of circumstance and tradition.

Once Creed has his jeans on, he grabs his shirt and faces me as he buttons it.

"You'll be okay?"

It's a loaded question. I'm not sure if I've ever been okay. Or if I ever will be. But that's too deep of a conversation for this late. Or early, depending on how you look at it.

"Of course. You?"

He smiles, but it doesn't reach his eyes. "Of course."

Once he finishes buttoning his shirt, he puts on his shoes, then steps toward me. My breath hitches when he leans down, stopping just shy of my mouth.

"Give me one last kiss. One last taste. Before we go back to being who we are to each other. Please. One last kiss goodbye."

When he puts it that way, I'm completely powerless to refuse him.

Even though I fear this one last kiss will shatter me.

Nodding, I whisper, "One last kiss goodbye."

"One last kiss goodbye," he repeats as he presses his mouth to mine, dragging my body against his, his arms swallowing me one last time.

Too soon, he drops his hold on me, increasing the distance between us. He meets my gaze, lips parting, as if about to say something. Make some emotion-filled plea about why we don't have to walk away after experiencing something so incredible.

Instead, he sighs, turning and disappearing from my room without a single glance back.

PART II

Secrets

*There are no secrets that
time does not reveal.*

~ Jean Racine

CHAPTER FOURTEEN

Esme

They all know. I'm convinced of it.

It's probably just a result of my guilty conscience, but I can't shake the feeling that everyone on my household staff is aware of what I did in the early hours of the morning with a man other than the one I'm supposed to be in love with.

How I invited Creed into my bedroom.

How I let him whisper his darkest desires to me.

How all it took for me to fall under his spell was a touch of his hand and the warmth of his lips.

How I didn't even think twice about the possible consequences of our secret tryst.

Until this morning, now that the haze of my two earth-shattering orgasms has finally cleared.

In the light of day, I can't help but feel like my indiscretions are written all over my body.

And these paranoid feelings of suspicion are amplified

further the instant Anderson storms into my dining room, determination in his expression and fire in his eyes.

Ignoring my butler's question of whether he'd like any coffee, my brother plops into the chair opposite me, gaze unwavering.

Watchful.

Accusatory.

My pulse increases, hands going clammy as I wait for him to speak. There's obviously something on his mind.

I fear I already know what that is.

"I need to get away," he finally announces after what feels like an eternity.

"Okay…" I draw out, doing my best to hide my relief.

If Anderson knew about Creed, he would have led with that.

"And you're coming with me." He gives my butler an appreciative smile as he places a cup of coffee in front of him.

"Coming where?"

"To the coast. I just…" He tugs at his hair, making it even messier than it already is.

Despite protocol, Anderson's still in the clothes he passed out in last night, shirt wrinkled, jeans disheveled, happy to ignore the rules. On the other hand, I'm wearing a conservative dress and heels, makeup applied, hair flowing to my mid-back in soft waves, prepared for a day of speeches and public appearances, this time with Jameson at my side.

Truthfully, I made sure my appearance this morning was in line with the rules, considering I pretty much broke every rule in the book last night.

"I need a break." My brother's voice is strained. "Need to go somewhere I can have some semblance of normalcy. We can go to the coast like we used when we were teenagers.

Go sailing. Sit on the beach. I don't care what we do, so long as we do it away from prying eyes watching our every move."

I study my brother as he brings his coffee up to his mouth, taking a long sip. I can't remember ever seeing him this frazzled. This…frustrated.

"Do you honestly think the royal household is going to allow me to just take off and head to the coast?" I retort, mindful to keep my voice somewhat lowered.

I know better than anyone I'm never truly alone in this place, even if it *is* my apartment. Another reason last night was a horrible idea.

"Not likely." I stab my fork into a piece of melon. "Not when Jameson and I just announced our relationship. My schedule for the next month is filled with engagements."

"What better way to show the world how in love you are than on a beach, enjoying some time out of the spotlight? Gianna would salivate over the idea of the media posting candid shots of the young lovers sharing a romantic kiss on the beach. That's much better than a bunch of staged photographs at some ribbon cutting or diplomatic dinner."

"So you want to go away, but you want Jameson to come, too?" I square my shoulders, posture straight as I've been taught my entire life. It's a stark contrast to Anderson, who remains slouched in his chair.

"Why not?" He steals a few berries from my plate. "He's a decent bloke. I'm sure he wouldn't mind some time away from all this bullshit, too. Especially since he's been thrown into the lion's den, so to speak."

I part my lips, about to feign ignorance and ask what he means, but I can't disrespect my brother like that.

When we were thrust into the spotlight after my uncle's death, we made a promise that we'd always tell each other everything. That we'd never keep secrets.

I can't pretend I want to be with Jameson, that our relationship is real. Not when Anderson is more than aware royal marriages aren't based on love, but on who has the most to offer the monarchy.

And Jameson Gates' family made the winning bid.

"Won't you feel...awkward? Especially if, as you put it, it's supposed to be a romantic weekend away for Jameson and me. You'd be a third wheel."

"We'll invite more people. I'm sure Harriet and Marius would like to get to know Jameson better, too. I'll also reach out to Jasper, Maggie, Cody, and Penny. The usual suspects." He winks.

"So that's it?" I ask somewhat hesitantly. "No one else?"

"No one else," he confirms. "Oh, and Creed, of course. But that goes without saying."

I grit out a smile, pretending as if the mere mention of his name doesn't cause a fluttering low in my belly. The memory of the way he moved inside me is still fresh in my mind, the heat of his touch still warming my skin.

Everything about last night was unexpected. From Creed barging into my apartment and telling me he changed his mind. To the way our bodies seemed to be perfectly in tune. To the words that came out of his mouth. The things he murmured, praising me for taking his cock as good as I did, only added to the experience. And that's what sex with Creed Lawson was.

An experience.

But it's an experience I need to forget.

Something that won't be possible if we're in the same house. Granted, our family's villa on the coast is quite large. But I'd hoped my hectic public appearance schedule would limit my interactions with him.

If I go with Anderson, I'll not just see Creed daily. We'll be under the same roof.

That's a disaster waiting to happen.

"Listen…" Anderson clutches my hand, pulling my eyes to his, "I'm getting out of here regardless of whether you join me. I've been stationed out of the base here since last year. You've only been back a few weeks, so this place may not have sucked the life out of you yet. It will. It always does. So, I'd really like for you to come with me."

"Anders, I don't—"

"Imagine if something horrible happened on my next deployment." He gives me his puppy-dog eyes, everything about him pathetic. "You'd have to live with the regret of not granting me this one final wish for the rest of your life. Is that something you want to put yourself through? I know I wouldn't."

I roll my eyes, playfully shoving him. "That's pretty low, using your deployment to your advantage. You truly are a horrible person."

"But you love me," he sings.

"I can't deny that."

Grabbing the napkin from my lap, I dab at my mouth before placing it over my plate, signaling I'm done eating. My butler swoops in, removing my meal in mere seconds.

A reminder that someone's always watching.

Since arriving home, I've longed for the freedom I had in Paris. Sure, my security detail kept a watchful eye on me, but it wasn't like it is here. Constantly being catered to by the royal staff.

Or more appropriately, being suffocated.

I see it in Anderson's eyes.

I feel it in my heart.

We need a break.

Before it's too late.

"Okay." I push out a sigh. "I'll see what I can work out. You're right. I'm sure Gianna would move mountains if it meant getting photos of Jameson and me enjoying a romantic getaway on the coast." I try to hide the sour taste in my mouth at the thought.

"You're the best." He jumps out of his chair, wrapping his arms around me and kissing my temple. "I promise to give you a holiday you'll never forget."

I meet his smile, feigning enthusiasm. But I can't shake the feeling this holiday has the potential to blow up in my face.

CHAPTER FIFTEEN

Creed

"You're going to the coast?"

I stop as I'm about to climb into my SUV, looking up to find my brother standing on the sidewalk outside of my building in what was once an industrial area on the outskirts of the city. Most of the warehouses have been turned into apartments and lofts. While the rents are starting to rise, since this area is becoming much more desirable, it's still affordable for someone on a military salary.

"I am," I tell him, doing my best to keep my voice even. The last thing I need is for Adam to pick up on my reluctance or unease.

Hell, I'm surprised Anderson didn't pick up on it when he told me about his plan to head to the coast for a holiday. Any other time, I would have jumped at the opportunity to go to the beach, considering I haven't taken any time for myself over the past eight years. And I most likely won't be able to take much time for myself once I'm sworn into the guard.

That was before I learned Esme will also be there.

As well as Jameson.

I haven't seen her since I walked out of her bedroom over a week ago. It's probably a good thing. I don't know how I'm supposed to act around her.

Well, I know how I'm *supposed* to act.

I'm just not sure if I *can* act that way.

If I can be around her and resist the urge to wrap her in my arms and kiss her.

If I can resist the urge to break every single bone in Jameson's hand when he touches her.

"How long will you be gone?" Adam crosses his arms in front of his chest, his biceps stretching his black t-shirt, his physique as fit as mine.

"Why?" I lean against my car, mirroring his posture. "Are you going to water my plants for me?" I chide.

"I'm just curious. According to Her Highness' private secretary, she cleared her schedule through the end of the month."

"Which is ten days. I postponed my induction date so I could spend some time with Anderson—"

"Gabriel," Adam corrects, as much a stickler for the rules and protocol as my father.

While I endeavor to adhere to the rules myself, something that was ingrained into me even before I enlisted, I still struggle with referring to my friend as his given name. What will be his regnal name once he's coronated.

He went by Anderson before his life changed and he jumped from seventh in line to second, then first. And he still prefers to go by Anderson, since his father is Gabriel. Until

I'm under an obligation to refer to him as Gabriel, I'll call my friend the name he prefers.

Because he's still my friend, royal bloodline be damned.

"That's what I'm doing," I continue, ignoring my brother. "I'm heading to the coast to spend some time with him."

"And his sister."

Brows furrowed, I study Adam, wondering what he's getting at. Why did he specifically bring up Esme when several other people will also be there?

"Yes." I straighten my spine, arms dropping to my side. "And his sister."

"Are you sure this is a good idea?" He narrows his dark eyes on me.

My mouth grows dry, a nervous fluttering in my stomach. I keep my gaze trained on him, not wanting him to notice a single hint of trepidation.

"Why wouldn't it be?"

Uncrossing his arms, he steps toward me. "I see the way you look at her, Creed," he whispers.

"Who?"

"Don't play dumb. You've had a thing for the Princess Royal for years."

"I haven't *seen* her in years," I argue in my defense. "Not until a few weeks ago."

"I saw the way you looked at her when you were younger."

"I was a horny teenager. I looked at anything with boobs like I wanted to hump them."

"And I see the way you look at her now, too."

"I've barely seen her since she got back," I scoff, averting my eyes so he can't peel away the lies and reveal the truth hidden underneath it all.

Did one of the guards at Gladwell notice me leave in the early hours of the morning and tell my brother? If that were the case, Adam would have brought it up the second he learned about it. He wouldn't beat around the bush like this.

Hell, if that were the case, I would have already received an earful from Anderson.

Instead, my friend all but coerced me to come to the beach with him for the next ten days, where I'll have no choice but to live under the same roof as Esme and Jameson.

"But you *have* seen her. You might be able to fool everyone else. Hell, you might even be able to fool yourself." He steps closer. "I'm your brother. I know you better than anyone. Don't forget who you came to whenever you needed advice about girls. Pretty sure I'm the one who bought you your first box of condoms."

I run a hand over my face, unable to deny the truth in his statement. With five years between us, Adam's always been there for me, especially regarding things no hormone-crazed teenage boy would ever want to discuss with his father. Like girls and sex. That would require my father to have been around. He wasn't, always putting his obligation to the royal guard above everything else, even to this day.

"It's nothing," I say finally, hoping to placate him. "Just a stupid infatuation that's probably the result of being surrounded by an overabundance of testosterone in the military."

His analytical gaze sweeps over me for a beat before he relaxes his posture and pushes out a laugh. "I know how lonely it can be out there." He gives me an understanding smile before schooling his expression once more.

"But don't forget who you are. I don't need to remind you that the caste system is still alive and well, even in the twenty-first century. Esme's a princess. And she's dating the equivalent of a goddamn prince. The public loves them, so if I were you, I'd forget any of those adolescent notions you once had. Even if Jameson Gates weren't in the picture, the royal household would never approve.

"Just because Dad is His Majesty's chief protection officer, and you're close with the heir apparent, it doesn't mean we have the same privileges they do. Prince Gabriel and Princess Esme are not your friends. Not anymore. They can't be. Not when it's our job to serve them. The sooner you come to terms with that, the easier it will be when you're inducted into the guard and officially become nothing more than the hired help."

"You don't need to lecture me, Adam," I shoot back in a harsh tone, his words stinging more than I thought they would.

Because they serve as a reminder that any foolish dreams I've had are just that... Foolish.

"I get it. Okay?"

"I don't mean to lecture you." He squeezes my shoulder. "I just don't want you to get hurt. And that's precisely what will happen. You're the one who will get hurt. Who stands to lose everything you've worked for."

"But I won't. There's nothing going on between us."

It's not a complete lie. Technically, there *isn't* anything going on. We shared one night, then walked away.

Like we agreed.

Except since that night, I haven't been able to stop thinking about her. About the way she moved. The way she felt. The way she responded to my touch.

Which is why I should stay here. Call Anderson and tell him something came up so I can't make it. Spending ten days in the same house as Jameson and Esme will be torture.

"Good." Seemingly satisfied with my reassurances, Adam gives my shoulder a final squeeze. "Enjoy your time away."

"You should take some time off, too. Maybe get away with Rory before the baby comes this fall."

He shrugs. "I may not be going with Her Highness, since Prince Gabriel's protection team has it covered, but I still have work to do. With Esme dating Jameson Gates, it requires more preparation to advance her public appearances. This will give me a chance to work on that."

This time, Adam's the one who doesn't look directly at me. It could be nothing, but I can't shake the feeling there's more to his statement. That he's hiding something.

But what?

The thought nags at me as I hop into my SUV and begin the three-hour drive along the coast to the royal family's villa.

I just pray whatever my brother's hiding doesn't involve my one forbidden night with the Princess Royal.

CHAPTER SIXTEEN

Creed

As if I'm not sufficiently aware of the gross disparity between Esme and me as it is, when I navigate the tree-covered cobblestone driveway and park in front of a sprawling three-story villa set on several acres of prime beach-front property, I'm reminded yet again how vastly different our lives are.

When we were younger, it was never on the forefront of our minds. Probably because Anderson and Esme didn't *want* to think about it. Now that we're all adults, we have no choice *but* to face the reality of our places in this world.

And mine isn't here.

Grabbing my duffel bag from the passenger seat, I step out of my SUV and into the bright sunlight. The sea breeze wraps around me, kicking up the aroma of plumeria, bringing back memories of coming here with Anderson, Esme, and the rest of our friends during our teenage years.

The same group of friends Anderson invited this week, with one addition.

I try to tell myself it won't be that bad. That it'll be just like old times.

But when I enter the house and follow the sound of laughter into the high-ceilinged living room, the far walls slid open to reveal an infinity pool overlooking the ocean, I know it *won't* be like old times.

Not when Jameson stands next to Esme, an arm slung around her shoulders.

To make matters worse, it seems as if everyone *likes* him, all the people I once considered close friends hanging onto his every word as he tells some story about almost getting shot while exploring old military barracks during a humanitarian mission in Vietnam. I temper my remarks that only an idiot would go snooping around a military compound in Vietnam. If anyone else was telling the story, I'd probably find it fascinating. Being a military history buff myself, I wouldn't have been able to resist the temptation, either.

But because it's Jameson, the man Esme's supposed to marry, it irks me.

He irks me.

"It's about time you got here, you wanker!" Anderson exclaims upon seeing me, taking the attention off Jameson.

Good.

Everyone looks my way, smiles lighting up their faces. It's almost like a grade school reunion, at least for me. I haven't seen most of these people since I left for basic training. But it appears they all see each other often.

Which makes the feeling that I don't belong here even stronger.

I try not to let my brother's words eat at me. Regardless

of what he says, I'd like to think my friendship with Anderson goes beyond any class lines.

But as I take in everyone I once considered friends, it's obvious one of these things is not like the other.

Me.

I went into the military immediately after graduation. They probably traveled, saw the world.

I don't come from money. While my father has a respectable job and has always provided for his family, we're middle class. Everyone else, apart from Jameson, holds some sort of peerage title. Although in a few months, he won't merely hold a peerage title. He'll become a prince.

But as Anderson approaches me, Jameson's story now long forgotten, none of our differences seem to matter. He embraces me like I'm one of them. Like I belong here just as much as he does. They all do.

Maybe this is why Anderson was so desperate to get away. Despite his position in the line of succession, no one here has ever treated him any differently. Hell, they typically refuse to even bring up the fact he's royalty. They act as if he's just another schmuck off the street.

Another schmuck whose family owns a ridiculously opulent beachfront property.

"Fuck me as I live and breathe. Creed Lawson grew up."

I smile at the petite redhead as she saunters up to me. "Hey, Mags." I lean down, kissing her cheek. "How've you been?"

"Good. Working at an investment firm in London these days. But when Anderson reached out and guilt-tripped me into taking time off to come to the beach, I figured I was due a vacation."

"That bloke pretty much guilt-tripped *all* of us," a lanky blond interjects, slapping Anderson on the back.

"I'm sorry to inconvenience you, Jasper," Anderson jokes. "Feel free to leave anytime."

Jasper shrugs. "I'm already here. May as well make the best of it."

"Because this place is *so* horrible," a tall brunette says with a wink before looking my way, pressing a friendly kiss to my cheek. "Great to have you back, Lawson."

"Thanks, Penny. It's good to be back. At least for a minute."

She furrows her brow. "I thought you were back for good. Didn't you finish your military service?"

"I'm done with special teams," I confirm.

"But—"

"He's slated to be inducted into the guard soon," Marius pipes up, heading toward me and shaking my hand before pulling me in for a quick bro hug. "Good to see you, Lawson." He steps back. "Although technically, Harri and I saw you a few weeks ago when we were having tea with Esme. Didn't we, Harri?"

The slender woman with nearly jet-black hair joins us. "We sure did." Harriet gives me a mischievous grin before glancing over her shoulder. "Isn't that right, Esme?"

When she calls her name, I swallow hard, heat prickling my skin. Several protracted moments pass, and it feels like everyone is watching to see how we handle being in the same room again.

Which is absurd, considering no one knows the truth of what happened between us.

Esme turns from Jameson, strides slow as she glides toward me, the picture of poise and grace. I try not to gawk at the bikini visible through her sheer coverup. Try not to remember tasting her flawless skin. Try not to focus on her long, tanned legs, how amazing they felt wrapped around me.

But damn. It's impossible.

"Creed," Esme greets with her head held high, not looking directly at me.

"Esme," I respond somewhat stiffly.

Thankfully, I haven't been around most of these people enough for them to pick up on the awkwardness stifling the air. Still, Harriet and Marius stare at us with scrutiny, their eyes ping-ponging between us.

When I feel like I'm on the brink of suffocating, Esme clears her throat, forcing a smile as she nods at the man by her side.

"You remember Jameson Gates, don't you?"

I'd spent the entire drive here preparing myself to see her again. Convinced myself it wouldn't be that bad, not when Anderson invited plenty of other people to distract me from the fact that Esme's here with the man who, for all intents and purposes, she's supposed to be madly in love with.

But no amount of distraction can subdue the jealousy bubbling inside me when Jameson pulls her close and kisses her temple. It's not the fact that he touches her that eats away at me. It's that he *gets* to touch her without a single care for who's watching. Something I'll never be able to do.

Jameson extends his free hand toward me, his other one remaining firmly planted on Esme's hip.

As if he's staking his claim.

It makes me want to break every bone in his manicured hand.

"Creed, not Adam, right?" He beams, displaying a mouth of perfect teeth.

Of course he'd have perfect teeth. Everything else about him is bloody perfect.

"Yes," I respond, not cracking so much as a hint of a friendly smile. "Creed. Not Adam." I place my hand in his, shaking it.

And much like the day at the stables, I don't let him off easily, maintaining a harsh grip as I stare him down.

I shouldn't act like this. Openly displaying my animosity will only draw attention our way. I can't help it. Need to get out my frustration somehow.

"That's some handshake you've got there," Jameson jokes, his laughter giving away his nerves. "I think you could use a drink."

Esme steps between us, forcing me to drop my hold on Jameson. Then she levels a glare at me. "I definitely think drinks are in order. We've been here for hours already. Time to play catch up, Lawson."

She lifts her empty champagne flute, the blush on her cheeks making me think that's not her first glass, either.

This is just what I need. To watch Esme put her hands all over Jameson because her inhibitions are lowered.

Or worse, to watch Esme allow Jameson to put *his* hands all over *her* because her inhibitions are lowered.

Maybe Adam was right.

Maybe this *is* a horrible idea.

Maybe I should have stayed home.

Maybe the sooner I distance myself from Anderson's world, the easier it will be once I'm sworn into the guard.

"What can I get you to drink?" Jameson pats my back and steers me toward the wet bar, as if we're old friends. That act may work on everyone else here, but it won't work on me.

"Actually, I'm not all that thirsty." I push out of his hold.

"We're here to have fun, Creed," Anderson reminds me, popping the top off a fresh bottle of beer and guzzling it.

"Away from prying eyes who will report everything we do and say to the bloody establishment. Even made sure my protection team sticks to the perimeter only."

"I had a long drive."

"Which you would have avoided if you came on the plane with us. We were here in forty-five minutes."

I ignore his statement, not wanting to tell him the reason I insisted on driving was because I couldn't stand the idea of being in such a confined space with Esme and Jameson. It's bad enough we're under the same roof. Albeit, it's a massive, exorbitant roof. But it's one roof, all the same.

"I just need a few minutes to freshen up and change into my swim shorts. Then I'll join the festivities."

"Fine. But here." He reaches into the refrigerator and pulls out a beer, using the counter to pop off the top. "Take one for the road."

I grab it from him, and he holds up his bottle.

"To a week we'll never forget."

I clink my beer against his. "To a week we'll never forget."

Although I have a feeling when this week is over, I'd give anything to forget it.

CHAPTER SEVENTEEN

Esme

"Creed seems a bit...off," Marius remarks once Anderson drags Jameson away for a round of billiards with Maggie and the resident bookie, Jasper.

While I'm happy Jameson and my friends are getting along, it's still leaves a sour taste in my mouth.

After my one night with Creed, I thought I'd feel better about this...arrangement.

I thought it would be easier to see Creed. Thought we'd be able to leave our one night in the past. Pretend it never happened. Go back to the way things were before we had sex.

Instead, every time Jameson kisses me, all I think about is the way Creed kissed me. How my body hummed to life. How my skin yearned for his touch. How my core ached to feel him everywhere.

People have one-night stands all the time and move on. Creed and I should have no problem doing the same.

But I'm starting to realize that what Creed and I shared wasn't just a one-night stand. It couldn't be. Not when it was so electrifying.

"What do you mean?" I plaster a smile on my face, feigning ignorance.

"Exactly what I said, Ezzy." Marius leans closer, dropping his voice so no one can overhear. "I saw the way you guys were all but eye-fucking each other."

"Not normal eye-fucking, either," Harriet adds. "It was more like...hate eye-fucking."

"Hate eye-fucking," Marius agrees. "And the daggers he shot at Jameson."

"He's just protective." I take a sip from my fresh glass of champagne.

Now that I'm officially feeling the effects of the alcohol, the last thing I should do is drink even more. But it helps diminish the anxiety filling me.

"Protective enough to try to break every finger in the poor bloke's hand?" Marius arches a brow.

What am I supposed to tell my friends? It's not that I don't trust them enough to share what happened. Harriet and Marius are the only two people I *do* trust with this secret.

But telling them would make it real. Would require me to admit I haven't been able to stop thinking about Creed since I watched him walk away.

Would require me to admit I nearly ran after him to ask if he wanted to come back the next night, too. And the next. And the next.

"I'll go talk to him." I place my flute on a nearby side table, the alcohol emboldening me to do something I know is a bad idea.

"And what do you need to talk to him about?" Harriet playfully nudges me, giving me an over-exaggerated wink.

"I just want to make sure he's okay. Truth be told, Adam gave Jameson a weird look when I first introduced them." I lean closer. "He may have mentioned something to Creed about never seeing us together during all his time as my CPO."

It shouldn't be this easy to lie to my friends, but it *is* a good cover story for why I need to put on my big girl panties and talk to Creed.

We're both here for the next ten days. I don't want every day to be like this. Don't want the tension to become so awkward everyone else picks up on it.

Including my brother.

"I just…" I push out a breath. "I want to make sure he understands that, even though this thing with Jameson may not have been my decision, we still have to keep up appearances. No one's supposed to know the truth." I grit out a smile, smoothing a hand down my coverup. "If you'll excuse me."

"Enjoy your 'talk'," Marius retorts with a snicker.

I roll my eyes, then turn, making my way through the living room, champagne and beer now being consumed as if it's the last days before prohibition. My flip-flops echo against the marble tile in the foyer before I ascend the elaborate staircase to the second floor, the décor all crisp whites against bamboo accents, natural light filling the space.

I'm not sure which room Creed chose, but I suspect it's the same one he always stayed in during our teenage years.

Which will only make things even more awkward, considering Jameson and I are in the suite right next to him.

When I'd invited Jameson to join me on this beach holiday to appease the 'establishment', it didn't even dawn on me that he'd expect to share a room. After realizing I didn't have the same expectations, he offered to stay in a separate room. But most normal couples share a room when they go away together. Once we're married, we'll be expected to *live* together. I may as well get used to sharing my space with him now.

The notion was much easier before I realized Creed would be sleeping in the room right next to mine.

Pausing in front of his door, I inhale a calming breath, taking a moment to collect my thoughts. Then I raise my hand and knock, listening for any movement.

After several seconds pass and I don't hear anything, I say, "Creed. It's me. Esme. I just… I wanted to talk to you."

I rest my ear against the door, but it's still silent, the only sounds coming from the frivolity downstairs.

It's possible Creed chose a different room, having no desire to sleep in the room next to mine. But I sense he's in this one. That he's simply ignoring me in the hopes of avoiding me as much as possible.

I don't want that. Want to have some semblance of normalcy between us, regardless of how difficult that may be.

My hand on the knob, I give it a twist, expecting it to be locked. To my surprise, it's not. When I steal a glimpse inside, I spy Creed's duffel bag on the ottoman at the foot of the bed. The sliding glass door on the far side of the room is open, the sheer curtains blowing in the ocean breeze.

Figuring he must be drinking his beer on the balcony, I slip inside and close the door behind me before making my way across the room. But as I'm about to step outside, a familiar voice calls my name from elsewhere within the suite.

And it's not just a familiar voice.

It's a familiar *moan*.

And he's moaning my name, the sound strained. Desperate.

Wanton.

Pausing, I slowly turn, gaze falling on the bathroom door that's slightly ajar. I don't immediately move toward it. Instead, all I can do is stare, my heart thrashing in my chest at what I suspect Creed's doing in there.

All the more reason I should walk away and pretend I never heard his guttural moan.

The same one I've heard in my dreams every night since he took my virginity. Since he showed me more pleasure than I thought possible.

The same one I've replayed in my mind whenever I've touched myself, struggling to recreate the high I experienced when Creed fucked me.

When he moans my name again, this time even more needy, I can't help myself. It's like a siren's call, beckoning me to the depths, even though there's nothing but danger within.

I carefully pad across the room, pausing outside the bathroom before I peek inside. As my gaze lands on Creed Lawson in the shower, all the air rushes from my lungs.

This isn't the first time I've seen him naked. A week ago, I was lucky enough to feel his flesh on mine.

But as my eyes feast on the water cascading down his distinguished face and along his sculpted body, licking every ridge and valley while he strokes himself, his head thrown back, a look of ecstasy on his face, I don't think I've ever seen anything so hypnotizing. So mesmerizing.

So erotic.

I shouldn't watch this. Should leave right now.

There's just something so beautiful about the fast and feverish way he works his large erection, my name like a prayer on his lips. I've never watched much porn. Hell, I've never watched *any* porn. But I would happily subscribe to

Creed Lawson's self-care extravaganza. I just wish I could be the one to make him feel good.

To touch him.

To drive him wild with need.

Like I did the other night.

I'm so captivated by the sight of his muscles straining and flexing, I forget where I am and that I shouldn't be watching this...

Until his hand stops moving, his body going rigid.

And not because he's about to come undone.

But because he's finally realized he's no longer alone.

CHAPTER EIGHTEEN

Creed

I blink, remaining perfectly still, praying if I open and close my eyes enough times, I'll learn this isn't real. That Esme's not standing in the doorway of my bathroom, watching me jerk off in the shower as I moan her name.

That this is all simply a manifestation of my fantasies. Nothing more.

But no amount of blinking makes her disappear.

Instead, she remains unmoving, eyes hooded with desire as she sucks in that bottom lip I'd give anything to taste again. Her chest rises and falls in a quicker pattern, skin flushing from more than just some time in the sun.

What do I do? Do I turn off the water? Grab a towel and try to explain this away. Tell her it killed me to watch Jameson touch and kiss her. That I came up here to figure out how to deal with these emotions warring inside of me.

That the second I stepped under the water and closed my

eyes, memories of our one night together came rushing back, my cock instantly stirring.

That I figured releasing some of my pent-up frustration might help me not be such a grumpy bastard.

That I never expected to open my eyes to see her watching me.

And I certainly don't expect her to step farther into the bathroom and lift her sheer coverup over her head.

But that's what she does.

I swallow hard, gaze transfixed on her as she loosens the ties of her bikini top, allowing it to fall to the floor. I hiss out a breath, my dick throbbing, begging for attention. I give him what he needs, slowly stroking myself again.

Esme shows her approval by sliding her tongue along her lips, smoothing her hands over her chest. When she pinches her nipples, mouth parting in pleasure, it takes everything I have not to come. Or storm out of this shower, force her to her knees, and plunge my dick between those red lips.

The mere thought has me on the brink of exploding, so I slow my motions, holding my breath as she slides a hand down her torso, grazing the waistband of her bikini bottoms.

Fully aware of the effect she has on me, she gives me a sly smile, arching a brow, as if asking if she should take them off, too.

Without a single moment of hesitation, I eagerly nod my reply.

Sultry eyes trained on mine, she removes the rest of her bikini, kicking it to the side along with her flip-flops.

I resume my motions, pulse racing. I don't even care that my skin's starting to prune. I'll stay in here forever if I can feast my appreciative stare on her body.

She props herself on the vanity and spreads her legs. Even with the obstruction of the foggy glass wall, I can see how wet she is for me. My cock pulses, wanting to bury itself inside her. And as much as I'd love to feel her convulse around me, I want this more. Want to watch as she gives in to her desires. Something I know she struggles with after a lifetime of always doing what's expected of her.

As she runs her hand down her stomach, her fingers traveling toward her apex, I can no longer remain silent, a groan thundering from my throat. I lean my forearm on the glass of the shower, working my erection with more intensity at the sight of Esme sliding a finger in and out of her sex.

I'm not ashamed to admit I've been with my fair share of women, most of whom I met at bars while on short periods of rest and recuperation between missions.

But this may be one of the hottest moments I've ever experienced in all of my twenty-six years.

Succumbing to the sensation, Esme leans her head back, closing her eyes. While I love the expression of bliss crossing her face, I need to feel the connection I've missed since I walked out of her bedroom.

"Don't.

At the sound of my gruff voice, she snaps her gaze to mine, stopping her motions, brows furrowed in confusion.

"Eyes on me. I need to look into them as you make yourself come, princess."

Her lips curve into a salacious grin, and she nods. She returns her fingers to her center, pushing one inside before adding another, motions increasing with every second, not breaking her gaze from mine for even a heartbeat.

Following my instructions.

Like the good girl she is.

Matching her rhythm, I jerk myself harder as I imagine my hand is her pussy wrapped around my cock. That alone pushes me to the brink of oblivion.

With a roar, I release my grip on myself, resting both forearms on the glass enclosure as I struggle to get my ragged breathing under control.

Struggling to get *myself* under control.

Esme stops her motions, straightening as she peers at me in confusion.

"Don't you dare fucking stop." I snap my fierce eyes back to her, nostrils flaring.

"But why did you? Did you already come?"

I shake my head as I draw in a deep breath. "If I didn't stop, I would have."

Her expression lightens. "Isn't that the point?"

"Yes." I flash her a mischievous smile before my stare turns heated once more. "But not until you do. I will always make sure *you* come first."

"Well, then…" Winking, she brings her thumb back to her clit, "I'd hate to delay your…happy ending any longer than necessary." Her lips form an O when she pushes two fingers inside.

"That's it," I exhale, fighting against the temptation to stroke my cock. "Make yourself come, Esme. Fuck your cunt with your fingers."

"Jesus, Creed," she moans. "Pretty sure you could make me come with your words alone."

"You could probably make me come just by looking at you. Hell, *thinking* about you."

"Oh, god," she moans as she fucks herself even harder.

What I wouldn't give to walk over there, plunge inside her, make her scream so loud no one in this house can question what we're doing.

Make her scream so loud *Jameson* knows what I'm doing to his innocent little princess.

But I'd be crazy to end to this. I've never seen anything

so beautiful. So fucking seductive. And it's not because Esme's naked. It's because she's comfortable enough to do this in front of me.

There's no bigger turn on.

"Please tell me you're close," I rasp, hands forming into fists as desperation consumes me.

"I am." She pulses harder against her fingers, mouth parting as she chases that high. "So fucking close."

"Thank god." I don't waste a second, wrapping my hand back around my dick.

At first, my motions are slow. I need her to come first. Need to watch her let go, even if it's the last time I ever see it.

"Oh, fuck," she gasps, chest heaving, skin flushing.

When she closes her eyes this time, I don't stop her, too captivated by the bliss covering every inch of her. She throws her head back, body convulsing, my name a benediction on her lips.

"Goddamn," I grunt, wasting no time in working my cock at a feverish pace as Esme writhes on the vanity.

I grit my teeth, barely breathing as I chase my own release. Release that finds me almost instantly. A quivering moan falls from my throat, muscles trembling as my cum coats the shower walls.

Needing something to ground me, I lean my head against the glass. The only sound that can be heard over our heavy pants is the water still cascading down my frame.

As I slowly come down from my high, I meet Esme's eyes. I feel like I should say something. Ask what this means for us. After all, she was the one who insisted we were only supposed to be a one-time thing.

Apparently not.

But what does she expect? That I'd help her get off, then happily send her back to Jameson?

That's a disaster waiting to happen.

Before I have a chance to bring up any of this, she slides off the vanity with a wicked smirk, collects her things, then pads across the tile floor toward the bedroom.

Just as she's about to disappear, she glances over her shoulder, meeting my confused stare.

"Thanks for always making sure I...come first." Her words linger in the air for a beat.

Then she slips out of the bathroom, leaving me wanting her even more than I thought possible.

CHAPTER NINETEEN

Esme

What the hell just happened?

I lean against the wall outside of Creed's room, my mind racing, body vibrating.

I'd hoped to talk to him, clear the air so things weren't so strained.

Instead, the second I heard him moan my name, saw him work his throbbing cock, felt his need, I became putty in his hands, a force outside my control taking over to the point that I did something I knew was incredibly wrong.

But god, it felt so incredibly right.

It still does.

I should regret it. Should regret stripping in front of him. Sliding onto the vanity. Spreading my legs. Fucking myself with my fingers while he watched.

The way he looked at me was intoxicating. Electrifying. Addictive.

All the more reason I need to end whatever this is right now.

Before it gets even more out of control.

Resolved to stay strong this time, especially now that I've worked off the sexual frustration that's built up over the past week, I'm about to storm back into Creed's room when Jameson's voice cuts through.

But it doesn't sound like him, at least not like the typical tone he uses around me. Instead, he sounds…angry. I didn't think Jameson Gates got angry.

Intrigued, I push off the wall and pad down the hallway, lingering outside our room, the door slightly ajar.

"I don't care what it takes," he growls, his voice low. Threatening.

Dangerous.

"We need those goddamn recordings so you'd better fix this, no matter the cost. I don't think you need me to spell out what that means."

There's a pause as whomever he's speaking to probably responds, my curiosity increasing with every passing second. Who is he talking to? What recordings? And why does Jameson need them, no matter the cost?

"Good. I expect an update in twenty-four hours, and it better be good news."

I inch forward, straining to listen to the next part of their conversation. Unfortunately, by the time I figure out he ended the call, the door flings open, Jameson coming to an abrupt stop when he sees me in the hallway.

On a sharp inhale, I stiffen, eyes going wide when I meet his gaze and see something I've never encountered during our short fake courtship.

Something…disturbing.

Or perhaps it's my own guilt and remorse over my most

recent interlude with Creed staring back at me, reminding me of everything at stake.

Instantly, his expression softens, making me question what I thought I saw mere seconds ago.

"Esme..." He runs his hands down my arms. "Is everything okay?"

"I suppose I should ask *you* that." I give him a knowing look, to which he briefly closes his eyes, hanging his head.

"You heard that, didn't you?" He drops his hold on me.

I cross my arms in front of my chest. "It certainly caught my attention, especially since I've never heard you use that tone of voice." I hold my head high, offering no excuse for why I was up here in the first place.

And thankfully Jameson doesn't ask.

"That's why I came up here to take the call." He gives me a sheepish smile, everything about him a complete 180 from the angry man I'd overheard moments ago. "Sorry to say that sometimes I let my temper get the better of me, especially when mistakes happen because of incompetence. I told you I wasn't perfect."

I stare at him for a beat, looking for any hint of deception. Any clue he's not being truthful. I don't find anything but sincerity in his gaze.

"We all suffer from that on occasion," I assure him, relaxing my posture. "Especially when things don't go our way. I've been known to be a bit of a drama queen from time to time myself."

"You?" he playfully chides, then winks. "Never."

I laugh slightly, berating myself for assuming Jameson was doing anything other than responding to a problem at work. Nothing he said during that phone call would indicate otherwise, and yet I was so quick to jump to conclusions, to the *wrong* conclusion, all because it would make me feel less guilty about my own behavior.

"Come on." Jameson slings an arm around my shoulders and steers me down the hallway. "Let's get back to the party. Although I'm not sure that's a great idea either, considering your brother seems hell-bent on getting me drunk."

"It's not just my brother." I flash a smile. "All my friends are. They want you to spill your deepest, darkest secrets."

"And how about you?" He leans closer, his voice husky.

"Me?"

"Are *you* trying to get me to spill my deepest, darkest secrets?" He waggles his brows, a flirtatious smirk curving on his lips.

Truth be told, I like this version of Jameson. He seems much more relaxed than he's been during the myriad of public events we've attended since announcing our relationship.

Then again, it could simply be because this is the first time we've spent any extended time together without the watchful eyes of the royal household scrutinizing our every move. We're free to be ourselves.

And maybe this is the authentic version of Jameson. Not the man he purports to be in public.

Like I'm not the woman *I* purport to be in public.

"The royal household already spilled those in that dossier they put together," I remind him.

He touches his hand to my elbow as we continue down the stairs. "I'd like to think there are some things even the 'Great and Powerful Oz' isn't able to find out," he says, using the nickname he's developed for the royal household.

I have to admit, it's growing on me. I've always simply called it the 'establishment' or the 'powers that be'. The Great and Powerful Oz has a nice tongue-in-cheek ring to it.

And is a much more accurate metaphor for the royal household. It's this mysterious entity everyone's so curious about. Has this connotation of being so powerful, so all-knowing.

In reality, it's a bitter old man who wants to control the inhabitants of Oz. Or, in our case, several bitter old men who want to control the members of the royal family.

"Then you don't know my friends very well. Put them in a room with the right person and they'll come out with not only the location of Jimmy Hoffa's body, but also who killed Kennedy. Oh, and what happened to Amelia Earhart."

He throws his head back and laughs, the raspy sound echoing against the high ceilings. "They do seem like quite the...persuasive group. And also good people." He pauses just outside of the living room, placing his hands on my biceps and forcing me to face him. "They care about you." A contemplative expression pulls on his brows. "I've never had friends like that. People who let me be myself and not give a shit about whom I am. Who my father is."

When I spy a motion out of the corner of my eye, I look away, gaze briefly meeting Creed's as he passes us, scowling at Jameson.

But if it bothers Jameson, he doesn't let on.

"And friends who seem quite protective of you," he states once Creed's out of earshot.

I part my lips, about to apologize for Creed's behavior. Insist he's like this around everyone he doesn't know well.

But before I can offer a lackluster excuse, Jameson places a finger over my mouth, silencing me.

"I'm glad you have people looking out for you, especially with, well...all of this. I'm more than happy to be on the receiving end of a few glowers and the occasional death stare from a frightening man who could probably kill me with his bare hands if it means he's looking out for you."

I swallow hard, tightness squeezing my chest.

Any guilt that plagued me about my previous indiscretions with Creed is amplified ten-fold now. Especially with Jameson mistaking Creed's cold attitude as him simply being a protective friend.

"Believe me when I say there aren't enough people like that. Maybe if I had…" He stops short, pinching his eyes shut.

"Maybe if you had…what?" I lean closer, my curiosity piqued once more.

Jameson draws in a deep breath, but there's no mistaking the pain and remorse covering the lines of his face. It's a complete change from the lighthearted man he was moments ago.

Memories of our conversation after I ran out of that first meeting rush back. How I'd questioned why he'd settle for someone he didn't love. I didn't read too much into his response. But now it haunts me.

I'm not holding out for another strike of lightning.

It makes me wonder about his first strike of lightning.

By his distraught expression, I sense it's not a simple breakup that pulled them apart, but something much more tragic.

"Nothing that matters anymore." He sighs, masking his grief with a forced smile. "Come on. Let's get back to your friends. Enjoy the freedom while we still have it."

"Of course."

He links his hand with mine, and we make our way through the living room and onto the patio, the sunlight causing the crystal blue water of the luxurious pool to glitter. I maintain my bright expression, not wanting anyone to read into the fact that I was gone for a while.

And that Creed rejoined the party only minutes before I did.

I doubt anyone's in the right frame of mind to put those two pieces together, not with all the alcohol that's been flowing since we boarded the private jet earlier this morning.

Then why do I feel like my misdeeds are written all over me?

Worse, why do I feel more guilty about the fact I'm holding Jameson's hand than I do about any of my acts of infidelity with Creed?

CHAPTER TWENTY

Esme

The bright moon casts a subtle glow across my darkened bedroom as I lay awake. The music of the nearby ocean waves normally lulls me to sleep whenever I'm here.

Not tonight, though.

Tonight, I can't quiet my mind enough to find peace.

And it's not because I'm sharing a bed with Jameson for the first time, even though he was a gentleman and put a pillow between us after sensing my unease. It's because my thoughts keep wandering to the man sleeping on the other side of the wall.

Needing to do something to settle my unease, I carefully slip out from underneath the luxurious duvet and tiptoe across the lush carpet, opening the door and stepping into the hallway.

As I pass Creed's room, I hesitate, debating whether I should knock, see if he's awake so I can tell him everything I'd wanted to earlier today.

Everything I *should* have told him earlier today.

Instead, I gave in to temptation.

It can't happen again.

It *won't* happen again.

If we stand any chance of keeping what happened between us a secret, we need to clear the air.

Not continue fooling around.

But I made the mistake of trying to talk to him in his room earlier and look at how that turned out. We need to have this conversation in neutral territory. Or at the very least, nowhere remotely close to a bed.

Or a shower.

Or a bathroom vanity.

It needs to be in the open where anyone could walk in.

Otherwise, I don't trust myself, the pull I feel toward him too strong.

So instead of knocking, I continue past his room, the wood floor cool on my feet as I pad down the stairs, the house quiet now that everyone's sleeping.

I make my way into the dimly lit kitchen and open the industrial refrigerator, grabbing a bottle of water. As I close the door, I sense a darkened figure standing by the island where no one was seconds ago.

My heart ricochets into my throat, hand flying to my chest as I try to get my pulse under control.

And it's not simply because I was startled.

It's because of the man standing gloriously shirtless in front of me, clad only in a pair of gray sweatpants.

I never knew such a dull color could be so sexy.

Until now.

Creed Lawson in a pair of gray sweatpants is one of the most sinful things I've ever seen.

And also one of the most dangerous.

"Sorry. I didn't mean to frighten you," he offers softly, his deep voice seeming to thunder in the stark silence.

"It's okay." I increase the space between us, clearing my throat. "I didn't hear you approach." I attempt to twist the cap off the bottle. But I'm so riddled with unease that it's a lost cause.

"Allow me." Creed steps toward me and extends his hand, expression unreadable.

As always.

I pass him the bottle, and he easily removes the cap before returning it to me.

I take a long sip, wishing it were something stronger than water. Then I place the cap back on, shifting from foot to foot as I toy with the necklace I wear whenever I can, a locket holding a photo of my mother. I wonder what advice she'd have for me if she were here.

Would I even be in this position?

Or would she have encouraged me to stand up for myself, instead of blindly following orders, like I have all my life?

What would she have done if she were in my situation, forced to marry a man she didn't choose all because the public adored him and loved the idea of them together?

I'd like to think she would have stood up for herself, but I can't say that with any certainty. I was only nine when she died. While I wasn't *that* young, with the passing of years and the fact no one really talks about her, my memories are foggy.

At a light twinkle, I snap my eyes to the floor, seeing my necklace has come undone and fallen.

Without hesitation, Creed bends to pick it up.

"The clasp is loose, but I can't bring myself to get a new chain," I explain. "Or a new locket."

He offers me an understanding smile, all too familiar with the importance this necklace holds. It was the last thing my mother gave me before succumbing to the multiple sclerosis that ravaged her body quickly and mercilessly in a few short years.

"May I?" He holds up the necklace, an end of the chain in each hand.

I nod, swallowing hard as he takes a step toward me. Then another. And another. Until he's standing a breath away, the heat coming off his body palpable. I try not to stare at his chiseled physique. Try not to recall the way his muscles strained as he brought himself to orgasm. But even keeping my gaze lowered doesn't do anything to slow my racing heart.

Not when Creed's delicious V obscures my vision.

He brings the necklace up to my collarbone, leaning toward me as his fingers work to secure the piece around me. The clasp gives him trouble, just as it does me. But for the first time, I don't curse that it's in need of repair. I revel in it since it keeps him closer to me a few seconds longer than normal.

"Almost got it."

"It's a tricky little bugger," I respond with a laugh, lifting my head slightly.

Which is a mistake.

Because it coincides with the precise moment he turns toward me, our mouths brushing.

I inhale a sharp breath, the jolt from his ghost of a kiss vibrating through me, even after I step away. All I can do is stare at his lips, desperate to feel them again. At the same time, I know they're a goddamn drug. If I don't break this habit now, I'll keep returning again and again until I'm so addicted I'd rather die than go a day without experiencing the high only he can give me.

And I *need* to break this habit.

That's easier said than done, especially when my next fix is within reach, tempting me with the promise of euphoria.

When he lunges for me, fingers digging into my hair, mouth crashing against mine as he pushes me against the wall, I do what all addicts do. Promise this will be the last time. That after this I'll get clean.

If this truly is to be my last hit, though, I need to make it count.

Make sure it's one I always remember.

My water bottle falling to the floor, I grip the back of his neck, rubbing my body against his. His tongue caresses mine, tempting and teasing, reminding me how talented that muscle is. How much pleasure it brings when used on other parts of me.

He slides his hands from my face, down the contours of my frame before they disappear underneath my tank top. When his fingers find my nipple and squeeze, a whimper falls from my throat.

"There it is," he muses against my mouth, pinching my nipple even harder, the combination of pleasure and pain almost too much, desire soaking my panties. "Do you know how much I love that fucking sound?"

I whimper again, giving him what he wants. What he needs. What he craves.

"God yes, princess. That's it," he grits out as he lowers his hand down my stomach, slipping it into my shorts.

Our first night together, he took his time, teasing me to the point that I was on the brink of losing my mind.

Not tonight.

Tonight, he knows we're short on time.

That we're taking a huge fucking risk.

When his thumb presses against my clit, I don't care about any of that, too high on this feeling to push him away.

He covers my mouth with his, swallowing my cries as he thrusts a finger inside, then another, his motions relentless.

"Do you know what sound I love even more?"

"What's that?"

"The sound of your wet cunt, knowing it's fucking drenched for me, and only me."

Hooking my leg around his waist, my eyes roll into the back of my head, body aching for release.

"Say it, Esme. Tell me I'm the only one who makes you feel like this." His wild gaze locks with mine. "Because you're the only one who makes me feel like this."

"Like what?" I circle my hips in time with his ministrations.

"Like I'm losing all bloody control." He buries his head in the crook of my neck, teeth clamping onto my skin.

Exhilaration jolts my core, and it only gets stronger the harder Creed bites me. I should tell him to stop. That it's too much. That he's going to leave a mark.

And that's probably why he's doing it.

After being tortured all day by watching Jameson hold my hand, brush his fingers against my skin, feather light kisses to my temple, he needs to stake his claim.

Needs to mark me as his.

Despite how wrong this is, I want him to do just that. Want his mark on me. Inside me. Everywhere.

"And I'm loving every second of it," he rasps, his thick erection pressing against my stomach, straining to be set free.

I trail my hand down his chest, reveling in the sensation

of his rippling muscles before sliding it into his sweatpants. When I wrap my fingers around his cock, thumb teasing the tip, smoothing the bit of pre-cum that escaped, he releases a hiss of pleasure.

But it's short-lived, his entire body suddenly becoming rigid.

I don't have a chance to ask what's wrong before he pushes away, eyes panicked, breathing shallow.

Then footsteps echo nearby, and I dart my head toward the living room just as Marius comes into view. Adrenaline replaces the lust that consumed me mere seconds ago.

Maybe he won't see us. Maybe he'll keep walking, head out to the patio for some fresh air.

But as luck would have it, he heads straight for the kitchen, stopping dead in his tracks when he sees us.

"Marius," I say in a voice that bears little resemblance to my own. "What are you doing up? Are you having trouble sleeping?"

"No," he draws out, his gaze ping-ponging between Creed and me. "Just came to grab a water." He walks to the refrigerator and retrieves a bottle, suspicious eyes never leaving us.

Marius isn't an idiot. All it takes is a cursory glance at our disheveled appearance to realize he walked in on something.

Or *almost* walked in on something if Creed's sharp hearing hadn't picked up his soft footfalls.

Between our labored breathing, flushed complexions, and kiss-swollen lips, not to mention what I can only assume to be teeth marks on my neck, it's more than apparent he caught us with our hands in the proverbial cookie jar.

Or nearly caught us with our hands down each other's pants.

"Me, too."

I swipe my bottle off the floor, unscrewing the cap, but offer no excuse for how it had fallen in the first place. Hoping he doesn't notice the tremble in my hand, I bring it up to my lips and take a healthy sip. This time, I *really* wish it were alcohol.

"Then my necklace fell off and Creed helped me put it back on."

A mischievous smirk crawls across Marius' lips. "Is that right?"

"Yes." I square my shoulders as I face Creed. "Thanks for your assistance."

Creed narrows his gaze on me. "It was my pleasure. As always."

A shiver runs down my spine in response to his sinful tone, the meaning behind his words not lost on me.

"Right then." I force a smile. "Goodnight."

"Princess," Creed says.

I turn toward Marius but don't look him directly in the eyes. "See you in the morning, Mari."

"You'd better believe it… Princess." He winks.

Spinning around, I hurry from the kitchen and up the stairs, slipping into my room to find Jameson in the same position as when I left.

I sink against the door, drawing in deep breath after deep breath, my body aching from the orgasm it was so cruelly deprived of.

And maybe that's what I deserve.

Creed and I were careless. Anyone could have walked in on us. In the throes of passion, I didn't care, but that was when I was enjoying the effects of my addiction.

Now that I've come down from my high, I can see how wrong it was.

How *reckless* it was.

Luckily, it was just Marius who interrupted us. It could have been a lot worse.

Which is why I need to keep my distance.

The next time, we may not be so lucky.

CHAPTER TWENTY-ONE

Esme

"God, I hope no one notices," I mutter to myself as I check my reflection in the mirror, examining my neck.

While the marks where Creed bit me last night aren't too pronounced, they still make me self-conscious. Especially considering I'm sharing a bed with another man.

When Jameson woke up this morning, I pretended to be asleep, keeping the duvet pulled tight up to my chin.

But I can't avoid him forever.

I also can't ignore my friends forever, a fact Marius reminded me of with the text he just sent, threatening to haul my ass down to the beach if I'm not out there in the next twenty minutes.

What do I say to him? Do I play it off and pretend it was nothing? Claim his imagination was just running wild?

Or do I finally confide in the only two people I trust with this secret?

I smooth a hand down my hair that I styled in a braid that falls over my right shoulder, another layer of protection against the mark Creed left on my neck. Placing my oversized hat on my head and slinging my beach bag on my arm, I draw in a deep breath. Then I make my way through the house and out the back door, the sound of laughter cutting over the crashing waves and the ocean breeze.

When I emerge onto the beach, a game of volleyball is already underway, Anderson and Creed on one team, Jasper and Jameson on the other.

The instant he sees me, Jameson calls a timeout and jogs toward me, a few beads of sweat visible on his chest.

And what makes it even worse is how happy he looks to see me, his smile bright, eyes dazzling with appreciation.

"There you are." His voice is breathless as he leaves a kiss on my cheek. "I was starting to get worried."

"I was just tired." I return a tight-lipped smile, ignoring the fire scalding my skin in response to the way Creed watches our interaction from a few feet away. "I can't remember the last time I didn't have anywhere to be. Figured I'd take advantage of it."

"That's understandable."

"Hey! Gates!"

At the deep rasp, both of us look toward Creed, his sweat-glistened body putting Jameson's to shame. While Jameson's fit physique makes it clear he takes care of himself, he pales in comparison to Creed.

Then again, most people pale in comparison to Creed.

"You in or out?"

Jameson looks back to me, hesitating.

"You go play," I insist.

"Are you sure? I'll stay with you."

"That's not necessary. I'll be fine. I'm going to lay out, read a book, maybe take a nap."

"A nap when you just woke up?" He arches a brow.

"When in Rome," I respond with a shrug.

"Okay then. Enjoy yourself." He presses another kiss to my cheek before re-joining the volleyball match.

Blowing out a long breath, I turn to my left, Harriet and Marius watching me with interest. Particularly Marius.

"Mimosa?" He raises a flute filled with a light orange effervescent liquid.

"You don't have to ask me twice," I respond, traipsing in the sand toward them and plopping down on the open lounge chair beside them.

I take the glass from him, swallowing several large gulps before setting it down on the small wooden table between us.

"Rough night?" he chides knowingly.

I flash him a warning look.

"What?" He holds up his hands in defense. "It's an innocent question. But a piece of advice for the next time you're caught doing something you don't think you should." He leans toward me. "The less information you willingly offer, the better. Guilty people tend to overshare. It's a dead giveaway they're lying or covering up something."

"What are you talking about?" Harriet scrunches her brows, her confusion authentic.

Which means he hasn't told her what he walked in on last night. Or *almost* walked in on.

"Didn't I tell you, Harri?" He smirks at me. "Last night, I was dehydrated after drinking a tad too much, so I went down to the kitchen to grab a bottle of water. 'And what to my wondering eyes should appear?'" he jests, quoting that age-old Christmas poem. "But an out-of-breath Creed with a rather flushed Esme, my dear."

I roll my eyes, leaning back in my chair, allowing the sun to warm my skin. "How long did it take you to come up with that little gem?"

"Only all night." He winks before his expression turns serious.

"So, you and Creed?" Harriet arches a brow, mindful to keep her voice low.

I doubt the guys can hear us over the ocean waves. Not to mention, they seem quite focused on their volleyball game. But Maggie, Penny, and Cody are lounging nearby. While they most likely wouldn't make a big deal out of it, I don't want a lot of people to know.

Hell, I didn't want *anyone* to know.

But that was when I thought this would be a one-time thing.

That we'd be mature about it. That we could *forget* about it.

Instead, whenever I'm near Creed, I succumb to my baser instincts, desperate for him to make me feel good one more time.

I truly am an addict.

I could feign ignorance. Tell Marius he's blowing it out of proportion. But after riding this wild seesaw of emotions these past few weeks, I need to talk to someone about this. Someone who understands how this world works and can give me advice.

Inhaling deeply, I square my shoulders. "Yes. Me and Creed."

"Did you?" Marius arches a single brow.

I nod. "We did. A week ago. I took your advice and asked him to help me take care of my little problem. It was just supposed to be one night. But then…"

"Yes?" Harriet prods as she and Marius lean closer, eyes focused.

"Well, yesterday was the first time we saw each other since that night."

"Hence the giant dick-waving contest when Creed arrived," Marius states in realization.

"I might be wrong, but I have a feeling Creed Lawson would win *any* dick waving contest by a mile," Harriet jabs, sipping her drink. "Or at least a few inches." She waggles her brows. "Am I right?"

"I don't have anyone to compare him to." Heat crosses my brow. "But I can tell you it *is* impressive."

"Can we not do this?" Marius winces, squeezing his eyes shut. "I'm happy to listen to your guy problems, offer the male perspective, but I'd rather not sit here while you two talk about his dick. Okay? Pretty sure it'll only make me feel even more inadequate in comparison."

"I'm sure you're quite adequate, Marius," I say, feeling relaxed for the first time since I arrived here.

"Great. That's exactly what every guy wants to hear. That they're adequate."

Harriet and I both throw our heads back and laugh as Marius pretends to be indignant. He knows it's all in good fun, though.

"Don't pout, Mari," I tease. "But if it makes you feel better, I'll endeavor to refrain from making any remarks about his gigantic dick."

Marius groans, then winks, his expression lightening.

"So what happened when you went to talk to him yesterday?" Harriet presses.

Heat prickles my skin, and not from the brilliant sun beating down on us, only a few clouds in the sky on a perfect summer day. Instead, it's from the memory of walking into Creed's room.

"I'd planned to bring up the awkwardness between us." I raise my glass to my lips and take another long sip. "Before we slept together, I'd specifically told him I didn't want any of that."

Harriet bursts out laughing. "Trust me, Ezzy. The second you sleep with someone, there's always going to be an inherent tension between you."

"I figured since we were pretty close before he left for the military, we'd be able to compartmentalize it. Obviously, I was wrong."

My gaze falls over Creed's body and I salivate at the sight of his rippling muscles. I could watch him for hours and never tire of the way he looks. The way he makes any sort of physical exertion seem effortless.

The way he made sex seem effortless.

Pushing down the memory, I snap my eyes back to my friends, who both smirk at me.

"When I walked into his room, I didn't see him, but the door to the balcony was open, so I figured he was out there. Then I heard someone call my name from the bathroom. But it wasn't really calling." I chew on my bottom lip. "It was more like…moaning."

Marius' jaw drops, eyes wide. "He wasn't."

"He was." I smirk. "When I peeked into the bathroom, he was indulging in a little self-care in the shower."

"Fuck…" Harriet fans herself. "That must have been a marvelous sight."

"Did you give him a hand?" Marius waggles his brows.

"No." I bring my drink back to my mouth, keeping it in place as I answer, "I gave *myself* a hand."

I study my friend's shocked expressions from over my glass.

"Are you telling me…" Harriet begins.

I place my nearly empty drink back on the table. "He got himself off. I got myself off. As we both watched each other. Then I left."

"Holy shit," Harriet exhales. "That's hot, babe."

"And last night?" Marius prods.

"We ran into each other in the kitchen. And let's just say things were going really good until Creed heard footsteps." I give Marius a pointed stare. "Cock blocker," I joke.

"This is better than most of the lame stuff I read in my romance novels," Harriet muses. "Which settles it. I need you to keep fucking him so I can get better material."

"And also, because you deserve to be happy," Marius adds.

"Even if it's fleeting?"

"Do you remember your reason for wanting to lose your v-card?" Marius asks.

"That was *your* idea," I remind him.

"That may be so, but you acted on my idea. Why? Why did you ask Creed to sleep with you in the first place?"

I heave a sigh. "Because I wanted to make one decision for myself."

"Exactly. You made the choice to lose your virginity, and with Creed. So what's stopping you from continuing to choose him?"

"Isn't it obvious?" I nod toward Jameson. "I'm supposed to be in love with someone else. Carrying on with Creed isn't fair to anyone, especially him. It was only supposed to be one night anyway. Nothing more. That way we didn't have to involve feelings."

"From the way I've seen him look at you," Harriet

chimes in, "you two are far past the point of not involving feelings."

"And the same goes for the way I've seen *you* look at *him*," Marius continues. "You obviously can't keep your hands off each other."

"I can't disagree with that."

"Do you really want to deprive yourself of something that makes you happy because you know there's an expiration date? Take this mimosa, for example." He lifts his empty glass. "I started drinking it fully aware I'd eventually reach the bottom of the glass, thus causing the happiness this delicious nectar gives me to wither and die. But I still poured it."

"That's not the same thing. You could always make another one. I can't make another Creed."

"You know what I'm trying to say," he argues. "The royal household loves taking away anything remotely resembling joy. Don't let them. Why punish yourself in the present for what the future holds? Live in the moment. Who knows? Maybe in the end, you'll not just experience some great sex, but also an amazing love."

I narrow my gaze. "I have no desire to fall in love. I can't. Not when I'm essentially betrothed to another man."

"Believe me," Harriet says. "You can try to resist all you want, but the heart has a mind of its own. Love happens whether or not we want it to. No amount of refusal or denial will change that."

I part my lips to argue against their crazy idea that I should not only continue sleeping with Creed, but also keep my heart open to the possibility of something more than purely physical.

No words come, though.

Instead, I allow myself to entertain the fantasy, regardless of how impossible it is.

CHAPTER TWENTY-TWO

Creed

Sleep escapes me for yet another night as I toss and turn in the luxurious bed, the high thread-count sheets soft against my skin. Despite my comfortable surroundings, I have a feeling this week will be filled with restless nights, my mind consumed with thoughts of the woman sleeping on the other side of this wall, another man sharing her bed.

I don't want to like him. Don't want to find anything remotely redeemable about him. That would make this easier. Would make me feel better about the fact that I can't stop thinking about Esme. Can't keep my hands off her whenever I'm alone with her.

But from everything I've seen, he *is* a good person. He treats Esme with respect. Doesn't touch her inappropriately, even though something as innocent as a brush of his finger against her skin causes jealousy to bubble inside me.

Because I can't do that.

Because I'll *never* be able to do that.

And it's killing me.

The sound of a door opening and closing cuts through the quiet stillness, and I snap my eyes toward my own door, holding my breath.

Then, much like last night, I make out faint footsteps tiptoeing from the room next to mine. I throw the covers off me and pad across the room, putting my ear against the wood.

Like last night, I sense Esme pause just outside.

But unlike last night, she doesn't sigh, then continue down the hallway. Tonight, she knocks.

I don't immediately open the door. Just stare at it, unsure what to do.

The last few times we were alone together, things got out of hand. That's only added to the awkward tension between us. If we keep going down this path, it's only a matter of time until someone figures it out.

Until *Jameson* figures it out.

I may not know him well, but I doubt he'd take kindly to the idea of Esme and me fooling around behind his back.

But despite how wrong it is, I can't seem to resist her.

So instead of returning to my bed and pretending to be asleep, I open the door.

Light filters in from the hallway as I rake my appreciative eyes over her. Long blonde waves are piled on the top of her head, her body clad in a loose t-shirt and pair of boy shorts. She barely resembles the put-together, fashionable princess the public knows her to be. I love that I get to see this side of her. The side most people don't know.

"Esme, are you—"

"Can I come in?" she asks, fidgeting with the hem of her shirt. "I... I need to talk to you."

I nod, stepping back.

She offers me a forced smile as she crosses the threshold. There's a nervousness about her that's never been there before, even when she propositioned me to sleep with her.

"Is everything okay?" I ask once I close the door.

It's a stupid question. Nothing is okay. It hasn't been since we slept together. I still don't regret it.

She lifts her eyes to mine, blinking, lips parting. But no words come.

Tearing her gaze away, she spies a bottle of scotch on the dresser and stalks toward it, pouring some into a rocks glass before gulping down more than I could probably stomach.

She winces through the burn, face scrunching. Then she exhales, taking another swallow, this one smaller. Gripping the glass as a baby would their favorite toy, she paces, obviously attempting to collect her thoughts.

"I've spent the past several weeks convincing myself this arrangement with Jameson won't be that bad," she finally begins. "I've done my research, like I always do so I can be properly informed about an issue." She stops, fully facing me. "Do you know what the divorce rate is for arranged marriages?"

"Can't say that I do."

"It's less than four percent." She takes another sip of the scotch. "And do you know what the divorce rate is for marriages where people marry for love? Where people get to *choose* who they marry?"

"What's that?"

"Over forty percent. So statistically speaking, an arranged marriage is better." She paces again. "Especially when I have an entire team of statisticians and researchers telling me that, all things considered, this is a good match, even if it's more of a business relationship. Regardless, we get along well. We share some of the same interests and hobbies.

And that pesky little muscle in my chest doesn't risk getting broken." She stops, facing me once more, her voice growing more and more impassioned with every word she speaks. "It makes so much goddamn sense, Creed."

I step toward her, my gaze unwavering. "And you're okay with that? Without having any passion? With sentencing yourself to a lifetime of mediocrity?"

She stares at me, her shoulders rising and falling in a quicker rhythm. Then she spins from me, heading back to the dresser and pouring more scotch into her glass.

"I thought I was," she says softly, staring at the wall as she sips the amber liquid. "And then you had to come along and make me question everything. Make me question these statistics. These facts. And it's driving me fucking crazy." She tips back the glass, taking another long pull before returning her gaze to mine, silently pleading with me to give her an answer that will help all of this make sense.

But I don't think there *is* an answer here.

Approaching her, I take the glass out of her hand and set it on the dresser.

"Well, here's what *I* know for certain. What *I* know to be facts."

I widen my stance, crossing my arms in front of my chest. Her eyes briefly float to my biceps before she forces them back to my face. I can't help but smile at the obvious magnetism she still feels toward me, even if she wishes she didn't.

"I know it's tradition in the royal family for marriages to be arranged, at least between those in the immediate line of succession, as you are. And those marriages are just glorified business transactions, a way to ensure only those with the preferred upbringing be allowed to pass their DNA down to future generations."

She nods. "That's correct."

"I also know that, unless you want to lose your place in the line of succession, essentially becoming persona non grata, the Royal Marriages Act requires you to receive the monarch's approval. In practice, however, the monarch will only approve if the royal household does. Since the royal household has already selected a spouse for you, there's no way they'll approve of someone else. Someone they didn't select after careful examination."

"Precisely."

"And I also know Jameson Gates is a good man, as much as it pains me to say so."

"He's as much a pawn in this game as I am."

"Right." I nod curtly. "So these are all things we know. That we can agree on as being completely factual in nature. Correct?"

"I believe we can."

"Good." I pull my lips together and turn from her, stepping toward the dresser.

Now it's my turn to attempt to get my thoughts under control. To need some liquid courage.

I bring the rocks glass to my mouth, tasting a hint of Esme as I sip the scotch, debating my next course of action.

I could tell her we'd be foolish to continue down this same path. That we're just setting ourselves up for heartbreak. Based on our circumstances, it's the reasonable thing to do.

But if I've learned anything over the past several days, it's that I lose all sense of reason when it comes to Esme.

After another long swallow of scotch, I slam the glass on the dresser and face her, my gaze determined as I sweep my eyes over her.

"But here's what I also know to be true." I grip her

biceps, not wanting her to escape what I'm about to tell her. "I know I hate the idea of anyone else kissing you. Know the thought of you marrying someone who will never love or appreciate you makes me more jealous than I imagined possible. Know I could need you more than I do my next breath, but that won't change who we are to each other. Won't change that there's no scenario in which the two of us could ever have a future together, so if we give in to these desires, it will only end badly for all involved. Which is why we should walk away right now."

"I can't think of a single valid reason we shouldn't," she responds evenly. But regardless of her words, she doesn't try to free herself from my hold. If anything, she moves closer, tilting her head back.

"I've always been a very rational man," I continue, my heartbeat thrumming in my ears. "All my life, I've been guided by rules, even more so once I joined the military. Everything's black or white. You either follow the rules or break them. There's no room for gray."

"And whatever this is can only be described as gray."

"That's true." I brush a wayward strand of hair behind her ear. "But lately I've come to realize something."

She swallows hard, chest rising and falling in a quicker pattern. "What's that?"

I bring my hands to her cheeks, clutching them in a firm grip.

"Gray's my favorite color," I growl.

Then I crush my lips to hers.

CHAPTER TWENTY-THREE

Creed

E sme doesn't react at first, frozen in place.

Based on everything she just told me, this isn't what she was looking for when she knocked on my door. If anything, she probably came by to make sure this *never* happens again.

All day, I've tried to convince myself this shouldn't happen again, too, especially after Marius nearly walked in on us.

But I can't resist this inexplicable magnetism that keeps drawing me back to her.

After a few seconds that feel like an eternity, she can't seem to resist it, either.

Relaxing into my kiss, she pulls me closer, threading her fingers through my hair. I coax her lips open, our teeth crashing as I kiss her deeper, hands frantically exploring her body.

"I told myself last night would be the last time," I

murmur against her mouth before peppering kisses along her jawline, nipping at the soft, delicious skin of her neck. "That I wasn't going to keep doing this."

"You can't get enough," she exhales, obviously more than aware of what I'm going through. "You're addicted to this feeling."

She cranes her head, allowing me better access. A flash of possessiveness fills me when I see the subtle outline from where I marked her. It was careless, especially since she's sharing a bed with Jameson. But my god, I love seeing my mark on her.

"Not just this feeling." I move from her neck, my eyes locking with hers. "I am hopelessly addicted to you, Esme. And no amount of time in a rehab facility will cure me of it." I dig my fingers into her hair, holding her tightly. "I don't *want* to be cured of it."

She parts her lips, her response on the tip of her tongue. I expect her to tell me we don't have a choice. Something I've reminded myself of since that day in the stables. Hell, since that kiss all those years ago, which is where my addiction first started.

But she doesn't force me back to reality. Doesn't insist I work on getting sober.

Instead, she hoists herself onto her toes. "Then why don't you take another hit?"

Without hesitation, I yank her against me, mouth covering hers in a kiss that consumes every inch of me. Her tongue swipes against mine, exploring and submitting to me. My hand on her hip, I steer her toward the bed, only tearing my lips from hers to rip her shirt over her head before kissing her again.

When the back of her legs hit the mattress, she reaches for the waistband of my pants. But before she can push them down, I grab her wrist, breaking away to stare into her eyes.

"There's no going back after this," I tell her. "If we do this, I need to know you're all in. I won't have you ignoring me."

She searches my gaze, then sighs, pushing away from me and sitting on the edge of my bed. "You know I can't give you what you want. You just said it yourself. I have no choice but to marry Jameson. I have to act as if I'm in love with him, at least whenever I'm at public events and in front of the royal household. Not to mention, you're about to be sworn into the royal guard. I won't put your career at risk. Your *legacy* at risk."

Joining her, I grab her hand in mine, brushing my thumb along her knuckles. "I understand that."

"Then what are you asking of me, Creed?"

I'm not sure *what* I'm asking of her. It's not like either of us can change our circumstances. But I need to know I'm more than an act of rebellion. That she's willing to give me more than just her virginity.

"I'm asking you to be mine in all the ways you can."

She opens her mouth, but I swallow her protest with a kiss.

"I know you'll have to be affectionate toward him. There's no way around it, not unless you want to raise some serious eyebrows. Just promise you won't let him do anything more than kiss you. And that you only let him kiss you when absolutely necessary. Otherwise, I may lose my fucking head."

"Is that possessiveness I hear in your voice, Lieutenant Lawson?" she jokes.

"With you, always." Hand cupping her cheek, I urge her mouth to mine. "Or more accurately, jealousy. I hate the idea of sharing you with anyone, even some arranged spouse. But if it's the only way I can have you, I'll suck it up. I don't want him knowing the intimate parts of you. Not yet anyway. Not until we have no choice but to walk away."

She considers my request for a protracted moment. It should feel strange to establish ground rules for what is essentially an affair. My rational side screams at me to walk away now. That this is a disaster waiting to happen.

But there's a certain amount of bargaining most addicts engage in as a way to rationalize their behavior.

Like I'm doing right now.

"Okay," Esme finally answers with a determined nod. "He doesn't get my body. Only you do." She edges toward me, lips hovering over mine. "I'm yours to do with as you please."

"I like the sound of that." My cock twitches in my pants, my sex-crazed brain thinking of all the different ways I could interpret her words. "I *really* like the sound of that."

I'm about to kiss her, but she presses a finger to my lips before I can. "Now I want *you* to promise *me* something."

"What's that?"

I'll promise her anything so long as it ends with being able to bury my cock deep inside of her. To watch as she comes undone. To hear those little moans of pleasure that drive me wild.

This is the power she has over me.

That she's *always* had over me.

She draws in a deep breath. "I need you to promise you won't fall in love with me."

I blink, taken aback by her words. I thought she'd ask me to be as discreet as possible in public. Or make sure I don't let anything slip around Adam.

But this request... I don't know how to respond.

It's not a promise I can make without feeling like I'm deceiving her.

"If this arrangement's to work," she continues when I don't immediately agree, "I think it's best we set…boundaries. And that's mine. My hard limit, so to speak."

"*Love* is your hard limit?"

"In my life, it has to be. There's no place for love in a monarchy," she says, repeating the words her grandmother has told her time and again. You hear something enough, you eventually believe it.

And I hate that Esme doesn't think she can have it all. That she doesn't think she can allow anyone to love her like she deserves.

But if this is what she needs in order to agree to this arrangement, I'll give it to her.

Eyes locked with hers, I nod. "I promise not to fall in love with you."

"And I won't fall in love with you."

"Okay." I pretend the thought of never possessing her heart doesn't pain me like it does.

"Now that *that's* settled…"

She stands, heated gaze trained on me as she hooks her fingers into her shorts, sliding them down her legs. Then she extends her hand toward me. I place mine in hers, allowing her to pull me to my feet.

"As much as I love a man in gray sweatpants, I think they'd look much better on the floor."

I chuckle, warmth and affection radiating through me.

While I love the sexy and sultry side of Esme I'm lucky enough to see on occasion, there's something about these lighthearted moments I absolutely adore. Love seeing her smile. Love knowing I'm one of the few people who gets to know the playful woman beneath the glittering jewels and tiaras.

"I'll always give you everything you desire, princess." I push my sweatpants down my legs, grinning to myself when she shifts her gaze to my erection, pupils dilating. "Now tell me…"

I loop an arm around her waist, dragging her body against mine. When I slowly circle my hips, her lips part, breaths coming quicker. Gripping her face with a single hand, I force her eyes up.

"What exactly is it you desire?"

"You, Creed. I desire you."

Growling, I capture her mouth, pulling her with me as I fall onto the mattress, her body crashing on top of me.

I yank her hair free from her messy bun, allowing it to cascade around us as she grinds her hips, the combination of her heat against my cock and her addictive mewls of pleasure driving me fucking crazy.

"I love those sounds you make. Those little whimpers." I scrape my mouth along her skin, nipping at her neck. "Those little cries of relief when I finally touch you where you want me to." I slide my hand up and down the contours of her frame.

She straightens, moving against me with more desperation. When I cup her breasts in my hands, twisting her nipples, she demonstrates the precise sound I was talking about.

"But do you know what sound I like best?"

"What's that?" she exhales, increasing her motions.

It takes every ounce of willpower I possess not to flip her onto her back and ram deep inside her. My god, I'm so desperate to feel her again, especially after these last two days of torturing each other.

I grab the back of her neck, urging her closer. "My name on your lips as I make you come."

She closes her eyes, shuddering in response to my words. Then she returns her fiery stare to me. "Why don't you fuck me so you can hear that?"

With a grin, I crash my lips to hers in a demanding kiss, about to reach for my stash of condoms in the nightstand.

Except I'm not in my apartment. This isn't my room. And this nightstand doesn't have any condoms.

Pulling back, I curse under my breath.

"What is it?" Esme's concerned eyes search mine. "What did I do wrong?"

"What makes you think you did something wrong?"

She looks away, chewing on her lower lip. "I figured that since your demeanor shifted so suddenly, I did something you didn't like. I'm still figuring out all this stuff, which sounds pathetic, considering I'm nearly twenty-five and most people my age already have this sex stuff figured out. But—"

I caress her face, bringing her lips to mine. "Believe me. I'm still figuring it out, too. Still figuring out what I like. But I can say with absolute certainly that I don't have a single complaint in the sex department where you're concerned. If anything, you make me want to screw you every hour of every damn day."

"Fiend." She winks.

I feather my mouth against hers, even her soft kisses driving me wild. "For you, absolutely."

She sighs, melting into me before returning her questioning stare to me. "But then—"

"I didn't exactly prepare for this."

She blinks, still confused. Then realization sets in. "You don't have any condoms."

"I'm sorry." I glance at the clock on the nightstand,

noting it's a little before two. "I can run out, see if there's a convenience store open."

"You don't have to do that," she offers.

"It's okay. I don't mind."

I start to get up, hoping she doesn't view this as a sign that this is a bad idea. Hope she won't change her mind before I get back. I wouldn't fault her if she did. Hell, I should probably change *my* mind.

But before I can stand, Esme presses a hand to my chest, pinning me back to the bed.

"I said," she begins, demeanor shifting from somewhat disappointed to something different. Something much more…sultry. "You don't have to do that. It's not necessary." She gives me a knowing look.

"Are you on birth control?" I can't mask the surprise in my voice.

"One of the benefits of being born into a world that wants to control every part of my existence." Her expression falters slightly. "They started me on them several weeks ago. Probably in case Jameson wanted a sample before signing on the proverbial dotted line."

My jaw clenches, frustration tightening in my throat at the reminder of all the decisions that have been taken from her.

Including one very important decision, the consequence of which is currently sleeping on the other side of this wall. But I don't want to bring that in here. Not now.

"Well then…" I pulse against her, grinning mischievously as I coax her mouth back to mine. "I guess I'll be able to reap the benefits of that. Because I've been dying to know what you feel like with nothing between us."

She takes my bottom lip between her teeth and pulls. "Then what are you waiting for?"

My erection hardening even more at the promise of feeling her without a barrier, I reach between our bodies, lining myself up at her entrance. I meet her eyes, making sure she truly is okay with this, just as I did our first night together.

This time, she doesn't nod her permission. Instead, she takes control, lowering herself onto me, both of us moaning at the sensation.

I thought last time was incredible, the way she felt unlike anything I'd ever experienced.

But as Esme moves against me, using my body for her own pleasure, I've never been so damn turned on in my life. And not just because the feel of her without a condom is fucking heaven.

It's because she's comfortable enough with me to take charge. To explore what she likes. To tell me where to touch her to make her feel even better.

As we both come undone at the same time, our cries swallowed in a desperate kiss, one thing becomes crystal clear.

Esme is one habit I don't plan to quit anytime soon.

Even if it ends up being my downfall.

CHAPTER TWENTY-FOUR

Esme

"Good morning, you two," I sing as I plop down on a wicker couch overlooking the pool, Marius and Harriet sitting on a couch across from it, already awake and enjoying their morning coffee. I bring my cup to my lips, savoring the nutty taste.

Even the coffee tastes better this morning.

And I've always been one to enjoy my coffee.

But today, it has more flavor.

Everything about this morning is better. More vibrant. More intoxicating.

Last night was one of the best nights of my life. My body still hums and vibrates from the memory of the things Creed did to me. The pleasure he was able to pull from me. Pleasure I didn't think possible.

I hated having to sneak out of his bed before the sun rose so no one caught me leaving his room, especially Jameson.

All the more reason I never should have agreed to this crazy arrangement. We're just setting ourselves up for failure.

But like Harriet and Marius urged me to do yesterday, I need to live in the moment.

So that's what I intend to do. No more thinking about a future with Jameson that's been planned for me. Instead, I'm only going to think about right now.

And maybe last night with Creed.

"Oh, my god." Harriet hitches a breath, expression wide as she gawks at me. "You had sex last night!"

Marius darts his gaze toward me, scrunching his brows. "How do you know that?"

Harriet rolls her eyes, gesturing down my frame. "It's practically written all over her. She's got that post-coital glow. Don't tell me you've never shagged a girl good enough to make her look like that."

Indignant, Marius squares his shoulders, head held high. "I'll have you know, every lady who's had the privilege of joining me in my bed has left quite satisfied. My comment box has received nary a complaint."

"Maybe because they were too embarrassed to offer constructive criticism."

"Trust me. There's nothing to criticize."

"Anyway," Harriet draws out with another roll of her eyes, this one even more dramatic. "We're not here to talk about *your* sex life." She brings her attention back to me. "We're here to talk about Esme's." She drops her voice to barely louder than a whisper. "I'm right. You had sex last night, didn't you?"

I fight to reel in the grin that begs to be set free, but it's impossible. So instead of keeping this from my friends, I nod.

I can't remember the last time I've smiled like this.

I don't think I've *ever* smiled like this.

Don't think I've ever been so...happy. Then again, I'm not sure happy is an adequate word to describe the way Creed makes me feel.

I don't think there's a word in any language to describe the way Creed makes me feel.

"Based on that smile, I can only assume Lieutenant Lawson gave you another slip of the little general. Not a certain billionaire the royal household chose for you."

"Again, it's not *that* little, but yes. I slept with Creed." My cheeks warm as I take a sip of my coffee. "And it was even more incredible than the last time."

"Because that was your first time," Harriet states. "Everyone's first time sucks."

I straighten. "My first time didn't suck. Did it hurt? Initially, yes. But Creed was amazing through it all. Took things somewhat slow at the beginning. But last night..." I fan myself. "It was unreal."

"Well, I'm glad you're finally making your *own* choices." Marius covers my hand and squeezes, reminding me of my reason for going down this path. "Doing something for yourself."

"Thanks, Marius." I hold his gaze for a beat before he pulls back.

"Now tell us about last night."

"Yeah." Harriet's eyes light up with excitement. "Tell us everything."

"Maybe not *everything* everything," Marius adds. "I'd rather you not go into detail about size or girth. Broad stroke it for us."

"Pretty sure Creed broad stroked it for Esme last night. Or maybe she broad stroked it for him."

"There's not much to tell," I say, ignoring Harriet's remark. "We decided to stop torturing ourselves in the present for what awaits us in the future. We enjoy being with each other. So we're going to keep enjoying each other."

"And Jameson?"

"What about Jameson?" I ask her.

"What are you going to do about your eventual marriage to him? And Creed's impending induction into the royal guard?"

"We've discussed boundaries," I answer.

"Boundaries?" Marius asks. "Like what?"

"We've agreed this won't continue once he's sworn in."

"But what if one or both of you want it to?" he presses.

"We won't. I made him promise not to fall in love with me. And I promised not to fall in love with him. No feelings. Just sex."

The second I utter those words, my stomach sours, as if even my own body knows I'm full of shit.

"That sounds like a foolproof plan," Harriet shoots back sarcastically. "Agree not to involve feelings so neither of you end up broken hearted. That's a great idea, Ezzy. Truly. And not at all absurd."

"It's the only way," I sigh, shoulders dropping.

"I understand that. And I'm happy you decided to take this leap." She gives me a sincere smile and straightens, bringing her mug to her lips. "Just be careful."

"What do you mean? Yesterday you told me I should keep screwing him. Hell, pretty sure you *begged* me to do so."

"I did. And I still think you should keep screwing him. Not because I'm having a bit of a dry spell and want to live vicariously through you, but because you deserve all the toe-curling orgasms you can handle."

"But…" I arch a brow, sensing there's more.

She draws in a deep breath, then squares her shoulders,

the breeze blowing a few tendrils of her dark hair in front of her face.

"But we all know how things in this world can be."

"I'm well aware of how things can be."

"Which is why we want you to be careful." Marius lowers his voice, glancing over his shoulder to make sure no one's nearby to eavesdrop in on our conversation.

But like when I first stepped out here, it's just us, the only sign of life a few seagulls circling the shoreline in search of breakfast.

"Not for your sake, but for his. If anyone learns the truth, there won't be many repercussions for you. But Creed…"

"He could lose everything he's worked for," I finish Marius' thought, their warning yanking me down from the cloud I've been on the past few hours.

"Exactly." He nods. "So be careful."

"I will," I promise through the sinking feeling in my stomach.

I peer into the distance, wondering if we were too impulsive last night. If we failed to give this the deliberation it requires.

But I don't obsess over the idea for long, all my unease evaporating the second a familiar figure walks up from the beach, broad chest dotted with sweat from what I assume to be a morning run. The sight of Creed's chiseled body erases every single thought, except the memory of last night. How he used that body to push me to my limits.

Past my limits.

And I loved every second of it.

"You might want to start by not drooling every time you see him." Harriet leans closer.

I tear my gaze away, pretending to be unaffected. "I'm not drooling."

"Yes, you are. And I love this for you."

"Can we stop talking about this? He doesn't know you guys know anything."

"You got it." Harriet nods, pretending to zip her mouth. "Mum's the word."

"Good."

We fall oddly silent, my heart rate increasing with every passing second as I watch Creed stalk toward the house.

It's only been a few hours since I slipped out of his bed, much to his protest. But those few hours may as well have been months for how much I've longed to feel his hands on me. To be in his presence.

I hate that I can't wrap my arms around him and draw his lips against mine.

Hate that I can't offer to shower with him.

Hate that we have to pretend we're nothing to each other.

"Morning," he offers politely as he passes us.

"Creed!" Harriet greets him enthusiastically. "How did you sleep?" She waggles her brows.

"So not cool, Harri," I mutter under my breath, using my mug to block my moving lips.

Creed slows to a stop, confusion knitting his brow. "Um… Okay."

"I bet you did." Marius gives him an over-exaggerated wink.

I place my mug on the table, burying my face in my hands. "Remind me never to ask the two of you to help me cover up a crime."

"What's going on?" Creed looks from me to Harriet, then Marius, my two traitorous friends wearing shit-eating grins.

"I'm sorry." I offer him an apologetic smile. "I told them

about us. Well, they've sort of known all along. It was Marius' idea that I ask you to, well…sleep with me."

Marius raises his mug. "You're welcome, Lawson. I'd like it noted in the record that she did ask me to do the honors first, but I think it was more a case of right place, right time. So I steered her your way, with the promise to be her plan B if it came to that." He sips his coffee. "Apparently, no plan B is necessary."

"Umm…" Creed shifts nervously from foot to foot. "I don't know what I'm supposed to say to that."

"I'll accept a show of appreciation or gratitude."

"Don't worry," I interject before Creed has a chance to respond. "No one else knows." I level a glare at my two friends. "No one else *can* know."

"We're more than aware," Marius says, his eyes full of sincerity, something I don't see enough of in my everyday life.

"We've got your back." Harriet squeezes my hand. "Always."

I return her smile, then shift my gaze back to Creed, about to offer yet another apology, hoping he's not upset, especially considering he's the one shouldering the majority of the risk.

But when I look at him, there's not a single hint of agitation. Instead, he beams down at me.

"I figured you'd tell them at some point. If you ask me, it's a good thing they know."

"Why's that?"

"Because now I can do this." He leans down and feathers a soft kiss to my cheek. It's a light touch, one similar to the way my brother or friends kiss my cheek in greeting. But instead of retreating after the initial touch, Creed moves to the opposite cheek. This time, he kisses me so close to my mouth I can't help but salivate for more.

When he pulls back, he smirks at the way he has me so tightly wound from a simple kiss to my cheeks.

"There you are."

Hearing Jameson's voice, I stiffen, darting my eyes toward the house as he steps onto the patio wearing a pair of gym shorts and t-shirt. I do my best to act as casual as possible, unsure what he may have seen.

To be fair, even if he *did* see anything, I doubt it would have looked suspicious. Just a platonic greeting between friends.

But there's nothing platonic about the way I reacted to Creed's lips on my skin.

There never has been.

"Morning, beautiful." Jameson leans down, leaving a chaste kiss where Creed's lips were moments ago.

My reaction to the two men's kisses couldn't be any more different. One ignites a fire I fear will incinerate me before this is all over. The other does nothing for me.

"Good morning." I force a smile, hoping it will slow my racing heart.

"Did you already go for a run?" Jameson asks Creed, glancing at his watch that probably cost more than what Creed makes in a year. "It's not even eight."

"I was up at 0400 every morning in the military. Not getting up until six is sleeping in for me."

"I don't miss those days." He flashes Creed a smile. "Why don't you pour some coffee and join us?" he suggests as he assumes the vacant spot beside me.

In the casual way he does everything, he slings his arm along the back of the couch and around my shoulders, drawing lazy circles on my arm as if he doesn't have a care in the world.

Unlike Creed, who seems to constantly bear the weight of his legacy on his shoulders, quiet and brooding.

"Thanks, but I doubt I'd be very good company right now." Creed pins me with a brief glare before looking at Jameson. "Considering I just got back from a run," he adds, expression even. "The shower's calling my name. Enjoy your coffee."

My eyes remaining glued to him, I watch him disappear into the house, wishing I could join him.

Wishing he were sitting next to me, his hand caressing my skin.

But that can never be our reality.

Instead, we'll have to settle for our stolen moments in the dark.

"So…" Jameson's bright voice cuts through the silence. "What were you all talking about? Or do I not want to know?"

"Oh, trust me," Marius says mischievously. "You most certainly don't."

I bring my mug back to my lips, thinking how true Marius' statement is.

CHAPTER TWENTY-FIVE

Creed

I pace the length of the patio, glancing toward Esme's darkened room every few seconds for any sign of movement. When several minutes have passed and I still don't notice anything, I pull out my mobile and navigate to the message I sent, seeing it still shows as delivered, but not yet read.

This is stupid. She's probably asleep. I should just go back inside and hope she'll eventually sneak into my room. Texting her was careless. What if Jameson sees it? Or Anderson?

But being in that house, in the room right next to where Esme and Jameson are allowed to share a bed, is suffocating. I want nothing more than to leave this place so I don't have to watch them together. I'm also painfully aware that finding alone time with Esme will be even more difficult once she's back under the royal household's watchful eye.

This week may be our only opportunity to find any meaningful time together, regardless of how short.

I just hope she still *wants* to have time together. That she hasn't changed her mind.

Finally, I hear the back door slide open and I stop pacing. The instant my gaze falls on Esme, body clad in a tank top and shorts, I exhale a breath, shoulders falling in relief.

Not wasting a single heartbeat, I eat up the space between us and crush my lips to hers, not caring we're out in the open. It's risky, but at four in the morning, I doubt anyone's awake. Not after going to a club in town and not getting home until after two.

"God, I've been wanting to do that all bloody day," I murmur against her mouth once I bring the kiss to an end. But I don't pull away from her. I can't.

It was pure torture to keep my distance today. To watch Jameson touch her perfect skin. Kiss her plump lips. Dance with her at the club while people shot photos and videos of the happy couple to post all over social media.

"Do you know how many times I was on the verge of throwing you over my shoulder and hauling you into the bathroom at the club without a single care for who saw us?"

She bites her lower lip as she curves against me, her body fitting me so perfectly I swear she was made for just me. When she grinds up against me, my erection prominent, I groan.

"And what would you have done with me?" She runs her fingers through my hair, teeth tugging on my bottom lip. "Or perhaps I should ask what you would have done *to* me."

I wrap my hand around her hair and yank her head to the side, dragging my tongue along her neck. "I would have fucked you so hard and made you scream my name so loud, no one within the city limits could ignore the truth."

A visible shiver rolls through her, her shoulders rising and falling in a quicker pattern. "And what truth is that?" she asks breathlessly.

My gaze goes to her neck, her pulse throbbing as she swallows hard, desire flushing her complexion. I edge toward her, lips skimming her skin.

"That you're mine."

When I clamp my teeth onto her, she yelps, but it soon turns into a moan, impatient and desperate. Hypnotized by the lust clouding my brain, I suck on her neck as I steer her backward, not stopping until her back hits the exterior of the house. Bringing my hands to her waist, I yank her shorts down her legs before lifting her up, using the wall to support her.

"Do you want me like this?" I free my erection and line myself up at her entrance, teasing her. "Where anyone can see us?"

With fire in her green eyes, she skims her lips along my jaw before nibbling on my earlobe. "Fuck me, Creed."

Every muscle in my body hardens when I hear those words come out of her mouth. I doubt I'll ever tire of hearing my prim and proper princess succumb to her baser desires. Of hearing her follow her urges instead of pretending to be someone she's not, all because she's been told to behave a certain way.

Slamming my lips against hers, I give her what she wants and thrust into her, my motions relentless and frenzied as we submit to the hunger that's built between us all day.

This is incredibly out of character for me. Normally, I don't take risks. Not like this. I follow the rules.

But Esme's always been the exception for me.

Our bodies are wound so tight, the past twenty-four hours of not being able to touch each other akin to torture.

I'll take my time with her later. Make sure she's worshiped the way she deserves. But right now, I need to feel her. Need the reminder that she belongs to me, even if only in the shadows.

"Creed," Esme whimpers, squeezing her eyes shut, mouth falling open. I know this look. Know she's on the verge of coming undone and is trying to resist.

But I won't let her.

"Don't fight it."

I bury my head in the crook of her neck, inhaling her delicious scent as she digs her fingers into my back. The sound of our bodies slapping together echoes in the night, intermingled with our lust-filled moans, all cutting over the ocean waves crashing in the distance.

"I need you to come. Need your orgasm. Need to own them all, princess." I brace myself, picking up my rhythm. "Because you. Are. Mine," I grunt, each word punctuated with another thrust inside her.

"Fuck!" she exclaims, and I cover her mouth, swallowing her cries of ecstasy as her body unravels around me.

I increase my rhythm, desperate for release now that she's found hers. It only takes a few more thrusts and I lose myself in her and this moment of bliss.

"Wow," Esme says after several moments of trying to catch her breath.

"You can say that again." I nuzzle her neck, peppering gentle kisses that are completely at odds with the way I just fucked her. Then I pull back, carefully helping her lower her legs.

Reaching into the pocket of my shorts, I retrieve a washcloth and bring it between her thighs. She arches a brow.

"Was this your intention all along, Lieutenant Lawson? Lure me out of my bed to screw my brains out?"

"No," I answer, then pause. "Well, in a way, yes. I *had* hoped to have sex. Fucking you against the wall where anyone could have walked in on us wasn't part of my plan. I just..." I shake my head, shoving the washcloth back into my pocket. Bending down, I grab her shorts and help her into them. "I can't seem to control myself when I'm with you." I touch my mouth to hers, the caress of her lips on mine sending another rush of desire careening through me.

"Or maybe the little general can't control himself," she jokes.

"*Little* general?"

"Well, he's not exactly little. It's just the code name Harriet came up with for your penis, and it kind of stuck."

I groan, running a hand over my face. "I'm not sure I like the idea of your friend calling my penis little. Why can't he be the warrior king? Or the pussy conqueror? Or better yet, the pussy destroyer?" I waggle my brows.

She pushes against me, playfully punching my arm. "You're twisted."

"Only for you." I pull her back to me, treating her to a soft kiss. "Come on. I'll show you the *real* reason I asked you to meet me." Grabbing my backpack off the ground, I hook it onto my shoulders before linking my fingers with hers.

"And what's that?"

"You'll see." I wink, leading her away from the patio and toward a tree-lined path abutting the property.

As we stroll to the background music of the ocean, I keep glancing at our joined hands, wishing we could walk like this in daylight, and in front of crowds of people.

But it's just a fantasy. One that will never come to fruition.

Not in this life, anyway.

CHAPTER TWENTY-SIX

Esme

"Here we are," Creed says, emerging onto the bluffs overlooking what locals call Boneyard Beach, a collection of driftwood and uprooted trees resembling an elephant graveyard.

"This is what you wanted to show me? I *have* been here before." I place my hands on my hips. "We used to come here all the time when—"

"When we were kids and wanted to disappear where no one could find us. I remember."

Of course he does. After all, Creed often joined Anderson and me whenever we needed an escape, even at the villa.

That seems to be our M.O., though. Always looking for a way to escape.

And always falling short.

"I figured what better place to have some privacy than the boneyard?"

"You want to hike down there?" My eyes widen, mouth growing slack.

"Why not? We used to do it as kids."

"It's, like, two kilometers."

"More like three."

"What? Have you measured it?"

He shrugs. "This is part of the route I run in the morning."

I glance down at my flip-flops. "I'm not exactly wearing appropriate shoes."

"Then I'll give you a ride."

"Pretty sure you just did." I waggle my brows.

"Not that kind of ride." He pinches his lips together as a blush forms on his cheeks.

Creed Lawson getting embarrassed may be one of the most adorable things I've ever seen.

At first, he can seem a bit rough around the edges. But once you push through his harsh exterior, he's all warm and soft. I'm grateful I'm one of the lucky few people to know this side of him. Who he trusts enough to let in.

Even though a part of me thinks this would be easier if he didn't. If I were no more special than any of the other women he's invited into his bed in the past. The mere thought of him with another woman causes my skin to heat with anger. I have no right to be jealous, especially since he's forced to watch Jameson touch and kiss me. But the idea of another woman being able to have these pieces of Creed stings worse than I thought it would.

"I meant on my back. I'll carry you." He shrugs off the backpack hooked to his shoulders. "You'll just need to put this on."

"You can't be serious." I bark out a laugh. "You'd carry me all the way down there?"

"My gear pack weighs more than you do, princess."

Normally, I hate when anyone calls me princess. The word serves as a reminder of the prison I'm stuck living in every day of my life. It's akin to a convict being called inmate.

But I *like* when Creed calls me princess, his deep timbre causing a shiver to trickle down my spine. He's not doing so as a reference to my title, but as a term of endearment.

"Hop on." He turns away from me, widening his stance and bending at his knees to brace himself to carry me.

I roll my eyes, slinging his backpack over one of my shoulders and slapping his ass as I pass, causing him to jump. "I can walk. No need to carry me."

"But I'd do it. For you." He catches up to me and takes his bag from me, sliding it onto his back and linking his fingers with mine.

"I know you would."

The moon lights our way as we trek down the sandy trail toward the boneyard, reminiscing about our younger years and the adventures we shared along this very path. I'd almost forgotten about the games we played, the fun we had.

Things were so much simpler back then. Before I understood my place in this world. The responsibilities placed on my shoulders. What I wouldn't give to go back to that time, when my biggest problem was the one-legged pirate finding me and making me walk the plank, which was always one of the fallen trees along the beach.

Once we reach the end of the path and emerge onto the vacant beach, Creed leads us to an alcove between two rock formations we once pretended was home to buried treasure. Setting the backpack down, he pulls out a blanket and lays it on the sand, gesturing for me to sit. As I do, he joins me, retrieving two thermoses and holding them up.

"Coffee or tea?"

"Coffee. Tea is an afternoon only kind of thing. Although when I was living in Paris, my typical afternoon tea was replaced with an afternoon glass of champagne. Which sometimes turned into an entire bottle of champagne."

He chuckles as he hands me a paper cup filled with coffee, the color giving the impression he already prepared it the way I prefer. With sweetener and a touch of milk.

I bring the cup to my mouth, savoring in that first taste. And the fact I get to enjoy my morning coffee with a ridiculously gorgeous and compassionate man makes it all the better, even if we have to sneak away to do so.

"Did you like it?"

"The coffee's great. Exactly how I take it."

"No. Paris. Did you like living in Paris?"

"I adored it." I sigh, wishing I could go back there. But like Dorothy was forced to learn in *The Wizard of Oz*. You can't keep running away from your troubles. Or in my case, responsibility. Obligation. Duty.

"Then why did you leave?"

My expression falls, and I take another sip of my coffee. "I'd originally planned to come back just for the summer to spend some time with Anders before he deployed." I set my cup on the sand, then lean back on my palms, extending my long legs in front of me as I take in the beauty surrounding me, the first light of day visible on the horizon. "I had every intention of returning to Paris afterwards. Even got accepted into one of the top culinary schools in Europe, if not the world."

Creed's eyes widen at my confession, something I haven't told a single person until now. Why bother when it's yet another dream I'll never be allowed to pursue? I don't feel like I have to hide anything from Creed. Around him, I can be myself.

"Culinary school? That's… That's incredible. I didn't realize you could cook."

"Why?" I feign annoyance. "Because I have a waitstaff who caters to my every need?"

"I suppose." He shrugs. "Plus, I've never seen you cook." He stares into the distance, brows pulled together in contemplation.

It makes him look so serious. So…sexy.

I love the way thoughtful Creed looks.

And lustful Creed.

Hell, I like all his looks.

"A lot's changed since you left for basic training."

His devilish eyes scan my body. "Yes, it has," he remarks, his voice oozing with sin.

"Even so…" I attempt to ignore the way my stomach flips under his wanton stare, "I've always had an appreciation for the culinary arts. My grandmother used to yell at me all the time for sneaking into the kitchen to watch the chefs cook."

"Now that you mention it, I remember that," he muses.

"I was so fascinated, especially when they'd taste a sauce, then add a little more of some spice or seasoning. I wanted to learn that, too." I lower my head. "If for no other reason than to have some sort of independence or freedom."

"And culinary school would give you that?" he asks.

"Not culinary school, per se. But cooking. Anders and I were raised to depend on other people to do everything for us. Our meals are prepared. Beds made. Clothes laundered and pressed." I laugh to myself as I reflect on the past seven years of my life, some of the lessons I've learned humbling and eye-opening. "Do you know I couldn't even wash a dish before I joined the Humanitarian Corps?"

"You couldn't?"

"It sounds crazy. Something most people take for granted. Or most *normal* people. But I had no idea. Hell, I didn't know how to fold my own clothes, either. It was difficult enough to overcome the stigma of being a bloody royal when everyone at my camp already hated me. Thought I was only there as a publicity stunt. And here I was, eighteen years old, asking someone my age how to launder and fold my damn knickers. It was so embarrassing. I decided right then and there that I wanted to be as independent as possible. So I stayed up late. Learned how to do all these things I should have years ago. Over time, I became fascinated with cooking again."

"And culinary school?" Creed asks, although I can hear the hesitancy in his voice. "Where do you stand on that now?"

On a long exhale, I give him a sad smile. "I guess that will have to be filed away in the hopes and dreams category."

"So you're not going to pursue it? You must be quite good if you got accepted into a prestigious school."

"I'd like to think I am. I've come a long way since the days when I managed to burn water."

He laughs. "I'm not sure that's possible."

"Trust me. Anything's possible with me." I flash him a smile before the moment of levity breaks. "But at this point in my life, there are some dreams I have to let go of. Duty to the crown, and all that."

"Don't forget what you just said, though," Creed states after a moment.

I tilt my head. "What's that?"

He inches toward me. "Anything's possible with you. I

may not be an expert, but in the past forty-eight hours, I've come to believe that's absolutely true. Anything *is* possible with you." His lips feather against mine. "Or maybe I should say that *everything* is possible with you."

"Creed," I sigh, heart expanding in my chest, even though I wish it wouldn't. Wish I didn't respond this way to his sweet words. "You're not supposed to say these kinds of things to me. Not when…"

He presses his mouth firmly against mine, swallowing my protest. "Not here." He rests a hand on my hip, urging me onto my back as he slides his tongue against mine. "Remember the rules we made up whenever we came here as kids? The real world has no place out here. So I say, whenever we come here, we follow the same rules."

I run my hand through his hair as he plants hungry kisses along my neck, the combination of his tongue and teeth setting me ablaze.

"I could be wrong," I exhale, writhing beneath him, "but if memory serves, this was never part of our games when we were kids."

As he leans back, that wicked smile I can't resist tugs on his lips, a sinful gleam in his eyes. "Then we make it part of our games now that we're adults." He brushes his mouth against mine. "Because I *really* like playing with you."

He kisses me more fully, grabbing my thigh and hooking my leg around his waist, teasing me with his erection.

"And my god, I love when you play with me," I whimper as I surrender to Creed yet again, happy to ignore our reality, if only for a little longer.

CHAPTER TWENTY-SEVEN

Creed

I can't remember the last time I've smiled so much. That I've been so happy. I try to tell myself to keep my head on straight. To remember this will eventually end. I can't help myself, though. I never imagined being able to hold Esme's hand as we stroll under a canopy of trees, sharing our hopes and dreams.

Granted, we're not in public. Nor will we ever be able to do this in public.

But I'll celebrate the small victories when I can. Otherwise, I'm not sure I'll survive what the future holds. And I'm not talking about months down the road, but mere minutes, knowing once we emerge from the protective cover of these trees, Esme will be forced to pretend she's in love with Jameson.

Will have to let him touch her. Embrace her. Kiss her.

I should find comfort in the fact that he doesn't know her as intimately as I do. But he eventually will.

It's enough to make me want to disappear with her. To leave this place and never look back.

But that's not possible.

"Now I understand how Connie Reid felt," Esme states as we near the edge of the wooded area, our return to the real world imminent.

"Who?" I scrunch my brows, attempting to place the name. "Did we go to primary school together?"

A husky laugh falls from her throat.

God, I love that laugh. Love the raspy, sensual tone of her voice. She's like a modern-day Lauren Bacall. Even has the same mysterious eyes, pouty lips, and slender stature.

"Lady Chatterley," she states.

"Ah. Well, I've *heard* of the book, but haven't read it."

"It's quite scandalous. At least, it was at the time. It was published in the early twentieth century. There was even a famous obscenity trial brought against the publishing house because of the repeated use of two certain four-letter words."

"Which are?"

"One is fuck."

"And let me guess." I lean against a tree and pull her close, my arms encircling her. "The other is dick, although it *is* a name, so that seems a bit absurd."

Biting her lower lip, she shakes her head. "Guess again."

"Cock?"

"Wrong again."

I furrow my brow. "Pussy isn't four letters."

"But cunt is."

As if I didn't find Esme ridiculously sexy and alluring before, hearing her throaty voice say that has my erection springing back to life. Then again, it doesn't take much around her.

She whispers her lips along my jawline. "Told you it was quite scandalous."

"Imagine if they saw some of the books published these days."

Esme snorts a laugh. "They'd die of a heart attack on the first page."

"The first page? What kind of books do you have on that e-reader I've seen glued to your hand?"

She pinches her lips together, drawing my attention to them. Making me want to kiss them. Bite them. Devour them.

"Wouldn't you like to find out?"

"I'm not sure I would. Not sure I could measure up."

"Trust me." She hoists herself onto her toes. "You're better than any man I've ever met. Fictional or otherwise."

I press my lips to hers, addicted to her kisses. Not wanting to stop kissing her for anything.

Hating it'll be almost another twenty-four hours until I can kiss her again.

"Tell me about Lady Chatterley," I say, wanting to drag out this moment as long as possible. "Why do you understand how she felt?"

"Constance Reid became the lady of the house upon marrying into the aristocracy. It turned into a loveless marriage, so she had an affair with the gamekeeper of her husband's estate."

She rests her head against my chest and I envelope her in my arms once more, kissing the top of her head. I close my eyes, basking in the warmth of her fingers as she runs them up and down my back, exploring my body in a way that feels just as intimate as when I'm inside her.

"Whenever she snuck out to his cottage for some alone time with him, Oliver, the gamekeeper, would walk her back to the manor afterwards, stopping just out of view so no one would discover the truth." She cranes her head to meet my eyes. "So given the underlying theme of class difference and societal expectations, I can't help but understand how she felt. Why she did what she did." She leans toward me, lips poised on mine. "How she would have given anything to kiss him wherever and whenever she wanted, but society's rules dictated otherwise."

My chest squeezes at the despair in her voice, just as frustrated with the situation. But for her, it must be even more profound than merely continuing some family legacy, as it is for me.

For Esme, this goes much deeper, the chains the royal household has shackled around her much more difficult to escape.

I cup her cheeks, my stare penetrating. "But we don't have to let society dictate the rules when it's only us. Do we?"

She drapes an arm over my shoulder, enticing me with the promise of her kiss. "No, Lieutenant Lawson. We certainly do not. When it's only us, I say there *are* no rules."

"I like the sound of that."

I crush my lips to hers, tongue swiping against hers as I take my time to explore every inch of her mouth.

Normally, our kisses tend to be frantic, a desperate attempt to experience as much pleasure as possible before we're forced to part ways. This one is more drawn out, both of us wanting it to last forever. But we can't stay here forever. Can't stay in our fantasy world forever.

And I can't kiss her forever, even though I'd love to try.

On a long sigh, I break away, but still remain close, mouth hovering near hers.

"Same time tomorrow?" I ask, keeping her in my embrace.

"You're hell on my sleep schedule, lieutenant." She passes me a coy smile. "Don't you know a girl needs her beauty rest?"

"It's impossible for you to get any more beautiful."

She parts her lips, gaze searching mine, as if on the brink of chastising me for my sweet words. Telling me I shouldn't say these things, not with an expiration date looming in the future.

But she doesn't, her playful expression returning.

"When you put it like that, how can I say no?" She leaves me with one last kiss before stepping out of my hold. "Same time tomorrow," she throws my way before starting toward the villa.

I hang back to give her a chance to sneak into the house before me, watching her hips sway in time with her strides.

As she's about to disappear from view, I softly call out, "Hey, Esme."

Pausing, she glances over her shoulder, a single brow arched.

"How does it end? In *Lady Chatterley's Lover*, do they... Are they ever able to be together?"

She pulls her lips between her teeth, hesitation flashing in her eyes. Then she fully faces me, mouth curving slightly in the corners.

A sad smile.

Making me think I may not like her response.

"When her husband learns of the affair, he fires Oliver. And being the controlling prick he is, he also refuses to grant her a divorce, which back then was perfectly fine. To make matters worse, she was pregnant with Oliver's child, so you can imagine the difficulty she would have as an adulterer who was now pregnant.

"Even so, she left the estate and lived with her sister while

Oliver attempted to find work in order to support Connie and their unborn child. Eventually, she received a letter from him, inviting her to live with him in Scotland."

"Did she go?"

She exhales a long sigh, a wistful look about her as the ocean breeze blows her hair in front of her face.

"The book never answers that question. It ends with the letter. But I'd like to think they found their way back to each other. That they didn't let society dictate who they can and can't love." She holds my gaze, something unspoken passing between us.

Maybe I'm reading her wrong, but it feels like there's a deeper meaning in her words. That she doesn't want this society to dictate who she can and can't love, either.

But I'm not sure that's possible.

This isn't merely a piece of fiction.

This is real life.

As such, there are real consequences to what we're doing.

And I'm not sure she's ready to face them. Not like I wish she were.

CHAPTER TWENTY-EIGHT

Esme

A subtle glow finds its way along the horizon as I lay in Creed's arms. In this place that's become our own the past week. Our secret world of make believe and fantasy.

In a few hours, it will all come to an end.

I've tried not to think about it, choosing to live in the present instead. But I'm not sure how we'll be able to steal moments like this once we're back under the watchful eye of my protection team, led by Creed's older brother. Not to mention the royal household and the public at large.

It was difficult enough to keep our early morning *rendezvous* a secret from everyone, especially Jameson. Luckily, he only caught me out of bed once, and since Creed and I waited until four each morning, I told Jameson I got up to watch the sunrise. Claimed it was one of my mother's favorite things to do when she came here and it made me feel closer to her.

He offered to join me, but thankfully said he understood

when I declined his offer, allowing me a few hours alone with Creed as we welcomed the dawning of a new day.

Now that I'm heading back to the real world, where my days will be filled with public appearances, barely a minute set aside for my own needs, I don't know how Creed and I will make this work.

"What are you thinking about?" Creed asks lazily as he runs his hand along my hipbone, kissing the top of my head.

In the past week, I've been treated to so many of Creed's kisses. His lust-filled, desperate kisses. The more tender, emotion-filled kisses. And the playful ones, too. Despite all that, these are my favorite.

It's such an innocent gesture.

But the way his lips linger turns it into something so intimate.

"Today," I answer on a long sigh.

He's silent at first. Then he pulls me closer, wrapping his arms even tighter around me.

"Me, too."

I lift my eyes to his. "Where do we go from here?"

"What do you mean?"

"When we started this, I was out of the spotlight."

"And now that we're going back, it won't be as easy."

"It will be a lot riskier. A lot more dangerous. Especially for you."

"I know." He cups my cheek, pulling my lips to his. "But you know what they say, don't you?"

"What's that?"

"The greater the risk, the greater the reward." He smiles, but I don't return it.

One of us needs to keep their head on straight. Normally, Creed plays that role. But over the past week, he seems to have lost all sense of reason, at least when it comes to me.

"But also, the greater the fall," I remind him.

His expression sobers, eyes brimming with sincerity. "That's a risk I'm willing to take."

"Even if it's just for a little more time together? Mere weeks?"

"A few more weeks is better than nothing." His lips move against mine, the taste of him as addicting and intoxicating as it was the first time he kissed me. "I'm not foolish enough to think we'll be able to sneak away like we have been. We'll just need to find a reason to see each other."

"I could always ask Harriet or Marius to help," I offer. "Not sure how they'll feel about allowing us to use either of their places as a sex pad, though. Not sure I want to put them in that position."

"It would only be a matter of time until someone caught on." He shakes his head, lips pinched. "If we're to avoid suspicion, a legitimate reason is best. Something we can tell your protection team and private secretary."

I rest my head against his chest and play with a few tendrils of hair, allowing the gentle music of his heartbeat to settle the unease that mounts with every passing moment. When I'm with Creed, I no longer have any need to do my counting exercises. Instead, just being near him chases away the anxiety I've dealt with after a lifetime of being made to feel like nothing more than a circus performer. Something the public comes to gawk at without a single regard for the fact I'm trapped in a life I don't want.

A life I don't control.

Over the past week, I've regained some of that control. It may be fleeting, but Creed's given me an opportunity to explore my needs and desires without even a hint of judgment.

For the first time in my life, I've felt...free.

But a caged bird can never truly be free. She'll always be lured back to the security of the only life she's ever known.

Like I now have to return to *my* cage.

It may be a gilded cage, but it's a cage all the same.

"I could say you're helping me plan some charity gala," I suggest as he smooths a hand along my hair.

"Is that typically something you require help with?" He arches a brow.

"Not really." I roll my eyes. "I'm just expected to show up at a certain date and time."

He nods thoughtfully, staring into the distance. Then his eyes widen and he darts his gaze back to mine. "What if we planned a baby shower?"

"A...baby shower?"

Excitement builds on his face as he rolls onto his side, facing me. "Rory grew up in foster care so she doesn't have any family."

"I'm aware."

"Right. So, we throw Adam and her a shower. Or some sort of party to congratulate them on their baby. And since I don't have the first idea how to plan anything like this and you presumably do..."

"You do realize we'll *actually* have to plan one. We can't use it as a cover and nothing come from it."

"I'm fine with that. I've debated organizing something but have put it off because this kind of thing is so far out of my wheelhouse it's laughable."

I stare at the horizon as I ruminate over the idea, analyzing it for any potential pitfalls. Of all the possible solutions, this one seems the least risky. And also the most believable if questioned.

"I bet if I tell my private secretary what we're doing and that it's a surprise, he'll make sure to keep it from Adam, too. Everyone will."

Lips curling into a devilish smirk, Creed hovers over me. "I like the way your mind works, princess."

A shiver rolls through me from the carnal look in his eyes as he cages me in with his arms, making it impossible to escape him.

But I have no desire to escape Creed. Not now.

Maybe not ever.

He crashes his lips against mine as he crawls between my legs, raw need hitting me deep in my core, despite the fact it hasn't even been twenty minutes since my last orgasm. Around Creed, though, my libido is on overdrive, always desperate for that sensation of euphoria only he can give me.

"Almost as much as your body."

He brings his erection up to me, teasing me before sinking into me. My lips part on a moan as I succumb to everything he is.

To everything he makes me feel.

To everything he makes me believe.

All I can do is pray we're not being completely reckless. Not just with our bodies.

But with our hearts.

CHAPTER TWENTY-NINE

Creed

N ervous tension tightens my stomach as I navigate my car up to the security gate at Gladwell Palace, a path I've driven more times than I can count.

That was before I slept with the Princess Royal.

Before I agreed to have a secret affair with her.

Before I made the decision to put my career and integrity on the line.

Before I decided to do something for myself for the first time in my life.

"Here to see Prince Gabriel?" Steven asks as he steps out of the guard shack and approaches my car, not checking his tablet to make sure I'm on the visitor log.

His question isn't meant to pry. He's simply making small talk, considering in just a few weeks I'll be joining his ranks, more or less. Although I won't be tasked with guard duty like this. I'll be assigned to one of the teams responsible for protecting members of the royal family.

I could very well be assigned to Esme's team.

"Actually, Princess Esme."

"Why?" Steven straightens, my answer taking him by surprise.

"You know Adam and Rory are having a baby, right?"

"I heard. Are you looking forward to being an uncle?"

I push out a small laugh. "I haven't even thought about that. But since Rory doesn't have any family, I've taken it upon myself to throw them a party to celebrate." I make sure not to give too much information, not wanting him to become suspicious.

"That's thoughtful of you."

"Of course, I have no bloody clue *how* to plan a party that doesn't include shotgunning beers and watching football. So…"

"You asked for the princess' help?" He arches a brow.

"Aside from Rory, she's the only woman I know well enough to ask. I just spent eight years in the military. I'm not sure any of the guys in my unit know much about party favors and centerpieces."

He chuckles, shaking his head. "You're right about that." Stepping back, he presses a button, raising the barrier. "Good luck with the planning."

"I'll need it," I say with a smile. "Oh, and if you could do me a favor?"

"What's that?"

"This is a surprise, so if you see Adam…"

"You were never here." He winks.

"Thanks, mate. I appreciate it."

Applying pressure to the gas pedal, I blow out a breath and continue up the driveway, pulling in front of the entrance to Esme's apartment.

Once I bring my SUV to a stop, a valet emerges from the

lobby, opening my door for me. In a few weeks, I doubt I'll receive the same treatment, not when I'll officially be part of the staff. The hired help, as my brother puts it. But for now, I'm a visitor. A guest of a member of the royal family.

As I step out of the SUV, I give the valet an appreciative smile, then continue into the foyer, pushing down any resurfacing feelings of guilt when I glance at the door to Anderson's apartment and instead make my way to Esme's place.

I don't even have to knock, her door swinging open and her private secretary standing there to welcome me inside.

"Lieutenant Lawson," Lieutenant Hawkins says, his posture stiff, spine straight. "She's expecting you. Right this way."

Once I cross the threshold, he closes the door, leading me through the living room and toward the part of her apartment that's home to what she calls the administrative wing, since it's where not only her office is located, but also the offices of all of her support staff.

I shouldn't be surprised Hawkins is bringing me here. If she'd asked to meet me in her bedroom, it would only raise eyebrows. Increase suspicion. That's the last thing we need.

Hawkins comes to a stop outside a pair of closed wooden doors at the end of the hallway and knocks lightly before opening them.

"Lieutenant Lawson is here for your meeting, ma'am."

He steps back, allowing me to enter.

But Esme's not alone.

Jameson is perched on the edge of her desk as she leans back in her chair. His leg rests against hers, acting as if it's his right to be here, to touch her so casually. I suppose it is. It doesn't make the sight of them together any easier, regardless of the hours I was forced to witness them together over the past week. I'd hoped to avoid this once we were back here.

I was wrong.

"Lawson." Jameson beams, jovial voice filling the space.

It's obvious Esme tried to modernize her office as much as possible for a building that's been around centuries. There are still heavy wood accents throughout, but the patterned carpeting and dark wallpaper that was once in this room is gone. In its place are clean, light gray walls and wood flooring, the furniture having more of a mid-century modern feel, natural light flooding in through the large windows.

It's a stark contrast to many of the offices in Lamberside Palace, all drab, formal, and dark.

Another reminder that Esme doesn't fit in with this world. She's light and sunshine, where this life is all gray clouds and depressing weather.

"What brings you by?" Jameson asks as if this were *his* office.

Esme stands, smoothing a hand down her blouse. "Didn't I tell you? I agreed to help Lieutenant Lawson plan a party for his brother and Rory, since they're having a baby."

"But your schedule is packed as it is." He narrows his gaze on her. "Even more so now that the royal household has added many of my prior commitments to your hectic agenda. Do you think you'll have time to plan a baby shower on top of that?"

"I—" Esme begins.

"I'll speak to my personal assistant," Jameson interrupts, talking right over her, which only irritates me more than I already am after walking in on them together, even though I know nothing untoward was going on.

I just hate that he can stop by whenever he wants.

Can touch her whenever he wants.

Can be with her whenever he wants.

"She's a miracle worker, Lawson. Whatever you need,

she'll arrange for you. And don't worry about the cost. I'll take care of it." He encircles Esme's waist, pulling her closer. "It's the least I can do for the man who keeps you safe."

"I don't need your money," I growl, doing my best to temper the jealousy coming to a boil in my veins.

It takes every ounce of willpower I possess not to ruin his perfect face with a punch to the nose. It's not like he's in the wrong here, though. If anyone is, it's me.

"That's not what this is about."

"He's right." Esme steps out of his touch, picking up my growing resentment. "It's about doing something nice for someone important."

She glances my way, her lips curving in that sly way she reserves just for me. Then she faces Jameson once more, demeanor shifting from the Esme I'm lucky enough to know to the one the rest of the world does.

"Like you said. Sacrificing a little time to plan something nice for Captain Lawson and his girlfriend is the least I can do for the man who keeps me safe. He puts his life on the line for me daily. I can spare a few hours here and there to make sure he knows how appreciated he is."

"I didn't mean to come across as heartless, darling. Or as if I know what's best for you." Jameson approaches and wraps his arms around her once more, pressing a kiss to her temple.

But unlike when I kiss her, she doesn't melt into his touch. If anything, she appears stiff. As if his touch makes her cringe.

Good.

"I just don't want you to overdo it. There are only so many hours in the day. I worry you're spreading yourself too thin."

"This is extremely important to me. If I have to cancel

some of my other engagements, so be it. Adam and Rory deserve to know they're appreciated and loved."

He studies her for several long moments, as if hoping she'll change her mind.

Little does he know Esme's not one to change her mind easily. Not once she chooses a course of action.

Which makes me even more grateful she chose me.

"If you feel this strongly, who am I to stand in your way?" He smiles down at her. "I'll leave you to your planning." He curves toward her, lips seeking out hers. But at the last second, she turns her head, offering her cheek instead.

He kisses it, but his disappointment makes it obvious he'd hoped for more.

"I'll be back at seven to escort you to the opera," Jameson says, bowing slightly toward her.

"I'm looking forward to it."

He doesn't immediately retreat, the seconds seeming to stretch as he rakes his analytical gaze over her.

But after a lifetime as a royal, she's mastered the art of putting up a façade. Jameson would have better luck breaking into the vault containing the Vatican Secret Archives than he would at trying to read Esme's thoughts.

"It was good to see you again, Jameson." I extend my hand toward him, hoping he gets the hint that this is his cue to leave.

"Lawson." He places his hand in mine, a tense moment passing as we stare each other down.

Then he turns and makes his way out of the office.

CHAPTER THIRTY

Esme

The instant Jameson disappears down the hallway, I push out a relieved breath.

After he stopped by unexpectedly to take me to tea, only for Lieutenant Hawkins to inform him he'd set aside some time this afternoon for Creed, I feared Jameson would realize something was going on between us. And to make matters worse, Creed showed up before I had a chance to tell Jameson about the shower we're planning.

Regardless that he seemed to believe our cover story, I still can't shake off his suspicion. I'd like to think he'd be more than understanding about the situation. But something about the way he stared at me unsettles me.

Or perhaps it's my guilty conscience rearing its unwelcome head yet again.

Stalking over to the door, I close it and turn the lock as discreetly as possible, then face Creed.

"I'm sorry about that," I ramble as I cross the office back

toward him. "I wasn't supposed to see him until later. We weren't doing anything. We just—"

Gripping my biceps, Creed presses his lips to mine. "You don't need to explain yourself to me." His dark eyes swirl with sincerity and understanding. It's so different from the normal look of suspicion and indifference I'm used to. "I'm more than aware of what I was getting into when I signed up for this."

Expelling a long sigh, I wrap my arms around him, a weight lifting off me at the feel of his body against mine.

It's only been twenty-four hours, but it may as well have been twenty-four years for how much I missed him. If we were a normal couple, I could have called or texted him. I can't even do that without raising unnecessary suspicion.

"I understand how…frustrating this situation must be for you. If I were in your shoes and saw another woman kissing you…" I shake my head.

"Yes?" He pinches my chin, forcing my eyes to his.

"I'd hate it, Creed. I wouldn't have remained as calm as you seemed just now."

It's odd to harbor this sort of jealousy, considering I'd intended for this to be purely physical. To keep emotions out of it.

But from that first night, I knew it was a losing battle. Trying to keep emotions out of this is like trying to control the weather. Some things are a force of nature.

And this thing between us most certainly qualifies as a force of nature, brutal and unexpected, yet also beautiful in its simplicity.

I just pray the effects don't ravage us like the tornado I sense is forming in the distance now that we're back under the scrutiny of the royal household.

"Make no mistake, princess. I was far from calm when I

watched him touch you." His mouth descends toward mine, hovering so close but remaining just out of reach, teasing and tempting. "Touch what's mine."

The atmosphere shifts, the possessiveness in his tone sending a shiver through me. I never thought I'd like the idea of belonging to anyone.

That was before Creed.

Now, I'd give anything to be his. For him to claim me. Mark me. Own me in all the ways I yearn to be possessed by this man.

"You could have fooled me," I murmur, fingers threading into his hair, nails scratching against his scalp.

"It's because I was counting."

"Counting?"

He pulls back, but keeps me locked in his arms. "It's something I picked up in the military, especially when about to go on a dangerous mission." He chuckles under his breath. "Well, on special teams, they're *all* dangerous, but some are more so than others. So instead of getting stuck in your head in the minutes leading up to it, a counting exercise helped ground me. Five things you can see. Four things you can touch."

"Three things you can hear," I continue with a smile. "I'm aware. It helped me after Mum passed. After I walked into her bedroom and found her—"

"Of course," he interjects, preventing me from reliving the awful memory of being the one to discover my mother's body. Something no one should ever have to deal with, let alone a nine-year-old little girl. "That's what I was doing. But to be honest, the things I counted were a bit…inappropriate." His voice drops to a sinful timbre as he flashes a salacious grin.

I drape my arms over his shoulders, toying with a few

tendrils of hair. "And what did you count, Lieutenant Lawson?"

He moistens his lips, drawing my attention to how much I want them on every inch of my body.

"Well, first it was five things I could see."

"And they were?"

"Your eyes and pink cheeks."

He drops his hold on me, bringing his hand toward my face. But he doesn't touch me as he hovers his fingers over my skin. Warmth vibrates through me, making me want to move a fraction so I can feel him. But I don't, allowing the anticipation to coil through me.

Over the past week, I've learned the buildup is often as pleasurable as the main event. While I enjoy every moment of sex with Creed, I love the seduction the most.

Because he doesn't merely seduce my body.

He also seduces my mind.

It makes the moment we finally come together, our bodies joining as one, even more incredible.

"Your nose." He lowers his hand until his thumb lingers over my bottom lip, but he still doesn't touch me. "This mouth and that sinful tongue you love to tease me with whenever you slide it along your lips, which you do quite often, I might add."

My tongue darts out of its own volition, and he smiles. "Just like that."

He inches toward me, breath intermingling with mine, but at the last second pulls away, leaving me panting. Frustrated.

And so turned on I'm ready to combust.

"Then what?" I ask, desperate to get on with it, since I know what's coming.

"Four things I can touch," he croons, his deep voice

causing goosebumps to prickle my skin.

"And what were those?"

"Your hair." He moves his hand to my hair, collecting it in his fist and yanking it to the side, exposing my neck. "This neck." Using his free hand, he wraps his fingers around my throat, the hunger and longing in his touch lighting me on fire. Then he releases me, hands traveling to my chest and cupping my breasts. "These amazing tits, of course."

My eyes roll into the back of my head as he pinches my nipples through the unwelcome barrier of my blouse. I want to rip it off. Want *him* to rip it off. Want to eliminate anything standing between us.

"And of course, then I thought of touching your—"

"Wait a minute." I snap my eyes open, stepping out of his touch.

Now it's *my* turn to tease him.

"That's already four things."

He scrunches his brows. "Hair. Neck. Tits. That's three," he states, counting off on his fingers.

I point to my chest. "One. Two. Two tits. So that's four things."

"You didn't use the same argument for your hair. Or your eyes. Or your cheeks."

"That's because they're little. I'd like to think my tits aren't."

"That's not fair. Don't make me choose one tit over the other, because I find them both spectacular," he says in all seriousness, as if we're discussing his favorite movie or band. Not which one of my breasts he prefers. "Can I rephrase and categorize them as a *pair* of tits instead? Pair is singular."

I bite my lower lip, trying to reel in the grin lighting up my face. But it's impossible when Creed's like this. Most people only know the brooding, quiet man who's spent all of his adulthood in service to this country. I can't help but smile whenever I'm treated to this playful side of him.

Can't help but want more of this.

"I suppose I'll let it pass this once," I say coyly. "Mainly because I'm quite interested in learning what's fourth on your list."

"Truthfully, there were so many parts to choose from." His gaze darkens as he stalks toward me, forcing me against my desk. "I love your legs." He slides his hands along the outside of my legs before cupping my backside and lifting me up. "And this ass."

I moan as his erection hits that spot I'm desperate to feel him.

But he won't let me, setting me onto the desk and stepping back. My disappointment is short-lived, though. He grips just above my knees and hikes up my skirt, spreading my thighs.

"But the fourth thing I thought about touching," he begins, sliding a lithe finger up the inside of my leg, my breathing growing ragged as he nears my center. He leans into my neck, teeth skimming my skin. "Was your clit," he continues, pushing my panties to the side and pressing his thumb against me. "Making you fucking squirm."

I pant as I move against him, my body a slave to his touch.

"Of course that brings us to three things I can hear," he says very matter-of-factly, as if his thumb isn't rubbing mercilessly against my clit, driving me wild. "Which I think is quite obvious, particularly now."

"What is?" I swallow hard, trying to maintain the same unaffected demeanor as him. But it's pointless. Especially when he knows exactly where to touch me in order to push me toward the edge.

Over the edge.

"Your racing heart. Your labored breathing."

"And?" I circle my hips as I revel in the way he plays me like an accomplished musician does their instrument.

He slips a finger inside me, thumb still pressed against my clit. At the welcome invasion, I release a tiny whimper, too overcome with sensation to stop it.

"That," he murmurs against my lips. "God, I fucking love that sound."

I pulse against him, frantic and eager. "What's next?"

"Two things I can smell." He buries his face in the crook of my neck, rubbing his nose against my flesh. "The lavender powder of your body wash always makes me smile."

He lingers there for a beat, peppering soft kisses to my skin. Then he steps back, removing his hand from me.

I'm on the verge of protesting when he hooks his fingers into my panties. I lift my hips, allowing him to slide them down my legs.

His stare trained on mine, he slowly drops to his knees and spreads my thighs even wider, leaving me exposed and on display.

For him.

Closing his eyes, he inhales a deep breath, a look of bliss crossing his expression. "Your desire for me."

Holy fuck.

This may be the most erotic moment of my life.

Over the past week, Creed's helped me explore my sexuality in ways I never thought possible. Has opened my mind, given me a place to experiment in a nonjudgmental way.

But right now, him barely even touching me as he inhales my scent, seems so much more intimate and charged than when he had me on all fours as he pounded into me from behind.

And I love everything about it.

"Tell me what's next." I can only hope he's about to give me what I want. What I need.

"Well, next is one thing I can taste."

Leaning closer, he flicks out his tongue, spreading my legs wider still.

"Yes," I moan, closing my eyes as lust heats my veins, the inferno so strong I'm on the verge of combusting.

"It's what I've been thinking about tasting all damn day."

"Yes." I thread my fingers through his hair as he inches closer still.

But still not close enough.

"A delicacy I could eat every day for the rest of my life and never tire of."

"Yes, Creed. Tell me."

He teases me with a finger on my inner leg, so close to where I need him. I whimper as I thrust my hips, greedy for him.

"This delicious..." He presses a kiss to the inside of my thigh. "And juicy..." He kisses the other thigh, the anticipation about to shatter me.

When he doesn't say anything else for several seconds, I open my eyes, looking down at him as he kneels before me. A smirk crawls across his lips.

"Cunt," he finishes, burying his face between my legs, devouring me as if I were his last meal.

I release a moan, relief filling me as Creed gives me the pleasure only he can.

"So fucking good," he hums against me, his praise and appreciation sending me toward the brink of oblivion. "You taste so fucking good, Esme."

He pushes a finger inside me, and I dig my nails into his

scalp, which only seems to encourage him to increase his motions, a frenzied air about him.

I try to resist. Try to delay it.

But the man is a master at the art of oral sex.

Hell, sex in general.

Couple that with the way he prolonged the seduction when I was ready to jump on him the second we were alone, it takes no time for me to fall over the edge, wave upon wave of ecstasy washing over me. I quiver and shake on my desk, teeth clamping down on my lower lip so my cries of rapture don't bring any attention to what we're doing.

But right now, I don't even care about that, too blissed out to think about anything other than the man between my legs.

Once my tremors subside, Creed slowly rises to his feet, his lips shimmering with my desire as he smirks.

"See? Counting down works like a charm every time."

It's silent for a beat as I stare at him. Then I throw my head back and laugh. I can't remember ever feeling so at ease, so happy within these four walls.

"It certainly does." Fisting his t-shirt, I draw him closer, wrapping my legs around him so he can't escape. I tilt my lips toward his, seeking them out, as a buzzing cuts through the room.

"Sorry to interrupt, ma'am," Lieutenant Hawkins' voice sounds from the intercom on my desk. "Just a reminder that you have another engagement in about twenty minutes and Captain Lawson will be here to escort you. If you want to keep this a secret, I suggest wrapping things up for now."

The possible double meaning in my private secretary's words aren't lost on me. Thankfully, he thinks the only thing I want to keep a secret from Adam is the shower. Not the fact I'm sleeping with his brother.

"Of course," I say in a firm voice, praying it doesn't give away the fact my body still tingles from the aftereffects of a mind-blowing orgasm. "Thank you, Thomas."

"Anytime, ma'am."

Pushing out a breath, I squeeze my eyes shut, hating everything about this.

"It's okay." Creed wraps me in his arms and presses a soft kiss to my lips. "Thirty minutes with you is better than zero."

"I'm sorry it was all I could arrange today. And with Jameson showing up unexpectedly, it ate into the little time we had to begin with. Now I have to send you on your way without making sure you're taken care of, too."

"I don't care about that." His expression softens as he waggles his brows. "Still got to make you come all over my face. If you ask me, I made out in the deal." He winks, and I laugh slightly, but it's not enough to damper my frustration.

"But seriously," he begins once more, pulling me off the desk, reassuring hands gliding down my arms. "I know things aren't going to be perfect, that we may have to be content with a few minutes here and there for the time being. Maybe one day, we'll find a way to spend all the time we want together. Maybe even fall asleep in each other's arms and not worry about having to wake up early so no one catches on."

I close my eyes, swallowing hard through the knot in my throat, my heart squeezing. I'd love to subscribe to Creed's fantasy. Would love to wake up in his embrace and have nowhere to be. Would love not worrying about who might learn the truth.

That will never be our reality, though.

Regardless, I allow myself to live in the world of make believe we concocted back at the beach.

"I'd like that."

CHAPTER THIRTY-ONE

Esme

"Hey, stranger," Harriet says as she opens the door to her townhome in a row house overlooking the canals that snake through the city.

It's one of my favorite spots, and where I'd want to live.

If I had a choice about things like this.

"Good to see you, Harri," I reply with a smile, hugging her tightly. Then I follow her into her home, grateful for a night off.

With all the public engagements scheduled for Jameson and me this past month, it's been ages since I've had a night to myself. It's a miracle I managed to squeeze in as much time with Creed as I have. It still hasn't been a lot. Usually a half-hour here and there, an hour if we're lucky.

But like he told me our first day back. Thirty minutes is better than nothing.

We've gotten quite good about making the most out of what little time we have together, setting aside ten minutes to go over details for Rory's shower, then spending the remainder indulging in ourselves.

A part of me feels like I'm using him, especially when he makes me orgasm, then I send him on his way seconds later. Like the only purpose he serves is to get me off.

Whenever those feelings of guilt surface, I remind myself he knew what he was getting into when this began. Still, I can't shake the feeling he wants more than I can give him. That he wants more than a quick fuck before I leave for some formal event on Jameson's arm.

And Creed's scent on my body.

I've often wondered if I'm being selfish in keeping him to myself when nothing will ever come from this arrangement. I've debated ending things so he could find a girl with whom he *can* have all the things I'll never be able to give him. By staying with him, I'm simply delaying the inevitable. Making it more difficult to walk away when the time comes.

With Rory's shower in three weeks, that time is fast approaching.

Then I think how lonely my days would be without the promise of seeing Creed. The only thing that gets me through most of my obligations is knowing he'll eventually show up in my office. We may only get thirty minutes together at a time, but those thirty minutes have become everything to me.

"Where's Marius?" I scan Harriet's place, brows furrowed when my other friend is nowhere to be found.

They'd insisted I come over tonight for an early birthday celebration before the official dinner party at the palace next week.

Truthfully, a dinner party at the palace is the last way I'd want to celebrate my birthday, but such is my life. No one cares what I want. It's all about the spectacle.

And I'm just another trained monkey.

"There's been a slight change of plans."

"Oh." My shoulders fall. "So we're *not* doing an early birthday thing tonight?"

I try not to sound like a whiny child. With everything going on, I've been looking forward to spending the night with my friends. I even cleared it with my security team to stay here tonight, something I fear I won't be able to do much longer. Not with the royal household wanting me to be married to Jameson by this time next year.

This may be the last birthday I'll be able to celebrate the way I want. I hate that Marius isn't here for it. That he doesn't realize how important this is to me, which seems out of character for him.

"We are," Harriet insists. "Sort of."

"Sort of?" The furrow in my brow deepens. "I don't—"

Harriet grabs my hands, cutting me off. "Do you know how difficult it is to find a gift for a bloody princess who has a vault filled with priceless jewels?"

I roll my eyes. "I told you. The only gift I want is to spend one night with my two best friends, drink copious amounts of wine, and pretend we're normal. Or at least *I* can pretend I'm normal."

"And I love that was all you wanted." Harriet gives me a sincere look. "But Marius and I took a vote, and we both agreed we're a pretty shite gift, especially since there's nothing preventing you from seeing us whenever you want."

"You could never be a shite gift. You're two of the best people I know, and I adore you."

"I appreciate the sentiment, although that bit about Marius being one of the best people you know might go to his head." Her expression brightens briefly. "But we can give you something much better than a night with us."

"What could be better than a night with my two best friends?"

At the sound of footsteps, I glance toward the hallway, sucking in a breath as Creed's frame comes into view.

"Hopefully me." He smiles shyly, running his fingers through his hair that's grown longer over the past few months.

Mouth agape, I look between him and Harriet, confused, surprised, and a myriad of other emotions at once.

Harriet smooths her hands down my arms. "I know how...frustrated you've been. How you wish you could have more time with Creed. That's what Marius and I want to give you. Why we pushed your private secretary to clear your agenda for a solid twenty-four hours." She pulls back, glancing at Creed. "So we could give you what you want more than anything."

"I guess maybe I should have put a bow on my head or something," Creed says with a chuckle.

I shake my head, struggling to reel in my smile. Then I look back at Harriet. "I don't even know what to say."

"You can say thank you." She wraps her arms around me. "And promise to limit sexual activities to the confines of the guest bedroom. I'd prefer I be a participant the next time my bedroom sees some action."

I laugh, my heart expanding at my friends' gesture. While I'd love nothing more than to have a night with Marius and Harriet, she has a point. I *can* see them whenever I want. Or at the very least, when my schedule allows.

The same can't be said for Creed.

As much as I worry that spending the next twenty-four hours with him will make me want more of him, will make me want him *all* the time, it's not enough for me to decline such a thoughtful gift.

"Thank you," I tell her with a smile. "And you have my word. We'll only get freaky in the guest room."

"Good." She holds my gaze before turning toward Creed, slinging her purse on her shoulder. "Be good to my girl, Lawson."

"Always," he answers, his eyes never straying from mine as Harriet makes her way down the hallway and out of the house, leaving me alone with Creed for the night.

CHAPTER THIRTY-TWO

Creed

With Harriet gone, I study Esme, not sure how she feels about this change of plans.

When Harriet and Marius first approached me with their idea, I didn't hesitate in agreeing, the occasional thirty minutes I've been able to steal with her never long enough to satisfy me.

Then again, I doubt even a lifetime with Esme would be long enough to satisfy me.

But after I had time to think things through, I wasn't sure if Esme would *want* to spend an evening with me. Not when we agreed this arrangement was only supposed to be physical.

Nothing more.

Sure, she seemed pleased by this surprise when Harriet was here. She could have just been polite, not wanting to upset her friend.

But as she takes several determined steps toward me,

grabbing my face in her hands and crushing her lips to mine, I get the confirmation I've been hoping for since sneaking into Harriet's townhouse earlier today.

That Esme's more than happy to spend the next twenty-four hours with me.

Enveloping her in my arms, I melt into her, relishing in the fact I get to take my time kissing her. That I can explore every inch of her and not worry about anyone walking in and discovering us.

"Is this really happening?" she asks as she cranes her head back to meet my eyes.

I nod, lips slowly curving up in the corners. "It's really happening."

"This may be the best birthday gift ever."

She covers my mouth with hers, tongue swiping against my lips, begging for entry. Never able to deny her what she needs, I open for her, our kiss becoming desperate as we succumb to everything we've been deprived of for too long now. She molds her body to mine, a moan falling from her throat.

As she trails her fingers down my chest, I lose myself in her touch, circling my hips against her, desire heading my veins.

When her hand lands on my belt and she starts to loosen it, I snap out of the haze of lust consuming me and grip her wrist.

"Hold on, Esme," I pant, struggling to catch my breath.

"What's wrong?"

"Nothing's wrong. I just…" I lick my lips as I draw in a deep inhale. "I want tonight to be different from every other time we've been together. When we've had no choice but to jump straight in for a quick fuck before we lost the opportunity. Don't get me wrong," I add quickly when I see the crease on her brow. "I'd love nothing more than to be inside you right now. And every minute of the day. But we have all night."

Narrowing my heated stare on her, I enclose her in my embrace "And trust me, princess…" My voice a low growl, I nuzzle the crook of her neck, tongue tracing delicate circles behind her earlobe as I inhale her delicious scent. "I plan on making every damn second of tonight count." I curve back, eyes locking. "But not until it's time. Okay?"

She studies me, not immediately responding. Then a sly smile pulls on her mouth. "Well then…" She drapes an arm over my shoulder, lips skimming mine. "What would *you* like to do first?"

Her tease of a kiss causes my dick to throb in my pants, but I refuse to cave in to my desires so soon.

Esme came here with the promise of a night of normalcy. That's what I plan to give her. A taste of what it would be like if we were a normal couple sharing a normal evening together.

"Perhaps we should begin with *my* birthday gift to you."

"I thought that's what we were getting to before you told me to stop."

I chuckle. "Making you come isn't a gift. Well, I guess it can be. I consider every second with you a bloody gift. But I prefer to think of a gift as something unique that you don't receive a lot of. And I may not have been keeping track, but I believe I've given you quite a few orgasms this summer."

A pinkish hue covers her cheeks as she chews on her lower lip. "You certainly have."

"Right. So fucking you isn't your gift, although I will absolutely make sure you have as many orgasms tonight as possible."

"Then what is it?"

"Come with me."

My fingers linked with hers, I pull her into the kitchen area of Harriet's open floor plan and head toward the refrigerator, opening it. Dropping my hold on her, I retrieve the various ingredients I'd picked up earlier.

"I wasn't sure what kinds of things you liked to make, so I enlisted your friends' help. Just my luck, you have a long list of favorite dishes," I ramble nervously, hoping she likes my idea of a gift.

When I'd first thought of it, it seemed like the perfect thing to give her. Now that I'm here, I worry she'll hate it. After all, most people prefer being pampered on their birthday, going out to a five-star restaurant.

But Esme's not most people.

I just hope I didn't overstep.

"Since I never want to do anything to take away your ability to make your own decisions, I picked up ingredients for about five different possibilities. Scallops. Filet mignon. Lamb. Salmon. And even some duck."

I shift through the various wrapped cuts of meat and seafood that cost me a small fortune. But Esme's worth it.

"If I'm missing anything, let me know and I'll text Harriet. Obviously, it's best if I'm not seen coming or going, but I can make sure you have whatever you need."

Esme blinks, mouth agape, not immediately saying anything. Her expression is an exact replica of the one she wore minutes ago when she learned she'd be spending the night with me instead of her two best friends.

"If you *don't* want to cook, I can attempt something. I make a somewhat decent steak. At least I think I do. Probably not nearly as good as yours, but—"

"Your gift is for me to cook us dinner?"

I cringe, running my hand through my hair. "Now that

you say it out loud, it does sound like a pretty shite gift. Almost as bad as a vacuum cleaner, I suppose. I remember how you told me you wanted to go to culinary school and loved the independence cooking gave you. Since you don't get to do much of it, I thought—"

Before I can utter another syllable, she flings her arms around me, hugging me tighter than she ever has, her body trembling against mine.

"This is the fucking sweetest thing anyone's ever given me," she chokes out.

I pull her closer, grateful she doesn't hate my gift, but at the same time frustrated this is the first decent birthday she's ever had. I'm sure Anderson has tried to celebrate it in his own way, but Esme deserves to be thought of. Deserves to have everything she could ever want.

Even if I'm more than aware of how impossible that is.

"I'll never be able to compete with whatever flashy piece of jewelry Jameson plans to give you. I just—"

"I don't care about that." Pulling out of my chest, she swipes at her cheeks, eyes glassy with emotion. "This is infinitely better than even the most expensive piece of jewelry. Because it means you actually listened. Did whatever you needed to give it to me. That makes this gift much more valuable. Priceless, really."

My shoulders fall out of relief, and I hover my lips near hers. "I just want to make you happy, Esme. That's all."

"You do, Creed. You make me so damn happy."

It's a simple statement, one most people wouldn't think twice about.

But it's not a simple one for Esme. Not when she's been intentional about keeping her feelings locked up for most of her life.

Especially these past few weeks around me.

It may not be a declaration of love, but with Esme, I've learned to celebrate the small victories. Knowing I was able to make her happy is a victory I plan to celebrate for the rest of my life.

"And you make me so damn happy, too, Esme. The happiest I've ever been."

She doesn't chastise me for saying things I shouldn't. Instead, she touches her mouth to mine, allowing herself to succumb to the fantasy that we could be together. That we could be happy.

I know it's a bad idea. That we're setting ourselves up for failure.

Right now, I don't care about that.

All I *do* care about is this amazing woman I can't imagine not being in my life.

CHAPTER THIRTY-THREE

Esme

"My god, Esme," Creed moans, eyes rolling into the back of his head in bliss. "You're bloody incredible."

Heat covers my cheeks as I fight a smile.

I've never been one to seek anyone's approval, not after growing up in a world where acceptance is never given. But after being with Creed, I hunger for his compliments.

His praise.

It gives me a sense of satisfaction I never realized I needed.

And when he commends my cooking, it means even more.

While I adore hearing his gruff voice tell me how incredible I feel when I move against him, or how much he loves watching my red lips circle his cock as I take him in my mouth, Creed's praise for my cooking hits differently.

"You like it?" I pull my lips between my teeth, pushing down the fluttering that erupts in my stomach when I see the pure ecstasy on his face as he chews the roast duck with a fig and sage glaze I'd made for our main course.

"Like it?" He dabs a napkin against his mouth. Then he grabs my hand from across the table, thumb brushing my knuckles.

It's an innocent gesture, but feels intimate.

Everything about tonight has felt intimate.

It's not the first time we've been alone together. But it's the first time we've been able to take our time. To savor being in each other's company.

What I wouldn't give to have even more nights like this.

"It's bloody brilliant," he declares with a gleam in his eye. "Probably the best thing I've ever eaten."

"I doubt the military set the bar too high."

"That may be true, but don't discredit yourself." He squeezes my hand. "You are extremely talented, Esme. You deserve to follow this passion."

I give him a tightlipped smile, not wanting to let reality into tonight. Because the reality is that I won't be able to follow my passion.

Even if the royal household weren't intent on marrying me off, I wouldn't be allowed to do what I want. Not when my life isn't mine to live. It never has been.

"I couldn't have done it without you," I tell him in a chipper voice, ignoring the reminder of what awaits me when tonight is over. "You're quite handy in the kitchen yourself."

"I could barely manage chopping the onions and garlic."

"You did great." I wink, digging in for another bite of duck.

I couldn't have asked for a better way to celebrate my

birthday. Not only did Creed give me a chance to cook, he stayed by my side, helping where we could, asking questions about different spices and flavors, much like I did all those years ago.

In the end, I'd prepared a salmon dill *amuse-bouche*, an appetizer of bacon-wrapped scallops as well as beef wellington bites, all followed with our main course of roast duck. The entire evening felt so…normal. And during the last few hours, I've allowed myself a taste of what it would be like if I were able to be with Creed.

Of cooking together while we indulge in a bottle of wine, and occasionally each other.

Of sharing a romantic dinner as soft jazz music plays in the background.

Of stealing sly glances over the course of the meal, every second causing the sexual tension to mount until neither one of us can stand it another minute, and he hauls me into the bedroom, where we lose ourselves in each other all night long.

Of waking up in his arms and doing it all over again.

Every day.

For the rest of my life.

Most people think I live a fairytale existence. That's what the palace publicity team wants the world to believe. That I'm a princess in love with a pseudo-prince and we'll live happily ever after.

But that life isn't a real fairy tale.

This strange existence I've created with Creed is the closest thing to a true fairy tale I've ever experienced.

It's the most *real* thing I've ever experienced, too. I hate the idea of it all ending in just a few short weeks. But what choice do I have? Do either of us have?

"I don't think I can eat another bite." Creed's voice cuts

through my thoughts, and I tear my attention back to his plate.

"It's a good thing, considering there's nothing left."

"You're a damn good cook, Esme," he replies, his voice full of awe and sincerity. There's something else within, too. Perhaps a touch of frustration over the fact I'll never be able to pursue this passion. "But don't worry." He flashes me a sinful smile. "I still saved some room for dessert."

My eyes widen and I pull back, straightening. "Crap. I completely forgot to make something for dessert." I toss my napkin on the table and push back to stand. "I think I saw some fresh berries in the refrigerator. I can probably whip up a quick custard or something."

I'm about to head toward the kitchen when Creed shoots to his feet, wraps his fingers around my wrist, and yanks my body against his. I inhale a sharp breath, the abrupt motion catching me off guard.

"While that sounds incredible…" He dips his head into the crook of my neck, tone becoming carnal and sensual. "I had something different in mind for dessert."

When his unshaven jawline scratches my skin, I whimper, my core clenching, lust spiraling through me.

Since we started this arrangement, an intense sexual tension has always existed between us.

Right now, it's even more potent. More powerful.

More combustible.

"What would that be?" I ask coyly, pulse increasing as he trails a hand down the contours of my frame, lifting my blouse and brushing his fingers along my hipbone.

"You." He inches closer, my mouth watering at the promise of his lips on mine.

While I've stolen the occasional kiss throughout the

evening, I'm desperate for more of him. For him to consume every part of me in a way only he can.

In a way I fear only he will ever be able to.

When he touches his mouth to mine, a moan tumbles from me. He tastes of sage, mint, and something else I've never been able to place. A nectar I've only found in this man's kisses.

A flavor I will forever associate with Creed Lawson.

"You're sweeter than any dessert I've ever had," he murmurs against my lips. "More delicate. More refined."

He moves along my jaw, peppering kisses to my neck, tongue tracing delicious circles.

"An indulgence I shouldn't partake in, but I just can't bloody resist the temptation."

When he nibbles at my skin, I gasp, raw hunger consuming me for more of his words. More of his touch. More of anything he'll give me.

"Then don't resist." I grab his cheeks, forcing his gaze to mine. "Have me, Creed."

He smirks. "Gladly."

Before I can brace myself, he swoops me into his arms as if I weigh nothing.

"Creed!" I shriek, a lightness filling me. "What are you doing?"

"Having my dessert." With a sinful waggle of his brows, he stalks up the stairs and into the guest room, his steps quick, a man on a mission.

Once inside, he kicks the door closed, then lowers my feet onto the floor, the mood shifting from playful and lively to something deeper and more intense, Creed's gaze awash with a look of awe and something else.

Something I don't want to articulate for fear of what it'll mean for us.

My heart thrashes in my chest as he brings his hand to my face, slowly pushing a few tendrils of hair behind my ear. Flames from the dozen or so candles flicker, casting shadows on his distinguished face. Everything about this moment, from the ambience to the sensual background music to the way he peers at me, screams romance.

Devotion.

Love.

But this was never supposed to be about romance or devotion.

And it certainly was never supposed to be about love.

I don't have a chance to voice my concerns before Creed's lips are back on mine, his kiss hitting me differently in this space.

In this moment.

For the first time, there's no risk of someone walking in and cutting things short. Instead, we can take our time.

And that's precisely what Creed does.

He takes his time kissing me.

Undressing me.

Lowering me onto the bed.

Exploring every inch of my body, like a man mapping out uncharted territory, venturing somewhere he's never dared travel before.

As much as I know I shouldn't, I can't help but follow Creed down this path, succumbing to his sensual touch.

"Please, Creed," I beg as he hovers over me, his tongue teasing my nipple with slow and languid licks. Heat courses through me, more powerful and fierce than any other time he's done this same thing.

"What do you need, Esme?" he asks in a low voice that oozes sex and seduction.

"You, Creed. Need you inside me." I grip his face, forcing his mouth within a breath of mine. "Need you to fuck me."

Normally, those are the only words he needs before slamming into me, giving me what I crave.

But nothing about tonight is how things typically are between us, everything infinitely more charged.

"I'm not going to fuck you, Esme." He presses a soft kiss to my lips before pulling away, a look of peace washing over his face. Dark eyes stare back as he runs a soft finger along my cheek. "I'm going to make love to you."

I swallow hard, his statement ringing in the air around us.

I should remind him of the promise he made when we agreed to this arrangement. Tell him this was only supposed to be about sex. That if I allow him to make love to me, it'll give him hope this could be real.

It'll give *me* hope, too.

But despite all of this, I can't resist the desperation in his gaze as he waits for my response.

Wrapping my legs around his waist, I run my fingers through his hair, lips touching his. "Please, Creed. Make love to me."

The instant those words leave me, tension rolls off him, his body momentarily relaxing. He covers my mouth as he eases inside me, a whimper falling from my throat with the fullness consuming me.

There's no relentless pounding. No harsh slaps or punishing bites. Instead, he draws everything out as he rocks his hips into me, each deep and penetrating invasion pushing my body higher than it's been before.

He grabs my hands in his, our fingers intertwining as he

pins them on either side of my head. Not being able to touch him only serves to increase the pleasure coursing through me.

The emotion in his stare and the sensuality in his movements is so big, so sharp, it's almost too much to bear. I try to stay in the moment, try to keep my eyes locked on his, but I can't, worried what he'll see. Instead, I squeeze my eyes shut, wanting to block out the myriad of thoughts swirling in my mind.

Wanting to block out the truth I see in his own dark orbs.

"Look at me, Esme," he demands. But it's not as gruff and wanton as is normally the case when we have sex.

It's softer. More like a plea. Because tonight, this is so much more than sex.

And not just for him.

For me, too.

I didn't want it to be. Wanted to keep things easy. Casual. Superficial.

Wanted to keep all emotion out of it.

Now I realize it was a foolish plan.

Marius and Harriet tried to warn me this might happen. That I could resist all I wanted, but the heart can't be controlled or reasoned with.

And when I fall over the edge with Creed, pulling him closer as I ride wave after wave of one of the most intense orgasms of my life, I'm faced with the truth that my friends were right.

The heart can't be reasoned with.

At least *my* heart can't.

Not when it no longer belongs to me. Instead, it belongs to the man holding me and whispering sweet words as I fall asleep in his arms for what I fear may be the only time.

And that makes this entire scenario hurt more than I thought possible.

Regardless of what I want, what my *heart* wants, it doesn't matter.

Not when my fate was sealed the second I was born.

PART III

Legacy

No legacy is so rich as honesty.

~ William Shakespeare

CHAPTER THIRTY-FOUR

Creed

"Lieutenant Lawson." Hawkins jumps up from his desk the second he sees me pass on my way to Esme's office. "I wasn't expecting you."

"I apologize for not calling ahead, but a last-minute issue came up I need to discuss with Her Highness. Considering the shower's tomorrow, I thought it best to catch her before she leaves for tonight's event. It won't take long."

I smile, acting as nonchalant and innocent as possible.

Even though the things I've been doing to Esme these past few months have been anything but innocent.

Thankfully, all the time we spent together under the guise of planning a shower for Adam and Rory never raised any eyebrows. Because we wanted it to be a surprise, everyone knew to keep it a secret from Adam. Even the General of the Royal Guard himself was in on it. Made sure to give Adam other responsibilities that would take him away so Esme and I had time to plan.

At least, in their minds, that's what we were doing.

While we did put together what I hope to be a wonderful celebration for a great couple about to welcome a child into their lives, it certainly didn't require us to see each other as often as we have.

Even on days we weren't slated to meet, her schedule too hectic to put aside any meaningful length of time, I often stopped by her office, pretending I needed to discuss something regarding the shower. Such as choosing a place setting. Or a theme. Or the menu. All things we could have handled over email. But considering our time together is short enough as it is, I used any excuse I could to see her.

Like today.

Especially today.

Because tomorrow, it will become much more difficult to find an excuse to see each other in private. Harriet and Marius have offered the use of their townhomes, but I know Esme's hesitant to agree, not wanting to put a strain on their friendship.

Since her birthday, I've been dying for another night with her, especially with my induction date just three weeks away.

Three more weeks until she's off-limits.

Officially.

Although I could argue she's *always* been off-limits.

I've simply been content to ignore that fact over the summer.

"I'll see if she's available," Hawkins says, picking up his phone to call Esme.

I thank him, playing the part I have all summer in his presence. But I'm not worried. Esme's always available for me.

After a brief conversation, Hawkins places the phone

back on the receiver, then addresses me. "She's in her suite getting ready for tonight. You can find her there."

"Thank you." I start to turn.

"Oh, and Lieutenant Lawson?"

I pause, glancing back at him, his military training obvious in his formal posture, along with the way he keeps his dusty brown hair groomed, not so much as a single tendril falling over his collar.

"She's scheduled to leave for tonight's event with Mr. Gates in about fifteen minutes." He narrows his gaze on me. "Be sure to conclude your business before then."

I study him for a beat, the warning in his stare striking me as odd.

Has he figured out the truth?

He keeps Esme's calendar. Is aware of all her comings and goings. If anyone were to put the pieces together, it would be Hawkins.

Or Adam.

But I don't have time to dwell on the idea, although I should take this as a warning.

Even when addicts are cautioned about the potential dangers of their continued drug use, they can't find the willpower to quit.

Just like I can't find the willpower to quit Esme. Not yet anyway.

"I'll keep that in mind," I assure him as I make my way from the administrative wing and toward her private suite.

I knock on Esme's door, but don't wait for her to answer before I slip inside. The second I do, she turns from where she stands by the far windows, all the air leaving my lungs at the sight of her.

Her hair is pinned in perfect waves, the style reminiscent of a 1940s Hollywood starlet. Her lips are a bright red, the smoky shadowing applied around her green eyes making them pop, appearing even more sultry than they normally are.

But what has my boxer briefs feeling unusually snug is the emerald dress she wears. The silk material clings to every curve before falling to the floor, a slit running the length of a single long leg.

"Esme…" I exhale as jealousy squeezes my chest.

This isn't the first time I've experienced this emotion. It's plagued me quite often over the course of the summer, especially whenever I caught footage of Esme and Jameson together. Listened to people speculate about a royal engagement in the near future.

Tonight, it hits me harder than normal. Not because I hate the idea of anyone seeing how incredible Esme looks in this dress.

But because I want to be the man on her arm. Want to kiss her in public. Want to dance with her as everyone gushes about what a beautiful couple we make.

Instead, Jameson gets to do all of that while I remain on the sidelines, forever her dirty little secret.

"You're stunning."

She blushes under my appreciation as she saunters toward me and drapes her arms over my shoulders.

"And what's this pressing issue that couldn't wait, Lieutenant Lawson?" She smirks, happy to play the game we so often do whenever I show up unexpectedly.

I brush my mouth to hers. "You know, I believe I've already come up with a solution."

"I'm sorry you made the drive all the way out here." Her hand slides down my chest, settling on my groin, eliciting a moan from me. "Perhaps I can still make it worth your while."

Clutching her hips, I yank her against me. "And how do you propose to do that?"

She bites her lower lip, passing me a demure smile. It takes everything in me not to bend her over this couch right now. My god, I want to. Want to fuck her ruthlessly, bask in her screams as I thrust harder and deeper, make her tell me I own every inch of her, my scent covering her as I send her off with Jameson. It's so primal. So animalistic.

As much as I love these rougher and more carnal encounters, they're no match for the slower, more sensual moments we shared during her birthday celebration. I've tried to recreate that feeling since then, but it hasn't been the same.

Mainly because Esme's begged me to be rougher with her again.

Maybe she prefers it that way.

But a part of me can't shake the feeling she wants it harder and faster so she doesn't have to admit the emotions I saw swirling in her eyes as I made love to her.

"I have a few ideas," she says coyly.

"And what would those be?" I waggle my brows.

"I recall you mentioning how much you love seeing my red lips wrapped around your cock. And since my stylist went with red tonight, it would be a waste of an amazing opportunity if I *didn't* let you fuck my mouth."

I immediately harden, jaw tightening, muscles clenching. The mouth on this girl is going to be my undoing.

Then again, I'm pretty sure it already *has* been my undoing.

"And I'd be remiss if I didn't allow *you* to take advantage of such an amazing opportunity." I move my hand to her nape, giving it a harsh grip, the atmosphere shifting from playful to more erotic. "So get on your knees."

"Yes, sir." Deliberately dragging her tongue along her lips, she starts to lower herself as I reach for my belt, about to unbuckle it.

Until a knock sounds on the door.

We both stiffen, eyes flinging wide as we jump as far away from each other as possible.

But I fear we weren't quick enough.

Not when we look toward the door and see my brother standing in the doorway, his suspicious stare darting between the two of us as he assesses the scenario, a thousand questions on his face.

"Your Highness," he says finally, bowing toward Esme. "I apologize for being early. There's a bit of traffic, so I suggest we leave soon if we're to be on time."

She grits a smile, her nerves obvious in the way she continually smooths a hand down her dress, shifting from foot to foot.

"I'll be right out."

"Of course, ma'am." He nods, then looks at me. "Creed."

My name isn't a greeting. More like an order to follow him. As much as I wish I could stay, finish what Esme and I started, I can't allow any appearance of impropriety.

I lift my gaze to Esme's, hoping she can hear my silent apology. "Your Highness."

"Lieutenant," she replies cordially, but still with a hint of something flirtatious.

Drinking her in one last time, I continue out of her suite, acting as unruffled as possible in the hopes my brother won't read too much into it. I say a quick goodbye to him, but before I can make my escape, he grabs my arm, pulling me to a stop right outside of the living room.

"What the fuck are you doing, Creed?" he whispers, voice low but determined.

"Nothing."

He scoffs. "That didn't look like nothing. From where I was standing, it looked like you and the princess, who I know you've always had a thing for, were a little too close. And a little too guilty. Tell me the truth. What were you doing?"

I don't say anything right away. Instead, I glower at him, debating how I should play this. Thankfully, I've prepared for something like this happening. We both have.

"You want the truth?" I seethe, unsure if I'm more upset at myself for not locking the door or at Adam for being the one to catch us. "The truth is Esme's been helping me plan a shower for Rory. Considering she doesn't have much family, and it didn't appear any of her friends were willing to step up and organize something, I took it upon myself to do it. But since I know fuckall about planning something like this, I asked Esme to help. That's what we were doing. Discussing some last-minute details that just came up and couldn't wait since the shower's tomorrow. *That's* why I asked you both to lunch. We'd hoped it would be a surprise, but I guess that's ruined now."

He stares at me for several long moments, his expression unreadable. Then he asks, "Why Esme?"

"What do you mean?"

"Why ask Esme for help? You could have hired an event planner. Asked someone else who doesn't have a million other things on her plate. So why her?"

"Considering you risk your life for her every day, she wanted to do something nice for you. Plus, she's a friend."

The instant those words leave my mouth, I regret them.

"That's where you're wrong, Creed." Adam's expression darkening even more, he leans into me. "The Princess Royal is *not* your friend. I told you that in the beginning of the summer. And I'm going to tell you again. You *can't* be her friend. Or Prince Gabriel's. Not when you're mere weeks away from swearing an oath to protect them. You can't allow any sort of friendship to cloud your duty to protect the royal family at all costs. You'll soon learn that will often mean protecting them from themselves. You can't do that if you're their friend. Do you understand?"

"Perfectly," I reply through clenched teeth, both of us glowering at each other for what feels like an eternity.

Suddenly, the sound of a door opening echoes, and Adam and I snap our heads up to see Esme slip into the hallway, everything about the way she carries herself regal and poised.

As if my brother didn't walk in on her mere seconds away from sucking my cock.

"Are you ready, ma'am?" Adam straightens, expression lacking the suspicion it held moments ago.

"Yes." She smiles politely. "Thank you."

He nods, turning his gaze to meet mine. I try to get a read on him, determine if he bought the same excuse everyone else has.

But everyone else isn't my brother.

I worried if anyone figured out the truth, it would be him.

And when he catches Esme looking at me with those soulful doe eyes, I fear he didn't believe a word I just said.

CHAPTER THIRTY-FIVE

Esme

I do my best to keep my eyes trained forward as I follow Adam through my apartment and out to the waiting SUV. With every step I take past my staff, I can't shake the feeling they all know my secret. That I'm wearing a giant scarlet A. Even the portraits of this country's past monarchs and their families seem to know the truth I thought Creed and I had hidden so well under the auspices of planning a shower.

I should have known our luck would eventually run out.

To make matters worse, Adam doesn't even look at me. Says no more than a few words throughout the duration of the drive to the art gallery for this evening's event, an auction benefiting one of Jameson's charities, an organization that attempts to find missing people as well as fights against human trafficking. Sadly, as Jameson has informed me, many missing people, especially girls, become trafficking victims.

He wants to put a stop to it.

Another reminder of what a good and noble person Jameson Gates is.

Another reminder that he doesn't deserve what I'm doing to him.

But do I deserve being forced to marry someone I didn't choose?

Does he?

Will that ever matter?

Or will the cycle simply continue for generations to come?

As the SUV slows to a stop in front of the museum, I peer out the window, cameras flashing, reporters shouting questions. Despite all the commotion, Jameson stands at the top of a short flight of steps, smile lighting up his face as he waits for me to make my entrance.

The instant I step out of the vehicle after Adam opens my door for me, still seeming to avoid my eyes, Jameson's smile brightens even more.

"Wow," he exhales as I approach, allowing him to pull me into his arms and feather a gentle kiss to my cheek. "You look, well…" He pulls back, drinking me in.

But unlike when Creed took his time, imprinting every single inch of me to memory, Jameson's eyes on me do nothing. There's no shiver of anticipation. No sensation of longing. No desperate need to feel him on every part of me.

"You look…" He shakes his head, grabbing my hand and spinning me around.

I can only imagine the high-fives the palace publicity team are giving each other right now, especially when the camera flashes become nearly blinding, everyone fighting to capture the best shot of him twirling me around before yanking me against his body.

"Yes?" I playfully bat my lashes.

"Like Lauren Bacall came back to life. Did I mention I had a thing for her when I was a teen?"

"I thought most teenage boys fantasized about whatever model was on the cover of *Playboy*. Surely, that's better spank bank material."

He throws his head back and laughs, both of us content to tune out the crowd. That's the thing about Jameson. From the beginning, he's made these sort of events easy. Shouldn't that be enough?

I once thought it was.

"Hand to god. Lauren Bacall was *it* for me. That throaty voice. Those soulful eyes. And those pouty lips." He traces his gaze over my face, focusing on my mouth. "And let's not forget one of her most famous lines. Hell, one of the most famous lines of any movie in history."

"And what would that be?" I flirt back, knowing all too well what it is. "It wouldn't happen to be, 'You know how to whistle, don't you?'" I inch closer. "'You just put your lips together and blow.'"

Groaning, he cups my face in his hands and presses his mouth against mine, camera flashes and cheers surrounding us. I doubt our PR team even cares Jameson is kissing me longer than they deem appropriate. Then again, he's always done this. His subtle act of defiance. One I'd find enjoyment in if it didn't make me feel like I were betraying Creed.

But I can't exactly push Jameson away. If anything, I should be curving into him. Kissing him more enthusiastically. Leaving no question in anyone's mind that Jameson is the only man for me.

But he's not.

I fear he never will be.

Once he brings the kiss to an end, he treats me to the same dazzling smile he bestows on the public at large. With his hand to the small of my back, he steers me toward the gathering of reporters, photographers, and fans who came out to catch a glimpse of us or any of the other celebrities slated to be in attendance.

We greet a few people, engaging in polite conversation as much as possible, but do our best not to linger too long in one place.

"Hey, Gates! Over here!"

Normally, I don't pay much attention to a single person calling either of our names. At events like this, *everyone* calls our names.

For some reason, this voice catches my attention.

I glance toward where it seemed to originate, Jameson also looking away from the conversation he's currently having with a group of teenagers, the excitement on their faces similar to that of adolescent girls swooning over the hottest new boy band.

Further proof the palace PR team did their job.

Then again, Jameson Gates has always been a bit of a heartthrob. A European John F. Kennedy, Jr., without the mysterious family curse.

As Jameson follows my line of sight, his expression instantly drops, complexion paling briefly before he fixes a smile back on his face.

"Are you okay?" I ask in a hushed voice, pretending it's business as usual as I continue shaking hands and posing for photos. "Do you know him?"

"He's probably just another person who doesn't think I'm good enough to date their princess." He winks in an attempt to cut through the tension, but it doesn't work. I can see the worry creasing his brow. Spend enough time with someone, you start to pick up on their tells.

It's obvious Jameson is concerned.

And that he's lying to me.

I'm about to press him when the same voice calls out over the crowd once more, this time louder.

"Don't ignore me, you lying bastard. You can't ignore the truth forever. You can't hide the truth forever. Especially now that you're dating a goddamn princess. She'll eventually learn who you really are! That you're a fucking murderer!"

After that, everything happens in slow motion.

There's a gasp from the crowd, coupled with movement as a tall, lanky man fights his way through the hordes of people. The members of my protection team all rush toward us, but not before the man jumps the barricade and heads straight for Jameson, shoving a photo in front of his face.

"Look at her, you lying son of a bitch! Look at her face and tell me you didn't kill her, you fucking bastard!"

One of the members of my protection team tackles him to the ground, but he doesn't go quietly, resisting as he yanks his arms behind his back, securing zip-ties to his wrists.

"Her name was Callie Sloane. And Jameson Gates killed her!"

I stare in horror and pity at the photo of a beautiful young woman that had fallen to the ground. Then Jameson and I are rushed inside, reporters fighting to get a shot of not only us, but also the man who just accused Jameson Gates of murder.

I expect him to offer some sort of reassurance that these allegations are completely baseless. Those of a deranged lunatic.

Instead, he looks as if he just saw a ghost.

One he thought was dead and buried long ago.

CHAPTER THIRTY-SIX

Esme

"We need to have a chat," Adam announces as he sits behind the desk in the museum office his team commandeered to head their security operations for the evening. "I trust Gianna's been in touch?"

Considering Jameson still appears to be in a state of shock, I answer for him.

"She told us to use the fact we're at a charity event to brush off any questions for the time being. If we're pushed, to offer our condolences, but state that Jameson's involvement with this charity, the main objective of which is to bring home missing girls, doesn't mean he's responsible for this woman going missing." I swallow hard. "Or worse."

Adam nods. "That about sums up what she told me would be the palace's position until we know more about Callie Sloane and her connection to the man we detained, Hayes Barlow."

I furrow my brow, the name having a familiar ring to it. I

was so surprised by the commotion and accusations that I never stopped to look at his face.

"Isn't Hayes Barlow…"

"A driver on the European racing circuit. Earlier this summer, he made headlines, not for anything he achieved in his career, but because he claimed a female member of his pit crew had gone missing and the police refused to open an investigation."

Adam leans across the desk and glowers at Jameson.

"If I'm to keep you both safe, both *alive*, I need to know everything about Hayes Barlow and Callie Sloane. Including your connection to them. Something you should have brought up the *second* you saw him go on the national news, if for no other reason than to prevent something like this. I don't like surprises. And this right here is a giant fucking surprise. If he was armed, things could have been much worse." His jaw ticks, nostrils flaring. "So start talking, Gates."

Jameson pinches his lips together, as if debating his response. Then he sighs, shoulders slumping in defeat as he shakes his head.

"Callie Sloane was the love of my life," he chokes out.

If we were a normal couple, hearing Jameson say something like this would shatter me.

But we aren't a normal couple.

And my heart can't help but ache at the pain lacing Jameson's voice, the wound obviously still raw.

I'm reminded of the conversation we had at the start of our relationship. How lightning rarely strikes the same place twice and he wasn't holding out for another strike of lightning.

Was Callie his strike of lightning?

"How do you know her?" Adam asks, keeping his voice low.

Jameson wipes his palms on his crisp tuxedo pants as he draws in a steadying breath. I grab his hand in an attempt to offer him the same comfort he's often provided me. I may not have any romantic feelings toward him, but I still consider him a friend. And right now, I sense he needs a friend more than anything.

"She helped me change a flat tire."

Adam tilts his head. "Don't you mean *you* helped *her?*"

A nostalgic gleam covers Jameson's face, eyes glassy as he stares into the distance.

"No. She helped me. In my defense, I could have done it myself, but she drove by, muttered something about not ruining my expensive suit, and changed my tire with such efficiency and speed, it was as if she were on a pit crew." He turns his gaze back to Adam. "I later learned she *did* have experience on a pit crew. Hayes Barlow's pit crew."

"So, she changed your tire. Now her boss blames you for killing her?" Adam knits his brow. "What am I missing?"

Jameson exhales a long breath. "Months of history."

"Then tell me what happened."

"We fell in love. Not at first. I'm pretty sure she initially hated me. Hated everything my family stood for." He laughs to himself, shaking his head. "Loved to remind me how difficult it was for so many people to just put food on the table. She was always a bit of a spitfire, completely unlike anyone I'd ever met. Every other woman my parents threw at me were all from wealthy families. Had a 'proper' upbringing. Had the right education. Knew how to handle themselves in social settings."

Jameson gives me a knowing look. I'm all too familiar

with what it's like to have someone else think they know what's best for you.

And to want to be with someone who goes against all of it.

"How did you run into each other again after she helped change your tire?" I ask, not to clarify any details, but because I'm interested in their story.

"She was wearing a polo with the logo of a local pub. One night, I took a gamble and stopped by to see if she worked there. Luckily, she did. When she spun around and saw me sitting at the bar, she was confused. I'd just come from a cocktail party where women wore designer dresses, makeup perfect, hair without a single strand out of place.

"But as I drank her in for the first time in a month, I'd never seen anything so beautiful. Her hair was piled on top of her head. Her shirt was stained from a few mishaps behind the bar. And she didn't have a single lick of makeup on her face. But she didn't need any of that to be beautiful. Not in my eyes. Unfortunately, she didn't exactly return my feelings, considering she kicked me out and told me never to show my face there again.

"So, I made her an offer. I'd found a 1960 Alfa Romeo Giuletto that was in rough shape. Since only 200 had ever been made, I'd bought it with the intention of eventually restoring it. I hadn't found the right person who would appreciate what a unique and special car it was. All these custom shops wanted to modernize it, make it like the cars on the road today. But that's not what I wanted. Didn't want to destroy the history of the car.

"Of course, when I told her about my find, she didn't believe me. That car is *extremely* rare. So I scribbled my address on a piece of paper and told her to stop by after her shift so she could see for herself."

"And did she?" I can't help but grin, hanging onto Jameson's every word. It's such a simple and pure love story. Two people who never should have been together finding a way to make it work, despite the odds.

"To my surprise, yes. About fainted when she saw my car collection. I've always had an affinity for vintage automobiles. The history behind them. The care with which they were made. It's not like today when they're rushed through an assembly line process.

"And when she saw the 1960 Giuletto, she was in awe. Then I asked if she'd help me restore it. It was a shot in the dark, considering I wasn't sure how much she knew about restoring cars. I wasn't an expert myself, either. I just wanted to spend time with her. Hoped that, since she was obviously a car enthusiast, she wouldn't be able to turn down working on such a unique automobile.

"Luckily, she couldn't, so we worked on it whenever she wasn't at the pub or at the track with Hayes. At first, I kept my attraction to her under wraps, not wanting to make her feel awkward. But during the long hours we spent in my garage, what started as animosity turned into appreciation. And then love."

"You worked on a car together," Adam interjected, obviously wanting to get to the relevant part of their story. "Formed an attraction and fell for each other. Then what?"

"Considering who I am, things were complicated. I didn't want to subject her to the spotlight surrounding me and my family. Nor did she want to be subjected to that, so we kept our relationship quiet. I knew we'd eventually have to take that next step. For the time being, we were happy to see each other in secret. Then…"

"Yes?" Adam encourages.

"Then I was invited to the King's Day gala at the palace

last summer, where I was photographed enjoying a dance and polite conversation with a certain princess. After that, it didn't matter who my heart belonged to." He shifts his gaze to mine. "The public salivated over the idea of a romantic relationship between us."

"Was she upset about it?" I ask hesitantly.

"Actually, no. Callie was extremely level-headed. Understood there are certain expectations that go along with who I am. And she more than understood how important my charity work is. That sometimes it's necessary to rub shoulders with the upper crust of society to further my philanthropic endeavors."

"Last I checked, you're a member of that upper crust, too," I remind him.

"Maybe." He rolls his shoulders. "But I never felt like I belonged. I can't quite explain why. I just—"

I place my hand on his arm and squeeze. "I understand."

"Why does Hayes Barlow think you killed Callie Sloane?" Adam asks after a beat.

Jameson shakes his head. "I don't know. I haven't spoken to her since February. Haven't *seen* her since February. It's… Well, it's when things took a turn, starting with a visit from Silas Archer."

"Silas Archer?" Adam lifts a curious brow.

"He, um…" He glances at me, uncertainty swirling in his eyes.

"It's okay. I'm pretty sure Adam's already figured out the truth about us."

"What? That your relationship was arranged by the royal household?" he scoffs. "They like to think no one can figure out their secrets, but they forget that everyone they hire to guard the royal family is former special teams. We're not all brawn with no brain, as they like to believe. I knew from the beginning."

"Okay." Jameson pushes out a breath, obviously grateful he doesn't have to pretend in front of Adam anymore.

Truthfully, so am I.

"Silas Archer shared all the positive press surrounding my dance with the princess during the gala. Then he made a proposition. He'd guarantee additional governmental resources for several of my charities operating in the Middle East and Africa, especially for many of the refugees who've come to us without passports. In exchange, I would agree to marry you." His gaze meets mine. "I reacted as I imagine you did. I refused. Insisted I wanted to marry for love. That he could take his veiled bribe and shove it up his arse."

I laugh slightly. "I would have loved to see Silas' face when you told him that."

"It was priceless. Hell, it looked like he'd already taken my advice. That man looks like he has a stick permanently shoved up his backside."

"He certainly does," I say, my laughter growing. After the events of tonight, I need this moment of levity.

Unfortunately, it's short-lived, Adam soon pressing for more information.

"What happened after you turned down Archer's proposal?"

"My father was livid." Jameson's expression drops as he runs a hand through his perfectly groomed blond hair. "Archer not only offered to help cut through miles of bureaucratic red tape I've been fighting for years, but my father hoped having a son with strong ties to the monarchy would give his company preferential treatment when bidding on government contracts. These contracts are often worth billions of dollars, especially from the U.S. government. Even more valuable than that, Archer promised him a title upon our marriage."

"A title is more valuable than a contract worth billions of dollars?" Adam asks incredulously.

"To my father, absolutely. The thing you have to understand about him is that he grew up dirt poor."

"I know," Adam says. "My father served with him."

At this revelation, I dart my eyes toward Adam.

"In the army *and* the guard," he adds.

"He was royal guard?" My eyes widen.

Jameson nods. "For a few years before taking a risk and opening his own private security company. It paid off. My father's smart, but he's also a natural salesman. Convinced people to invest in his company when he barely had two pennies to rub together. Everything he built was because of hard work and determination, not because he was handed a hefty trust fund.

"Because of this, he tends to value certain things above all else. Like titles. And power. They're two of the few things money *can't* buy, although one could argue power is easily bought in most countries. That those with money are the ones with the power. Regardless, my father saw this as his opportunity to climb the social ladder even higher. He threatened to cut me off. Remove me from his company. Take away my inheritance. Which also meant taking away my means to not only provide for myself but also to support my various philanthropic endeavors.

"Still, I didn't care. I was determined to find a way to make things work with Callie." He sucks in a shaky breath. "Less than a week later, she showed up at my garage and told me she was leaving town. And me. That she didn't love me. That she never could. That she was just having some fun with a spoiled rich boy and it was time for her to move on.

Then she drove away. I tried to get in touch with her, find out what was really going on, but she cut off all contact." He squeezes his eyes shut, pulling his lips between his teeth. "Never in a million years could I have imagined it was because…" He trails off, unable to finish his sentence.

I reach for his hand, squeezing, knowing how hard it is for people in our position to show emotion. I went years refusing to show any for fear it would be used against me. Which is why I don't believe for a second Jameson had anything to do with what happened to Callie.

Maybe I'm being overly naïve, but I can't shake the feeling in my gut he's as much a victim as Callie is in this entire scenario.

"Not to sound insensitive," Adam begins after a few moments of silence, "but do you think your father may have put Callie up to it? Bribed her to walk away so you'd accept Archer's proposal?"

Jameson wipes his cheeks, clearing his throat. "I don't see how he'd even know about her. No one did. Neither one of us told anyone. We were careful to keep what we had private."

"Nothing stays a secret forever," Adam tells Jameson before shifting his attention toward me. "Someone will eventually uncover the truth, no matter how careful you think you've been."

His words may be for Jameson, but I sense they're also directed at me.

A warning to walk away now before Creed and I find ourselves in a similar situation.

Except I won't be the one who mysteriously disappears.

Creed would.

The mere idea of any harm coming to him guts me, a vice squeezing my heart.

"At what point did you learn Callie hadn't just cut off communication, but was missing?" Adam leans back in his chair, analytical gaze sweeping over Jameson. It's obvious he's not only curious about his answer but also in *how* he responds. His demeanor. His reaction. His body language.

"I saw Hayes' press conference earlier this summer when he claimed Callie had disappeared and the police refused to open a missing person's case because there wasn't sufficient evidence to prove she *was* missing."

"Why does he believe you had something to do with it? And that you actually killed her? Even though there's no evidence she's actually dead."

Jameson scrubs his hand over his face. "You'll have to ask him. I'm not lying when I said I lost touch with her after she ended things. I'd tried to reach out to her. But after so many unanswered calls and texts, I needed to move on. For my own sanity. I couldn't spend the rest of my life chasing someone who didn't want to be chased. Or found."

It's silent as we all process Jameson's version of events. On one hand, I view it as an unfortunate set of circumstances. That the fact Callie left around the time Silas Archer paid him a visit is merely a coincidence. I can't fault her for wanting to get away. Have a fresh start, especially if she knew she could never truly be with Jameson like she hoped. That if he chose her, he'd be forced to give up everything he'd worked hard for his entire life, so she made the decision for him.

Something I've debated doing myself with increasing frequency these past few weeks.

But I also can't ignore the peculiar timing behind everything. Based on what Jameson mentioned about his father always craving acceptance by the upper crust, I wouldn't be surprised to learn he bribed her to leave town.

If that were the case, though, wouldn't she have told Hayes where she was going? Or, at the very least, come out of hiding when she learned a continent-wide manhunt had been launched in the hopes of finding her?

But she didn't.

Could she truly be missing?

Or worse?

And why?

As my gaze meets Adam's, I sense he's asking these same questions.

Worse, I sense none of us are going to like the answers.

CHAPTER THIRTY-SEVEN

Creed

I've never been so on edge in my life, even when about to leave on some dangerous mission where I may or may not make it out alive. But after learning of Hayes Barlow's foiled attack on Jameson and Esme at the charity gala, I'd spent all night sick with worry.

And jealousy.

I should have been able to go to her apartment. Call to check on her. I couldn't do any of those things. My only source of comfort came from knowing my brother takes his job seriously. That he'd put his life on the line to keep her safe without a moment's hesitation.

Just as I would.

It still didn't diminish my need to be with her. That's what people who care about each other do. They offer each other comfort in a time of crisis.

And I'm not allowed to do that.

Which is why I practically run from my car and into the

restaurant where we're hosting Rory's baby shower in a few hours, not caring if any of Esme's protection team stationed around the perimeter observe me wrapping her in my arms.

She stiffens at first, uneasy about such an overt display of affection.

"I was so damn worried about you," I say to explain my rash behavior. "It was fucking torture." I pull back so I can peer into her green eyes. "I thought of calling, but after yesterday, I didn't think it advisable. Same with reaching out to Adam. Your brother insisted you were fine——"

"And I am," she assures me. But instead of stepping out of my touch, she cups my cheek, thumb brushing my skin. I cover her hand with mine, soaking in the comfort I've needed since yesterday. "It was all just a misunderstanding."

"Misunderstanding?" I choke out. "The man you're supposed to marry is accused of killing a woman and you expect me to believe it's just some misunderstanding?"

"You know damn well your brother wouldn't allow me remotely close to Jameson if he suspected anything off about him, to hell with what the royal household wants. He takes his vow to protect the royal family quite seriously, and that includes protecting us from the royal household, if necessary."

"I know," I respond, swallowing hard.

"Then you know you have nothing to worry about. Adam's good at his job. And he would never do anything to put my life in jeopardy." She moves her hands to my arms. "This is simply a case of an overly emotional man whose friend went missing, so he targeted Jameson because he founded a charity, the main objective of which is to find and bring home missing women. He's not involved. Okay?"

I pull my lips between my teeth, jaw clenching in frustration. There's something practiced about her response, as if it's the one she's been told to give.

And I hate it.

Last night brought into sharp focus exactly how much I hate everything about this situation. And it's not just the idea of Jameson in general I loathe. It's that I can't do the things most people in relationships take for granted.

Then again, we're not exactly in a real relationship, not when we agreed months ago this would eventually come to an end.

For the first time, I'm willing to admit I don't *want* this to end. Don't want to continue the family legacy. Not if it means having to walk away from Esme.

But even if I'm willing to give up everything to be with her, that doesn't mean *she* is. Doesn't mean she'll be *allowed* to.

"Okay, Creed?" she repeats when I don't immediately respond.

Not wanting to spend what little time we have together arguing about Jameson Gates, I offer her a tight smile. "Okay."

"Good." She pushes against me, voice brightening. "Now get to work. We have a lot to do before our guests arrive in an hour. You can start with arranging the centerpieces." She playfully swats my ass before returning to the long table at the head of the room where the gifts are to be placed. Then she glances over her shoulder and winks, the thick tension dissipating.

"Such a taskmaster," I remark, waggling my brows.

She purses her lips into a flirtatious scowl. "And I thought you liked it when I take charge."

I step behind her and skim the backside of her leg, lifting the material of her dress. "I don't just like it. I bloody love it." I scrape my lips against her neck. "Love watching you ride my cock. Love watching your tits bounce. Love feeling your nails dig into my chest."

"Creed." My name is a cross between a warning and a moan. "We can't."

"But you want to." I brush a light thumb against her panties, finding them warm and wet. "I can feel how much you ache for me, princess."

"I do," she whimpers.

I push her panties aside, sliding a finger through her slickness, wishing I could pin her to the wall and have my way with her, to hell with who might walk in on us. After the helplessness that consumed me all night, I need this connection. Need to feel Esme.

Need the reminder she's still mine.

Even if for only a little while longer.

And what makes matters worse is I don't know when we'll be alone again. This is the first time since we started down this path that there's no more scheduled meetings, leaving us at the mercy of her stacked agenda and the prying eyes of her household staff, as well as my brother.

"Who's on your detail tonight?" I ask as I continue teasing her.

"W- Walsh."

"Ask him to bring you to my place."

On a sharp inhale, she spins around, forcing my hand away as wide green eyes meet mine. "But—"

I bring the same finger I'd just used to tease her up to her mouth, silencing her. "I want to see you. Want you in my bed where I can take my time without worrying who might interrupt us. Just for a few hours."

"What am I supposed to tell Walsh? We don't have the excuse of the baby shower anymore."

"I know. I just…"

Licking my lips, I look around the restaurant, searching for a reason I'd need to see her. Something that won't raise suspicion any more than already seems to be the case.

"What if I brought everything back to my place after the shower? Flowers. Balloons. Favors. Anything left over. We can make up some excuse about putting together care packages to donate to children's hospitals in the area. Something like that."

She peers at me thoughtfully. "We don't have to make up an excuse. I actually think that's a good idea."

"Then say you'll come." Tugging her against me, I dip my head toward her, her breath hot on my lips. "I promise to make it worth your while." I lift the skirt of her dress again, my thumb teasing the heat between her legs. "More than once."

She moans, pulsing against me, her resistance slowly waning.

Everything inside me screams this is a horrible idea, especially after the warning we had last night. Yet I can't seem to help myself. Can't seem to listen to reason. All I can think about is spending every possible second with her before this all ends.

"Tell me, Esme." I shift her panties to the side, but don't touch her, torturing her instead. "Say you'll come."

Her eyelids flutter closed as she groans, expression tight in frustration. Then she finally whimpers, "I'll come."

"Damn straight you will." I press my finger to her clit, tension rolling off her as she loses herself in my touch. Then I abruptly pull back and smirk. "But not until later."

Turning from her, I get to work on the centerpieces, just as she asked me to. I can feel her frustrated stare trained on me.

"You'll pay for that, Lawson," she huffs out, pretending to be unaffected by me.

I look her way and wink. "I can't wait, princess."

Over the next hour, we work quickly and efficiently, making sure every detail is in place. When people start arriving, everyone wants to gossip with Esme about Jameson and his connection to that missing girl, many hoping for the inside scoop. It doesn't seem to faze her, though. Instead, she easily defers all comments and questions, stating she's here to celebrate Rory and Adam, and she prefers that to remain the focus.

To my surprise, when asked if Jameson will be here, she says he won't. I have to admit I'm relieved. While I look forward to any opportunity to be in Esme's presence, I haven't been too enthusiastic about spending several hours in the same room as Jameson.

It's one thing to run into him in passing, although Esme's done her best to keep that to a minimum. It's a different thing to be forced to sit in the same room as him. To watch him touch her. Kiss her. *Be* with her.

"Hey. Lawson."

When I hear a familiar voice, I snap out of my thoughts, glancing to the open doorway to see Archie Walsh, another member of Esme's protection team, peeking his head in.

"What is it?"

"He just pulled up."

"Thanks, mate."

With a nod, he retreats, hiding once more so Rory is none the wiser.

Adam may already know the real reason I invited them here, but Rory still deserves to be surprised. Deserves to know she's surrounded by people who support and love her.

Who will support and love her baby when he arrives in a few weeks.

I make my way through the room, finding Esme with Harriet and Marius, as I expected.

"Creed," Marius greets with a quick bro-hug. "Everything looks amazing. You two make a great team. If this whole badass bodyguard routine doesn't pan out, you could have a future in event planning."

"Thanks for your vote of confidence, but I'd rather set my balls on fire than do this for a living."

"Are you saying you didn't enjoy working with Esme?" Harriet asks in faux shock.

I smile, eyes floating toward Esme. "That part I did enjoy quite a bit."

"I bet you did." Marius nudges me.

"I noticed Walsh poke his head in," Esme states, ignoring Marius' comment. "Are they here?"

I nod. "Just pulled up, so we probably only have a minute or two."

"I'll rally the troops then."

Esme spins from me and gets everyone's attention with ease, telling them to all quiet down because the guests of honor will be here soon.

When Adam escorts Rory into the private room of the restaurant a few minutes later and she realizes she's not here just to have lunch, she's clearly surprised and overwhelmed by the gesture, tears welling in her eyes.

"Was this your doing?" She glances up at Adam, her short stature tiny compared to my brother's six-five frame.

He slowly shakes his head. "Sorry to say I can't take credit. This was all Creed's idea, with the help of Her Highness, of course."

There's something slightly antagonistic in his response.

Or maybe I'm just on edge after he walked in on us yesterday and my guilty conscience is playing tricks on my mind.

But as Rory flings her arms around both Esme and me, pulling us in for a group hug, I get the feeling my mind *isn't* playing tricks on me. Not with the intense suspicion swirling in my brother's dark gaze.

CHAPTER THIRTY-EIGHT

Esme

I rest my hands against the bathroom vanity, thankful to finally have a moment to myself for the first time all day. While I'm thrilled Creed and I were able to do this for Adam and Rory, I'm mentally drained.

What I thought would be a relaxing day spent with friends was anything but, especially whenever I noticed Adam's attention focused on me as Creed sat beside me during lunch.

As he stole a lingering touch along my leg.

As he used the distraction of Rory and Adam opening their mountains of gifts to slide his hand up my dress and tease me, bringing me to the brink of orgasm before cruelly retreating, depriving me of release yet again.

Which is why I excused myself in the first place. To catch my breath, not just from Adam's suspicion, but also from Creed.

I keep telling myself we need to be more careful. That

after our close call yesterday, I should keep my distance. That if we don't stop our reckless behavior soon, it will only end in disaster.

Not wanting to be gone for too long, I turn from the vanity and open the door, startling when I almost run right into Creed's formidable frame. All words escape me as he grips my hips and pushes me back into the bathroom, turning the lock before stalking toward me.

"What were you doing in here?" he asks in a quiet yet demanding voice, his eyes dark and dangerous.

"I… It's a bathroom."

He pulls me against him and skims his lips along my neck, the contact sending a thrill racing through me.

"You didn't make yourself come. Did you?"

I squeeze my eyes shut, trying to summon every ounce of strength I possess, reminding myself this is a bad idea.

I've said before that Creed Lawson is like a drug. The same remains true to this day. I know I need to stop using him. Need to break this habit before it turns into a lifelong addiction.

But the second he's in front of me, the promise of ecstasy staring back through his penetrating gaze, I lose all willpower, surrendering to him in the hopes of experiencing just an ounce of pleasure.

"I thought about it," I say honestly. "But no. I didn't."

A sly smile teases his lips. "Good. Because that's my job."

In one swift move, he lifts my dress, yanking my panties off.

"Creed, what are you doing?"

He covers my mouth with his, tongue swiping against mine in a kiss that erases every single thought… Including the voice warning me this is a horrible idea. My sole motivation right now is releasing the tension that's been building between us all day.

Hell, since last night when Adam interrupted us before we could chase that high.

"Giving you what you deserve, Esme," he answers as he hoists me onto the counter and pulls out his erection, spreading my slickness around. I barely have a second to brace myself before he thrusts into me.

I cry out, but he swallows my moans, crushing his lips to mine, his motions relentless. This is not how I saw the rest of my afternoon going. I certainly didn't expect Creed to fuck me while his brother sat in the other room. But I can't help myself.

Apparently, either can he.

"Tell me you're mine," he grunts, muscles strained, chest heaving.

"I'm yours." The words fall so easily from my lips. And not just because I know he wants my reassurance. But I truly feel like I *am* his. Body. Mind. Soul. This man possesses every last part of me.

"Tell me this pussy is mine."

I close my eyes, leaning my head back as he propels me higher and higher with every punishing thrust.

"My pussy is yours."

"Damn straight it is."

When he clamps onto my neck, I fight back a scream. Between his teeth on me and his cock pistoning inside me, I'm powerless, my orgasm seizing me mere seconds before he also succumbs to his own bliss.

Panting heavily, he brings his mouth to mine, kissing me so tenderly it almost makes me cry. It's one of the things I've grown to crave. How he can be in control and dominant one minute, then so tender and compassionate the next. It satisfies my desire to be cherished, but also my need to surrender to him, even temporarily.

"I couldn't wait until tonight," he explains breathlessly. "Probably not the smartest idea to screw you in the bathroom of a restaurant where my brother's currently sitting."

A chorus of *oohs* and *ahs* sound, the guests responding to yet another gift being opened.

"Sounds like they're all distracted."

He runs a hand over his face, a wariness about him I haven't noticed before.

Is he having the same reservations?

Given everything I know about Creed, how pragmatic and sensible he is, I imagine he's also sensed Adam's scrutiny. Feels the weight of it crushing him.

"I hope so."

He kisses my nose, then grabs a few tissues, using them to clean me up before helping me to my feet. He swipes my panties off the tiled floor, but instead of handing them to me, he shoves them into his pocket, winking.

"I'll give them back later."

This is the perfect opportunity to tell him I don't think I should go over his place. As always seems to be the case, I can't find the words I need. Not if it means depriving myself of the one thing I've come to crave.

"Fiend," I remark playfully.

"Only for you." He holds my face as he lowers his lips to mine. "Always for you."

My heart squeezes.

Since my birthday, some of the things he's said have become more affectionate. More romantic. More...loving. I try to convince myself it's the post-sex glow that has him uttering these sweet words, but I know that's not the reason. I'm not sure what to do with that.

Not anymore.

Not with our expiration date looming in the near future.

"You leave first," I tell him to avoid facing the reality of his feelings.

And mine.

"I'll follow shortly."

He brushes a soft kiss against my temple. "Okay." He cracks open the door, making sure the hallway is clear, and slips outside.

Once the door shuts behind him, I exhale a deep breath before checking my reflection in the mirror. As luck would have it, Creed left a few marks on my neck. They're not too obvious, but enough that someone might notice.

That *Adam* might notice.

Grateful for my long hair, I yank it out of the low bun I'd styled it in earlier and smooth it to one side. I spend the next few minutes applying makeup to my face and neck to cover up the more prominent marks.

Once I'm content my appearance doesn't scream "just railed by my bodyguard's brother", I open the door, transitioning into the picture of poise and grace as I return to my table, grateful that Creed's commandeered someone else's chair so he could chat with one of his brother's longtime military friends.

"Careful, E," Harriet mutters as she leans close.

I look at her, brows scrunched. "What are you talking about?"

"Is it a coincidence that, after you left to use the bathroom, a certain Lawson also did?" she whispers. "That you were both gone for a good ten minutes, then returned just a short while after him with your hair suddenly down?"

Facing forward, I grab my champagne flute, a subtle tremble in my hand as I bring it to my lips, a mixture of nerves and the aftereffects of my orgasm rolling through me.

"I gather he's a biter," Marius remarks from the other side of her.

Lowering my drink, I smooth a hand down my hair, ensuring it's still to the side.

"And if you think we're the only ones who noticed, think again," he continues, voice filled with concern. "Pretty sure everyone here did. Including a certain *other* Lawson."

I slowly look toward the front of the room as Rory opens a baby swing. But Adam doesn't seem the least bit interested in the number of different modes or the overhead mobile.

Instead, his eyes float between Creed and me, everything about his demeanor screaming distrust and incredulity.

I don't even have to ask the question.

He knows.

And I have a feeling my inability to overcome this addiction is about to end us.

CHAPTER THIRTY-NINE

Esme

I pace the length of my living room, chewing on my nails as I debate whether to do this. Whether I should call Walsh and request he take me over Creed's place, claiming we need to sort out gift baskets to donate to area hospitals with all the leftover balloons, flowers, and favors from Rory's shower.

I want to see him. Spend a few hours losing myself in him.

But at what cost?

All I hear is Adam's warning from last night.

"Nothing stays a secret forever. Someone will eventually uncover the truth, no matter how careful you think you've been."

Adam already knows. I can feel it whenever he looks at me. If I want to make sure no one else does, I need to do everything to remove any appearance of impropriety. And that means not asking one of my protection officers to drive me to see Creed.

I hate the idea of standing him up. Of him sitting in his apartment, staring at the clock, wondering where I am. But it's the right thing to do.

Then why does it feel so wrong?

A knock sounds, and I look toward the door, pulse quickening over the prospect that perhaps Creed sensed my unease and came to Gladwell under the auspices of visiting Anderson.

But when I make my way across the living room and look through the peephole, Creed isn't standing in the foyer.

Adam is.

On his day off.

When he should be spending time with Rory, assembling the myriad of baby gifts they received today.

He could have stopped by to give me an update on his investigation into Hayes Barlow's accusations. But if that were the case, he could have called. I sense this has nothing to do with Hayes Barlow, Callie Sloane, or Jameson Gates. Instead, it has everything to do with me.

And his brother.

Fixing a smile on my face, I smooth my hair over my shoulder to hide any lingering bite marks, then open the door.

"Adam," I say brightly. A little too brightly. "I wasn't expecting you."

"Your Highness." He bows toward me. "I apologize for the interruption. And for stopping by unannounced." He pulls his lips between his teeth, his demeanor slightly agitated.

Most people probably wouldn't pick up on it.

For a man who's always been calm and collected, even in the face of danger, it's quite noticeable. I've never seen Adam so off. So…distressed.

"No apology necessary," I assure him, stepping back. "Please, come in."

He nods his thanks as he enters my apartment. I close the door and walk toward the reading chair, lowering myself onto it.

"Won't you have a seat?" I gesture to the couch catty-corner to me.

"Thank you, ma'am." He sits, but his posture remains taut, as if at attention even while sitting.

"Would you like any tea?" I ask when he doesn't immediately say anything, the silence thick with tension.

"I won't be here long. I just hoped you could clear up a few things."

"Certainly." My face heats, nerves fluttering in my stomach. But I push them down to the best of my ability, not wanting Adam to be able to use his powerful sense of perception to observe how on edge I am. "What can I help you with this evening, Captain Lawson?"

He pushes out a sigh, his rigid and formal posture relaxing. He squeezes his eyes shut as he pinches the bridge of his nose. When he returns his gaze to mine, what I see within causes the feelings of guilt and shame I've battled all summer to boil to the surface, threatening to spill over.

"Are you sleeping with my brother?"

I part my lips, words escaping me. It doesn't matter how many times I've imagined or prepared for this scenario. Now that I'm here, I'm at a loss. I'd hoped I never *would* be in this situation. That Creed and I would be careful enough not to raise suspicion.

"Adam, I—"

Holding up his hand, he straightens, mouth pinched into a tight line. "Let me remind you I risk my life for you daily so please give me the courtesy of respecting all the sacrifices I've made by answering me honestly." He swallows hard, giving me an admonishing look. "Even if I may not like what that answer is."

I can't remember the last time I've felt so small. So uncomfortable. So ashamed. Which is quite a feat, considering the royal household loves to make me feel small. But that's nothing compared to how I cower under Adam's disappointed stare.

"Are you having an affair with my brother?"

His question echoes around me, taunting and shaming me for my indiscretions.

I have to suppress the urge to insist we're not. An affair would imply something wrong and dishonest. If anything, my relationship with Jameson feels more like an affair.

But that's not how anyone else would see it.

So instead of arguing on a technicality, I show Adam the respect he deserves.

I nod my confession. "I am."

By his response, face squeezing, muscles straining, you'd think I just admitted to murdering puppies in my free time.

"I had a feeling. Noticed the way you looked at each other. Heard rumors you were spending quite a lot of time together. But then I also heard the rumors about the surprise baby shower so figured it was just office gossip. Lord knows, there's heaps of gossip going around these days. But when I walked in on you together yesterday..." He pinches his eyes shut once more, shaking his head.

"I didn't want to believe it. Didn't want to believe the two of you could be so bloody stupid." His voice grows louder. Angrier. "And to carry on like you have been right here under everyone's noses." He waves his arm around before leaning toward me, eyes on fire. "Did you think you wouldn't get caught? That no one would talk?"

"I wasn't thinking that far ahead."

"That's fucking obvious."

He throws his hands up as he shoots to his feet, digging his fingers into his hair. Then he spins toward me. With his impressive frame towering over me as I sit in my chair, I feel like a small child being chastised for making a horrible decision.

It's not that far from the truth.

I knew my arrangement with Creed was a ticking time bomb, but I couldn't pull myself away.

"How did you think this would all play out? Did you think you could marry Jameson Gates, but keep screwing my brother in secret? Did you even stop to think about how this would affect him? His future? I don't need to remind you that *he's* the one who stands to lose here. Not you. *Him.* If anyone puts the pieces together and goes public, he could lose everything he's worked for. So could I. And my father. This kind of scandal has the potential to destroy so many people."

"It wouldn't go that far," I attempt to argue in my defense as I slowly stand, but my words seem weak and unconvincing. "We agreed it was just for the summer. Once I was engaged or he was sworn into the guard, it would end. No matter what. It was purely physical. Nothing more."

Adam throws his head back and barks out a maniacal laugh. I can't recall ever seeing him this emotional over something. He's typically even-headed, not allowing anyone so much as a glimpse of what he's thinking or feeling.

He has no problem showing me exactly what he's thinking now.

"Purely physical. That's rich. I'll let you in on a little secret. When sex is involved, it's never purely physical.

Someone eventually develops emotions. When that happens, it can only end in disaster. And if you continue this…"

He stabs a finger in my direction, much like the townspeople pointed at Hester Prynne when she wore that scarlet A, whispering their disapproval and shame.

"That's precisely what will happen. It will end in disaster. You need to end it. Immediately. And when you do, you need to destroy any hope my brother has of a future with you. Even if that means ripping his heart out of his chest and shattering it into a thousand pieces. That's what you need to do. Remind him there can't be anything between you. That he's just the hired help."

"You want me to make him…hate me?" I blink, his request stealing all my breath.

It's one thing to demand we end things a few weeks earlier than planned. But to ask me to obliterate Creed in the process?

"I know my brother. He's had a thing for you for years. Believe me when I say he won't let you go without a fight. You need to make sure he *won't* fight. Make sure he knows there's nothing *to* fight for."

My lips part, no response forthcoming. It doesn't matter I spent most of the day convincing myself that ending things is the smart move. I can't imagine hurting Creed. Not like Adam wants me to.

"Why are you talking to me about this and not Creed?" I ask in the hopes I can avoid doing what he's asking of me.

"Because he'll give the same excuses you just did. That it's not serious. That it's not going anywhere. But I've seen the way he looks at you. I saw it yesterday. Hell, I've seen it for *years*. This *is* serious. At least for him. He'd throw away everything if he thinks there's even a minuscule chance of having a future with you."

I open my lips to argue to the contrary, but I can't deny the truth in Adam's words. Especially after the past several weeks.

Especially after he begged to make love to me on my birthday.

"I'm also worried about what some people might do if they perceive Creed to be a threat to your relationship with Mr. Gates. After everything we learned last night, I don't think I have to spell it out for you."

I whip my eyes to his. "Did you confirm your theory that Callie's disappearance is somehow connected to my relationship with Jameson?"

Adam hesitates, seeming to toil his response over in his mind for a protracted moment.

"I'm still looking for definitive answers. But I do think the timing of everything is suspicious. That it's not entirely unreasonable to believe that someone may have forcibly removed Ms. Sloane from Mr. Gates' life because she posed a threat to a potential marriage between the two of you."

I'm about to argue it could just be a coincidence, but he holds up his hand, cutting me off.

"I understand there's no proof. It's just one possible explanation. But I won't take that risk where my brother's concerned. Which is why you need to end it. You said it yourself. It was just for the summer. Consider summer officially over."

I squeeze my eyes shut, fighting back the tears threatening to fall.

I want to tell Adam he's wrong. That it'll be okay. That his brother won't lose everything. That we'll be more careful.

But that's not realistic. I've known all along I wouldn't be the one to suffer any harm if the truth got out. Not like Creed would. It's irrelevant that he's not a member of the royal guard yet, even if we've used that technicality to support our indiscretions all summer. To the outside world, I'm supposed to be in love with Jameson Gates. And if anyone perceives any sort of threat to that relationship, I have no doubt they'll do whatever is necessary to eliminate the threat.

And I can't have that on my conscience.

Reluctantly bringing my eyes back to Adam, I nod. "Okay. I'll end things."

"And make sure there's no hope of a future?" He arches a brow.

I pull my bottom lip between my teeth, swallowing hard. Then I nod again.

"And make sure there's no hope of a future."

It's not what I want, but when have I ever truly been able to have what I want?

CHAPTER FORTY

Creed

I kick the door to my apartment closed, placing the bags containing all the items I'd grabbed at the market on the kitchen counter. While we won't have hours on end like we did on her birthday, I still want to do something with Esme besides a quick fuck. Sill want to do something that makes her smile, like cooking together.

Checking the clock on the stove to see it's not yet seven, I start toward my bedroom when I hear a knock.

Apart from Adam, I don't get many visitors. I doubt it's him. He's probably pulling an all-nighter assembling baby furniture. I consider ignoring it, but when I hear the knock once more followed by Esme's voice telling me it's her, I don't hesitate. With quick steps, I rush to let her in.

"You're early," I remark. "I haven't even had a chance to jump in the shower. Perhaps you'd like to join me?" I waggle my brows, expecting her to agree.

She doesn't. Instead, her expression remains even. Sullen.

"May I come in?" she asks with a formality I haven't heard in a while. Not like this. While we've been formal with each other at times, it was all in fun, a playful quality to her tone.

There's nothing playful about her right now.

"Of course."

I step back, allowing her to enter before closing the door and approaching her as she takes in the open living area of my apartment with an expression I can't quite explain. Longing maybe?

"Is everything okay?" I ask after several moments. "You don't seem like yourself. Did something happen?"

She pulls her gaze away from the oversized sofa that's a far cry from the designer furniture that fills her place. Everything in my home is a far cry from anything she has in her apartment. The coffee table has a few dings, sofa cushions worn from years of use, walls in need of a fresh coat of paint. But for someone who doesn't require much in terms of luxury, it suits my purposes.

With a deep, steadying breath, she squares her shoulders and brings her eyes to mine, steely resolve fixed on her expression.

"Based on recent events and certain rumors that are beginning to circulate, I believe it's in our best interests to, uh, well...end our arrangement."

I blink, unsure I understand what she's saying. I see her mouth move. Hear her voice, but the words don't register.

"Without the excuse of planning Rory's shower, it'll be much more difficult to find time together," she continues when I don't immediately respond. "It will be much *riskier* to find time together. Adam's already suspicious. He's not the only one. If we want to put an end to any rumors before they get out of control, we need to walk away. We knew from the beginning this had an expiration date. I think it's best we go our separate ways now and…get on with our lives."

"Get on with our lives?" I squeak out, testing the words on my lips.

Tightness squeezes my chest, making it impossible to breathe. I should have known something was off when she showed up earlier than planned. I thought she wanted more time together. I never expected she'd break up with me.

"Yes," she responds, as if this is little more than a business negotiation. As if she's not ripping me apart thread by tiny thread. "I enjoyed this summer." A smile cracks on her lips, a break in her stoic demeanor. "More than I thought I would." She clears her throat, all business once more. "Now that summer's nearly over, it's time we move on."

"Move on." I bark out a laugh, becoming more and more frustrated with every second she stands in my apartment. And not because she wants to end things.

But because this isn't the Esme I've spent time with over the summer. The Esme who finally learned to live for herself, to hell with the obligations placed on her shoulders.

Instead, this is the Esme she was before this all began. The Esme the royal household molded her into years ago, eliminating all joy and independence.

"Like I said, this is the best course of action."

"Why?" I advance on her. "So you can fuck Jameson and not feel any remorse?"

She blanches, the real Esme peeking through the cracks.

I don't believe for a second she's been anything but faithful to me. Or as faithful as possible in this fucked-up arrangement.

But the fact she wants to walk away now is tearing me up. I thought we still had time. Not much, but it was something.

Now she wants to throw it all away just because of some workplace rumors.

"You know you're the only one," she mutters, slowly lifting her eyes to mine. "It's only been you."

I clasp her hands, grateful when she doesn't pull away. "Let it still be me. Three weeks. That's all I'm asking for, Esme. Just three more wonderful, amazing weeks. Please, love." My voice catches on my words. "Don't do this."

Tears dot her lids, her lip quivering. "But I have to, Creed."

"No, you don't." I move my hands to her biceps, holding her in place as I fight the despair consuming me, making me dizzy. "We can still enjoy the time we have left. We'll find somewhere else to meet."

"People are already suspicious. All it takes is *one* moment of carelessness and it will all go up in flames. Everything you've worked hard for, all the sacrifices you've made for this country, would be for nothing. I just…" She shakes her head. "I can't have that on my conscience, Creed."

"I don't care about that," I insist, gripping her tighter. "I knew the risks when we started this. I accepted them back then. And I still accept them now." I frame her face in my hands, not allowing her to escape my next words. "I love you."

She sucks in a sharp breath, eyes widening. The room goes still as my confession hangs in the air.

"What did you say?"

A small smile curves on my mouth as I erase the distance between us, my lips so close to hers. "I said, I love you, Esme."

She squeezes her eyes shut, a single tear sliding down her cheek. "No, Creed. You can't. You—"

"Yes, I can," I answer calmly, at complete odds with the

frustration and devastation covering her expression. "And I do. Trying to will it away won't stop the way I feel about you." When she returns her gaze to mine, I repeat, "I love you."

"But you promised," she chokes out. "You swore you wouldn't fall in love with me. You broke that promise, Creed."

"I did no such thing."

"Yes, you did. You——"

"I promised I wouldn't *fall* in love with you. And I didn't. Because I was already *in* love with you, Esme. I have been for a very long time." I hold her face tighter as my mouth descends toward hers. "And I know you love me."

"No," she exhales, but loses her protest when I touch my lips to hers in a ghost of a kiss. She whimpers, but doesn't retreat, remaining in this place of indecision for several long moments before finally pressing her mouth more firmly against mine.

She can try to deny this electricity, this amazing connection. But I felt it the night we celebrated her birthday. And I've felt it every day since then. She loves me. She's just scared to admit it. Scared of what it could mean for her.

And me.

When I dig my fingers into her hair and deepen the kiss, our tongues sliding against each other, I groan. The sound must snap her out of her trance, because she stiffens, scrambling out of my hold as she wipes her kiss-swollen lips.

"We're not doing this, Creed." Struggling to catch her breath, she holds an arm out in front of her in an effort to keep me from coming closer. "Not anymore. We can't."

"I understand this is scary for you. It's scary for me, too. But I'm willing to jump. To take that risk. I know it's complicated, but we'll find a way to be together. To make it work.

You say you don't want to do anything that puts my future at risk. But I can't imagine a future without you. Without loving you."

"Creed, I—"

"One of my military buddies has been trying to get me to join his private security firm," I interrupt before she can turn me down. "I can go work for him. We can leave this place. Start over again somewhere else. Just… Don't push me away because you think you have to. You don't. We'll figure it out."

She pulls her bottom lip between her teeth, shaking her head. Then she draws in a deep breath, smoothing a hand down her perfectly tailored dress, the picture of poise and sophistication.

And like seconds ago, she transforms back into the old Esme, a puppet once more.

"There's nothing *to* figure out. I apologize if any of my behavior this summer gave you the wrong idea. Or if I led you to believe my feelings were anything…more. I've grown up accustomed to a certain lifestyle. One you could never give me. We had some fun. But that's all this was. Meaningless fun. Nothing more." She holds her head high, refusing to look at me as she moves toward the door.

"Bullshite. This isn't you talking right now," I argue, my words laced with desperation. "It's your fear talking."

"I'm not afraid," she throws over her shoulder.

"Yes, you are!" I roar, my voice thundering in my tiny apartment.

She whirls around, eyes wide at my tone. I doubt she's ever heard me this angry before.

"Sorry. I…" I pause, taking a moment to collect myself before speaking again, this time much more calmly.

"When you first asked me to sleep with you, I thought you were this amazing woman who had the confidence to go after what she wanted, to hell with what was expected of her. It made *me* want to say to hell with what was expected of me. In fact, it was what made me finally take a risk and accept your proposal, regardless of what was right. When you agreed to continue seeing me, despite the risks, I thought maybe you were willing to do something for yourself. To break from tradition and make a stand."

I approach her, eyes on fire, a boulder in my throat over the prospect of her walking out of my life and never looking back.

Of her actually *not* loving me.

"Where's *that* woman? The woman who stood up for herself?"

She meets my gaze, remaining the put-together princess she was groomed to be. "That woman isn't real. She's merely a fantasy you concocted. Nothing more. Now if you'll excuse me, Jameson is expecting me." She starts to turn from me.

"Of course." I throw my hands up. "Keep running away, Esme. It's what you always do, isn't it? Whenever things get real, you return to what's comfortable. To what's the least risky. But at least I know I *tried*. That I fought for what I wanted. For you. That I did everything I could to make you see that I don't care about all the reasons we could never be together. That I'd willingly walk away from everything. *All. For. You.*"

"But I'd never willingly walk away from everything for you. I'm second in line to the throne. And you…" Her voice briefly catches before she takes a deep breath, composing herself once more. "You're just the hired help."

Her statement lingers in the air for a beat. Then she spins on her heels and hurries out of my apartment, slamming the door behind her.

Of all the things she could have said, that hurts the most.

I could deal with her claiming she doesn't love me. That she doesn't think I'm worth the risk.

But to hear her call me the hired help feels like she grabbed the sharpest knife and plunged it directly into my heart.

All summer, I've struggled with feeling like I don't belong. That I don't deserve someone like Esme.

She just confirmed I don't.

That I never will.

That no matter what I do, it will never be enough.

I will never be enough.

CHAPTER FORTY-ONE

Esme

I stare at the walls of my father's conference room Monday morning, all the usual suspects sitting around the large table, discussing a plan of action regarding the "incident", as they now refer to what happened the other night between Hayes Barlow and Jameson.

Truth be told, I haven't paid much attention to what was being said in the media. It's been business as usual, more or less.

Except for the part of my daily life where Creed Lawson paid me a visit.

That most certainly hasn't been business as usual.

And I hate it.

Hate that every time I sit at my desk, I'm reminded of the many times he bent me over it and gave my body more pleasure than I thought I could handle, all while telling me how amazing I was. How needy he was for me.

No man ever made me feel the things Creed did.

And I fear no man ever will again.

I've tried to tell myself it's for the best. Our carelessness has already put Creed's future at risk.

Was a few more weeks of amazing sex really worth it?

Was it really just sex?

As I reflect back, it was never about sex. Not after that first time. It was about experiencing the things Creed made me feel. Tenderness. Admiration.

Love.

But as my grandmother has repeatedly told me. There's no place for love in a monarchy. Love makes you weak.

And she's right. Love *did* make me weak, so much so that I allowed myself to live in a fantasy world all summer. Imagined what a life with Creed could be like, despite the impossibility of it all. If we continued down that path, it would have only become riskier. And not just to Creed's reputation.

But to my heart.

I needed this. Needed to be snatched back to reality. Needed Adam to remind me what was at stake.

"As you can see by the recent media reports," Gianna's voice cuts through my thoughts, pulling me back to the present.

I glance at the large screen on the far wall, several headlines from the past few days popping up.

"We've countered any negative publicity Mr. Gates has received with concerns about Hayes Barlow's reported drug use. It appears he associated with quite a few methamphetamine addicts. Several medical professionals have suggested his reported behavior is in line with methamphetamine use. As such, nearly all of his sponsors have dropped him, and he's been placed on leave from his racing circuit pending an investigation. Based on all of this, the 'incident' the other night may have just been a meth-fueled outburst. Meth addicts often have episodes like that. Become violent for short bursts of time. Become…delusional."

"Do you recommend this is the position we take?" my father asks.

If this happened earlier in the summer, I may have fought harder to make my voice heard. Argued this entire scenario stunk to high heaven.

If I reached out to the reporters who wrote these stories, I'd most likely learn they were fed this information from an anonymous source. And that anonymous source probably came from within the palace walls, as is so often the case whenever a news article breaks that could paint anyone associated with the royal household in a bad light.

But I can't ignore the disapproving expression in Silas Archer's eyes every time he looks my way. As if waiting for me to challenge him so he can pull out his ace card.

I won't give him the satisfaction. It won't matter, anyway. I have no reason to fight this. Not anymore. I made sure Creed hated me.

After the lies I spewed so he wouldn't fight for me, I have no doubt he does.

If he'd said those things to me, called me nothing more than a spoiled princess who was only good for a bit of fun in the sack, I'd certainly hate him.

"I believe that's for the best," Silas answers for Gianna.

"Very well," my father says, granting his approval, although it's not necessary. The royal household has most likely already set this course of action into motion. This meeting is just a formality so my father can give his rubber stamp.

Further proof we're nothing but pawns.

"If I may suggest we schedule an appearance for Her Highness and Mr. Gates at an addiction treatment facility,"

Gianna states matter-of-factly, always playing the part of the royal household's fixer. "It would show they're sympathetic to the issues facing Mr. Barlow."

"That's a wonderful gesture," my grandmother interjects. "But I also think it would go a long way if Mr. Gates receives positive press in a way that *isn't* connected to Mr. Barlow."

"I agree, and have been brainstorming a variety of possible opportunities to present not just Mr. Gates in a positive light," Gianna glances my way before continuing, "but also his relationship with the princess. The incident with Mr. Barlow is still trending on social media with strong opinions on both sides, so I've come up with several scenarios, one in particular, that will bury any mention of Hayes Barlow."

I study Jameson. Like me, though, he's learned to mask his true feelings, remaining the same expressionless man he needs to be for fear someone will use his emotions against him.

"I'm intrigued," my grandmother says evenly, not so much as a hint of a smile curling her thin lips. I can't remember the last time I've seen her smile when not at a public event. Even then, her smiles are few and far between. "What kind of positive press are you talking about?"

When Gianna looks my way again, an unsettled feeling forms in my gut. She doesn't need to utter a single syllable. I know what she's going to say.

"In my experience, there's one type of news story that tends to be a golden ticket to block bad publicity. Or at least bury it so far down that it barely registers."

"You mean…," my grandmother begins.

"Yes." Gianna nods in her direction before looking at Jameson and me. "I believe it's in our best interests to announce an engagement. We were planning for it to occur in a few weeks anyway. With these recent developments, it's best to limit any possible negative publicity as soon as possible. An engagement will help toward that end.

"Truthfully, I believe this is even better than our original plan. After all, the first time you two danced together was at the King's Day gala. How romantic that Jameson would propose at that very event his year? Doing it at the gala also has the advantage of it not appearing to come out of left field, based on your history with the event. You'll dance to the same song, after which he'll get down on one knee.

"Once the engagement is announced, we'll be able to use the planning for the upcoming nuptials as media fodder for any additional issues that may arise."

I barely even register the squeeze on my hand, everything foggy, feeling like a dream.

But this isn't a dream.

This is real.

At the end of the week, Jameson will propose.

That should be enough to encourage me to fight for what I actually want.

But I have nothing *to* fight for. Not anymore.

I zone out as I listen to Gianna discuss plans for the proposal, every detail already decided, right down to the dress I'm to wear.

It's not until I sense motion out of the corner of my eye that I snap out of my trance, watching as everyone around the table stands, the meeting adjourned.

Jameson helps me to my feet, places his hand on my lower back, then steers me through the halls of the palace and into the SUV waiting to whisk us to our next engagement.

"Are you okay?" he whispers as Adam navigates the car away from the palace.

"Why wouldn't I be?" I shoot back with a quizzical look.

Jameson narrows his gaze on me, leaning closer. "Because of what was just discussed. Are you okay with this?"

I squeeze my eyes shut, pushing down the urge to scream. It won't do any good.

"This was always how it was going to end. No need to delay the inevitable." I force a smile. "Like you told me after that first meeting. You're a decent guy. It could have been a lot worse. For both of us."

He nods, something resembling pity in his gaze. "But it could have been a lot better, too. Isn't that right?"

I lift my eyes to his, my response caught in my throat.

He could be referring to his relationship with Callie, but I know he's not. He's talking about Creed. I can feel it in my soul.

Turning from him, I meet Adam's stare through the rearview mirror.

"It could have been everything," I choke out, allowing my emotions to show for the first time since I destroyed Creed.

Jameson reaches across the seat and squeezes my hand. "I'm sorry."

"Not as much as I am."

CHAPTER FORTY-TWO

Creed

"Now I know what you've been up to these past few days."

At the sound of Adam's voice, I look away from the TV where yet another action movie plays. I'd hoped by watching only movies with tons of explosions, I'd forget about Esme.

But even the most exciting action and adventure films have some sort of love story.

I hate it.

"Drinking all the liquor in Europe," my brother attempts to joke, but I'm not in a joking mood.

Haven't been for days.

While Adam may be exaggerating, I usually don't drink much and always keep my place rather tidy. To not only see evidence I've been drinking, but also take-out containers littering my living room, I can understand how this scenario might come as a surprise.

"I'm going out on a limb here and guessing this has something to do with Esme?"

I part my lips, about to voice the same argument I did when he nearly walked in on us, but I have nothing left to lose by admitting the truth. I've already lost everything.

"Esme doesn't matter." I sink back into the couch, running a hand over my face. "It's over now. In fact, it was over before it began. At least for her. I thought..." I pinch my lips into a tight line. "Actually, I don't know what I thought. It was just supposed to be for the summer, but the more time we spent together... I don't know." I shake my head. "I guess I was happy to forget about reality. Started to believe maybe we *could* find a way."

He steps closer, stopping just past the kitchen peninsula. Based on the dark suit he wears, I can only assume he stopped by on his way to pick up Esme for the King's Day gala.

"That's not how things work, Creed," he sighs, giving me a sympathetic smile. "Not in this world. You should know that by now. Esme was always going to marry someone with much higher social standing than either of us will ever have. We may have grown up around this life, but we aren't them. We never will be. I tried to warn you that we're not their friends. Not when we're the hired help."

"I know. I just..." I lean forward, attempting to push down the reminder of Esme telling me the same thing, the pain from the knife plunging into my heart still as excruciating.

And what makes it worse is that it was so out of character for her.

She's never been the type of person to view her staff as the hired help. In fact, she's one of the few people in the royal family who takes the time to learn the names of not just her staff, but also everyone working behind the scenes at the palace.

And that's not all. She also routinely shows an interest in their personal lives. Hell, she even gave one of her maids six months paid leave so she could be with her daughter during her cancer treatment and not worry about being able to cover the bills. Even made a point to visit her maid's daughter in the hospital. Acted as if it were her own family member who'd fallen ill.

That doesn't sound like someone who'd refer to any of the palace staff as the hired help. Who'd refer to *me* as the hired help.

But I know someone who *has* repeatedly referred to me as the hired help.

Someone who, twenty-four hours prior to Esme breaking things off, confronted me about her, to which I denied any wrongdoing.

I slowly shift my eyes to my brother, analyzing him. He doesn't look directly at me. Blinks more than usual. Rubs his thumb and forefinger together.

Most people wouldn't read too much into these quirks.

But Adam's my brother.

I know him almost as well as I know myself, including all his tells.

"It was you," I say, barely audible. Despite that, my words seem to echo in my apartment, reverberating against the walls.

"What?" Adam stiffens, licking his lips, pupils dilating.

"I said…" My voice grows stronger, nostrils flaring with my increasing breaths as I fight to suppress my rage. "It. Was. You."

"What are you going on about?" he scoffs, downplaying my accusation. "Or is this the alcohol talking?"

"It's not the alcohol talking." My words are even. Cold. Determined. "It's me. And I'm talking about Esme. You put her up to it."

"Up to what, exactly?"

I grit my teeth, fists clenching as the puzzle pieces snap into place, something that probably would have happened days ago if I hadn't allowed my anger and heartache to cloud my judgment.

"Everything, Adam." I slowly stand, widening my stance in an attempt to dwarf him, even though we're the same height. "You knew you couldn't manipulate me. So you manipulated her instead. What did you say to her? That you put your life on the line for her so this was the least she could do in return?"

When Adam doesn't respond, I know I've hit on something.

"My god." I dig my fingers into my hair, chest squeezing from the pain of his betrayal. "Did you really think I wouldn't figure it out? That I'd be *okay* with what you did?"

He doesn't respond. Simply stares at me, eyes darting back and forth as if deciding on a course of action.

Finally, he leans into me, jaw tense, nostrils flaring.

"It was for your own good, Creed," he bites out gruffly. "You weren't listening to reason. You were living in a fantasy world. People were talking. You may not like what I did, but I did it to *protect* you. To protect your legacy. There are things you don't know. Things—"

"I don't care about my goddamn legacy!" I interject, spittle forming in the corner of my mouth, rage blinding me to the point I reel back, my fist connecting with his jaw.

Adam doubles over, not immediately moving, my assault momentarily taking him by surprise.

"All my life, that's *all* I've heard about," I continue, voice thundering in my tiny apartment. "That this is my legacy. I would have given up everything to be with her. To hell with some family legacy."

"And what about her?" he shoots back as he straightens, rubbing the side of his face and wiping a few drops of blood from his bottom lip. "Do you really think she'd be allowed to ride off into the sunset with you? Jameson Gates was *chosen* for her. They'd sooner kill you before letting Esme even consider marrying you. Trust me on that."

I clench my fists tighter, resisting the temptation to punch him again. Then I spin from him, quickly yanking on my shoes before swiping my keys off the kitchen counter.

"Where are you going?"

"Where do you think?" I bark. "To talk to Esme. To set things straight."

"It won't make a difference. It's too late."

"No, it's not. It's never too late. I can—"

"Jameson's proposing tonight."

His words stealing my breath, I skid to an abrupt stop.

"What did you say?" I manage to squeak out as I glance over my shoulder at him.

I don't want to believe him. Need him to tell me I'd misheard him. That this is just another ploy. Another act of manipulation and betrayal.

His stern expression falls as he steps toward me. "It's been decided that, based on recent events, an engagement might quiet some of the noise."

"It's not true. It can't be."

"It is."

"Then I'll just make sure that doesn't happen."

"And how do you intend to do that? Do you have an invitation to the gala I don't know about?" He tilts his head, advancing toward me. "Oh, that's right. You don't, even though you're supposed to be close with the Crown Prince. Did you ever wonder why you're never invited to any of these formal events thrown by the palace?"

I swallow hard, heat washing over my expression.

"Because you're not one of them, Creed. If you need further proof, there it is. You've *never* been one of them. And the sooner you come to terms with that, the better off you'll be."

"You just can't stand the thought of anyone being happy," I say through the lump in my throat. "Of *me* being happy. Can you?"

"That has nothing to do with it. I did this to—"

"Yeah, yeah," I scoff. "To *protect* me. But I don't *need* your protection, Adam. I'm not a child anymore. I can make my own decisions. So can Esme."

"And you honestly think she would have chosen you?"

"I hope she would have. But you took that choice away from her. From both of us. Worse, you betrayed both of us. You're my brother. Someone I've always looked up to and admired. And now..." I shake my head, disgust churning my stomach.

Adam's behavior shouldn't surprise me. After all, my father put his duty to the crown as the king's chief protection officer above everything else in his life, including his own family.

I thought Adam was different. Thought he remembered all those times our father made a promise to come to a football game, a swim meet, or recital, only to look into the crowd and not see his face.

Thought he didn't want the same thing for Rory and him.

Thought he was better than this.

I was wrong.

"And now," I begin, swallowing through the frustration in my throat over the idea that my brother chose his career over me. "I don't want to know you anymore."

"You'll eventually come around. Understand I did you a favor."

"A favor?" I bark out a laugh. "If this is your idea of a favor, I don't want it. I don't want *you* in my life. Not anymore."

I turn from him, strides determined as I head toward the door, unsure where I'm going. He's right. It's not like I can just show up at the gala. Hell, I wouldn't even be able to get near the palace tonight, the entire compound locked down, security tight. But I can't stay here, either. I need somewhere I can breathe.

I can no longer do that in my own home.

Just as I'm about to yank open the door, I pause, glancing over my shoulder.

"Remember when we were kids and wanted to go to the football finals? Begged Dad to take us, since it was rare the local team here ever made it that far?"

He subtly nods, throat working in a hard swallow.

"He finally agreed. Even worked out for us to sit in the royal box. The morning of the match, we were more excited than we were on Christmas."

"I remember," he replies somberly.

I fully face him. "Then you also remember how devastated you were when he never bloody showed up to take us. Mum tried to make it up to us, took us to race go-karts and overindulge in ice cream. And when Dad finally *did* show up the following morning, did he even apologize?"

Adam shakes his head. "No."

"Exactly. He offered no explanation. Said it couldn't be helped. That there are more important things than a football match. But we both know what he was really saying. That there are more important things than his own sons. His own *family*." My words come out strained as the feelings of inadequacy return.

"You may not remember it, but I do, Adam. That was the day you swore you would never turn into him. That you would never put your career first." I pull my lips between my teeth. "But that's *precisely* what you've done. You've turned into him. In fact, you're *worse* than he is."

I allow my words to linger for a beat.

Then I storm out of my apartment, slamming the door shut behind me.

CHAPTER FORTY-THREE

Esme

I study my reflection, barely able to recognize the person staring back. And not in a good way. My eyes may be the same, my hair unchanged. But I've never felt like such an imposter. Like a doll that's being dressed up in clothes belonging to someone else.

Most women would probably love to be adorned in a designer gown, draped in expensive jewels, a priceless tiara carefully woven into their hair.

Not me. These jewels are a shackle, the clothes I've worn my entire life merely a straitjacket I'm powerless to free myself from.

Or maybe Creed was right.

Maybe it's because I'm too *scared* to free myself from this life. Too scared to take a risk and chase what I want.

"Is there a reason you look like someone just died?"

I glance up from the full-length mirror as Anderson

strides into my living room, tall frame clad in a crisp tuxedo, hair slicked back, face clean-shaven.

"I don't look like someone just died," I attempt to argue, but it's unconvincing. I can't even fake a smile. Not when, in a few hours, Jameson will get down on one knee in front of hundreds of people and my fate will officially be sealed.

Then again, wasn't it sealed the day I was born?

"Is this about Creed?" Anderson asks in a low voice, narrowing his gaze on me.

My eyes widen. "What are you—"

"Did you think you could hide this from me, of all people? I know the two of you better than anyone." He laughs under his breath. "Sometimes I feel like I know you two better than I do myself. When I noticed that, one day, my sister wasn't so morose about her forced relationship with Jameson, and my brooding best friend was much less brooding and actually smiled, I put two and two together."

I exhale, a weight lifting off my shoulders now that my brother knows. It killed me to keep it from him for so long. But it doesn't matter. Not anymore.

"I'm sorry, Anders. I should have told you."

"You *are* my sister. And he's my best mate. The fact you both kept it from me stings a bit. And not because you went behind my back. But because you didn't think you could trust me with the truth." He lowers his voice as he runs his hands down my arms.

"Remember the promise we made to each other when Uncle Nicholas died? How we vowed to always be honest with each other? To always trust each other with our secrets, no matter what?"

"I thought…" I shake my head, at a loss for words, which seems to be the norm these days. "I don't know what I thought. It doesn't matter. It's over now." I push past him and walk toward the window, the entire city out to celebrate the founding of our country.

"You sure about that?" Anderson asks, his voice filled with skepticism.

"Of course I am." I face him, shoulders squared. "In case you missed the memo, Jameson will be proposing tonight. And I'll be accepting."

He steps toward me. "Is that what you want?"

"It doesn't matter what I want." I look away as another lump lodges in my throat. "He told me he loves me," I say wistfully, fighting back the tears threatening to fall at the memory. I should have been so happy to hear those words.

Instead, it only made our circumstances even more painful.

"I know," he replies, not even asking about whom I'm referring. He doesn't need to.

"You do?" I dart my eyes to his as he approaches.

"He's had a thing for you for years, Ezzy."

"He asked me to run away with him. Leave this life. Start over again."

"And you turned him down."

"What choice did I have?" I choke out. "It's not as easy as he made it sound. Not for me. I can't abandon you."

"Esme…" He grips my biceps. "You wouldn't be abandoning me. I'm a big boy. I can take care of myself. And while I find some of the things about this life abhorrent, I also know it's much harder to change things from the outside." He holds my arms tighter. "You may think you're powerless to do anything, considering certain members of the royal household like to pretend they're in control, but you're not powerless, Esme. You've always had a choice. As long as you're willing to stand up for it.

"All your life, I've watched you stand up for everyone else.

Minorities. The poor. Children. You name it. So long as it's not some rich, white man, you lend your voice to their cause." He pauses, tone softening. "When are you going to stand up for yourself? When are you going to lend your voice to *Esme's* cause?"

"Anders, I—"

A loud throat clearing cuts through the space. I look toward the doorway, Adam standing there in his dark suit, expression stoic, as always. But there's something different about him. I can't help but notice some redness along his jaw, his bottom lip swollen a bit.

"Your Highnesses." He bows slightly before directing his attention toward me. "Are you ready to go?"

"Of course," I reply, although I doubt I'll ever be ready for what awaits me at tonight's gala.

"Then we should be on our way. Don't want you to be late."

"Certainly not." I lift my eyes toward Anderson's, wishing I'd find the answer I need within his blue orbs. What I wouldn't give for my mother to still be alive. To wrap me in my arms and tell me what to do. To assure me I'm on the right path.

Leaning down, my brother presses a soft kiss to my temple. "No matter what, I'll always support you."

I close my eyes, his assurance exactly what I need right now. "Thank you, Anders."

"Love ya, Esme."

"Love you, too." I hold his gaze, grateful to have a brother as understanding and level-headed as him. Then I pull back and walk toward Adam, following him out of my apartment and into the SUV waiting to take me to the palace.

And my future with Jameson Gates.

But as I look out the window at the palace lights in the distance, I question whether this is the future I actually *want* for myself.

Until now, I've never dreamt of anything different. Knew it was futile, so why even try?

But is it?

Or have I just been conditioned to always do as I'm told and not make waves? Not question centuries of tradition. Not stand up for *my* needs. *My* dreams.

For years, I've done everything to be a voice for the voiceless, sometimes at the disapproval of the establishment, considering the royal family is supposed to remain apolitical. Regardless, that didn't stop me from championing these causes.

Still, there's one cause I've never championed.

My *own* cause.

"Can I ask you something?"

I tear my gaze away from the window, meeting Adam's eyes as he turns around in the front seat of the SUV, seemingly in no rush to get to the gala.

"What is it?" My words have an icy quality they've never had with my chief protection officer.

Then again, things between us have been strained since he forced me to break up with Creed. I debated requesting a new CPO. What would be my reason? That I was having sex with his brother and, when he found out, he made me end things? Not sure that would go over well, especially since Adam *is* very good at his job. There are no reasonable grounds for his reassignment.

"If you weren't who you are, and he wasn't who he is——"

"But he is," I interject, to which he holds up a hand.

"Just indulge me, ma'am. If neither of you had these duties and obligations, if there was absolutely nothing standing in your way, who would you choose? Jameson Gates?" He pauses before finishing, "Or my brother?"

"Creed," I answer quickly, not needing time to deliberate. "I'd choose him today and every day for the rest of my life."

He nods, shoulders falling, then asks, "Do you love him?"

I part my lips, contemplating my response.

When I made Creed promise he wouldn't fall in love with me, I thought by making it part of our agreement, we'd keep emotions out of it.

Be able to protect our hearts.

I didn't want to fall in love.

Resisted it at every turn.

But there are some things in life we *can't* control. Some forces more powerful than sheer willpower or stubbornness.

"I love your brother in a way I never thought existed in the real world," I admit finally as a tear slides down my cheek. "If I'm being honest, that makes what we share so remarkable." I pull my lips between my teeth and swallow hard. "What we *shared* so remarkable," I correct before continuing, "I never thought this kind of love was possible."

With every word, my heart warms in my chest, a fluttering low in my belly at the mere reminder of Creed. Of these intense emotions I never thought I'd experience. But I have. For much longer than I was originally willing to recognize.

Creed was right.

He didn't break his promise to me. He was already in love with me when we started down this path.

Now I realize I've been in love with him for years, too.

"Your brother showed me what love is. True, unconditional love. For that, I will always be grateful, regardless of what my future holds. Regardless of the fact I may never be allowed to love him openly. But that doesn't matter. Not when I know the truth. And the truth is that Creed Lawson will always own my heart, regardless of some halfhearted vow I may be forced to make in front of God to appease the royal household. They may dictate who I marry. But they can't dictate who I love. I will always love your brother."

Adam nods dejectedly, a mumbled curse falling from his lips. Then he faces forward and shifts into drive.

"I'm sorry if that's not what you wanted to hear, but I'm not going to hide my feelings. Not anymore."

"It may not be what I wanted to hear," he sighs as he navigates the SUV toward the gates protecting Gladwell Palace from the outside world. "But it's what I *needed* to hear."

After the barrier gate lifts, he proceeds forward, but instead of turning left and toward Lamberside Palace, he takes a right.

"What are you doing?" I ask, brow winkled in confusion.

"Most likely getting myself fired. And disowned. But if Creed thinks you're worth the risk and you're willing to give all of this up for him, who am I to stand in your way?"

I stare at him, speechless, heart thundering in my chest.

"Unless you want me to take you to the gala so Jameson Gates can propose?" He brings the car to a stop, looking at me through the rearview mirror, a question within.

This is crazy, not to mention out of character for Adam. It was one thing to want to be with Creed when I knew it was an impossibility.

Can I *actually* follow through with this?

Can I actually take this risk?

"I told you I'd choose your brother today and every day," I finally say. "So that's what I'm doing. Making my own decision."

A hint of pride fills Adam's eyes as he eases on the accelerator. "Good for you."

Excitement bubbles in my veins as I settle into the back seat of the SUV, watching as the familiar streets of my country's capital city pass by. I've driven along these streets most of my life. But today, they seem brighter. Livelier. More colorful. And it's not simply because it's the celebration of our country's independence. It's because I'm finally ready to reclaim *my* independence, too.

Normally, the drive to Creed's place on the outskirts of town doesn't take too long, maybe twenty minutes.

But tonight, those twenty minutes may as well be a year each, especially with Adam's cell phone vibrating every few minutes, most likely someone demanding to know where he's taking me.

But he doesn't answer. Nor does he turn the car around and take me to the palace. Instead, he ignores the calls, regardless of the consequences he'll suffer when this is all over. It makes me question why he'd have such a sudden change of heart.

Mere days ago, he demanded I end things with Creed, not only because of the risk to Creed's future but also because of the potential risk to Adam's own career with the guard, as well as their father's.

Now he's willing to do something that will undoubtedly lead to his discharge?

"Why are you doing this for me?" I ask as he pulls down a dimly lit street, barely another car in sight.

"Let's just say someone smacked some sense into me." He rubs his jaw. "Or, more accurately, punched some sense into me."

"Creed?"

He nods. "Accused me of turning into our father. Forgetting what's most important."

"And what's that?"

"Family," he responds with a deep exhale. "I'm not sure this will fix things between us. At least not right away. But hopefully it's a step in the right direction."

I reach up from the back seat, giving his shoulder a squeeze. "Thank you, Adam."

He lifts his gaze to the rearview mirror and gives me a serene smile. I don't think I've ever seen him so calm. So… tranquil. As if he's finally made peace with his role in life, too.

But in a heartbeat, it all vanishes, his expression filling with something else. Something akin to alarm.

I glance behind us, panic tightening my chest when I see a dark car chasing us at a high rate of speed.

"Get down!" Adam shouts as he engages in several evasive maneuvers, but he's no match for whoever's driving the other vehicle.

Just as I peek out the window to see how close it is, we're hit from behind. The impact forces us off the road and into a tree, my head slamming into the seat in front of me.

The last thing I remember is the stench of gasoline filling the SUV.

Then everything goes dark.

CHAPTER FORTY-FOUR

Creed

"Creed? Are you here?"

When I hear my father's gruff voice, I groan, grabbing a pillow and covering my throbbing head.

Drinking as much as I did last night probably wasn't the smartest idea, but with the knowledge that Esme would be getting engaged, that there was nothing I could do to stop it from happening, especially when I couldn't even get in touch with Anders, I needed something to make it hurt less.

So, I went to a dive bar in a seedy area of town, one I knew wouldn't be showing any footage from the gala on the television. I couldn't stomach any reminders, choosing to tune out the world.

Including the repeated calls from my father, prompting me to turn off my mobile. We're not little kids anymore. We don't need our father to intervene in our disagreements.

I told Adam there was no coming back from this betrayal.

T.K. LEIGH

Not even asking Dad to come to his defense will help. If anything, it will only make it worse. Further prove my point that Adam did the one thing he swore he never would.

He turned into our father.

"Get up, Creed."

When he yanks the comforter off me, I turn over, about to berate him for barging into my apartment, then attempting to order me around.

But when I see the red rimming his eyes, I know something's not right.

That something must have happened.

I sit up, running a hand over my face. "What's wrong?"

He lowers himself onto the edge of the bed, shoulders slumping, a look of despair on his face.

My father's always had a very serious demeanor. I can count on one hand the number of times I've seen him show any emotion, and only once that I've seen evidence he's been crying.

The day we learned Anderson and Esme's uncle, along with his wife and all their kids, perished in a tragic skiing accident.

Dread settles low in my stomach.

"Did something happen?"

"I'm afraid so." Drawing in a deep breath, he attempts to collect himself before turning his dark eyes to mine. "Last night, there was an accident."

"An accident?" I swallow hard. "What kind of accident?"

"Adam and Her Royal Highness Princess Esme were attacked. Their vehicle was followed, then forced off the road, at which point it was doused in white gas and lit on fire." He pulls his lips between his teeth. "Adam didn't make it."

His statement is like a punch to the gut, stealing my

breath, my heart physically aching as I struggle to comprehend my father's words.

This can't be real. I must still be dreaming, my conscience playing tricks on me for the way I treated Adam, reminding me what's important.

"And Esme?" I begin in a shaky voice, unsure I want to hear the answer.

Unsure I can *handle* the answer.

"Is she… Did she?"

"She's in stable condition, albeit suffering from smoke inhalation and minor burns."

I stand, feeling a modicum of relief that Esme is okay. But that has nothing on the guilt plaguing me over the fact that my brother's gone.

And it's not simply because he's gone, because I'll never hear his voice again.

It's because the last words I ever said to him were those of hate. Disgust. Outrage. I essentially told him he was dead to me.

And now he really *is* dead.

I may not have been the one to pull the proverbial trigger.

But I feel just as responsible. Just as culpable.

I'll never be able to apologize. Never be able to tell my brother I love him. That I didn't mean what I told him. I'll have to live with that for the rest of my life.

"Who did this?"

"Hayes Barlow. If you've been following the news—"

"I know who he is," I interrupt. "I thought he was arrested."

"He was held for questioning, but was eventually released on a promise to appear." He swallows hard.

"Who was the target? Was it Adam? Or was it Jameson? Is *he* okay?"

My father nods. "Luckily, he wasn't in the vehicle. I'm not sure of the specifics, and they're still looking into motive, but it appears Adam…" His voice momentarily catches when he says his name.

Pausing, he takes a few moments to collect himself. Then his expression evens as he turns back into the stoic man he's been all my life.

"It appears Adam took a bit of a…detour on their way to the gala. They were attacked by Grace Park."

I furrow my brows, something not adding up. "Grace Park? That's nowhere near Lamberside."

"Based on their proximity to Her Majesty's final resting place, they believe Adam was taking Princess Esme to visit her mother's grave. They were a few blocks away when they were attacked," my father continues. "The investigation is still underway, but the General of the Royal Guard has shared a few details with me. As has the Chief of Royal Police. They pulled surveillance video along the path Adam took, based on his car's GPS.

"Approximately five kilometers before the scene of the crash, an Audi registered to Hayes Barlow was spotted exiting the parking lot of a nearby church. The vehicle followed them, but stayed far enough back so as to not alert Adam to its presence. At least until he was ready to attack, at which point he increased his speed and forced the SUV off the road. Adam used defensive techniques, but he ultimately lost control and crashed into a tree."

"So he forced them off the road, then…" I trail off.

"He approached the vehicle, poured accelerant over it, and lit a match. The doctors say it's a miracle Princess Esme survived, albeit with severe smoke inhalation and some second-degree burns. What little information she was able to give investigators before needing to be sedated further was that she'd lost consciousness because of the initial impact, but then the flames had woken her up. She managed to open the back door and escape. She tried to get to Adam, but the front of the car was already engulfed in flames." He pinches his lips together. "It was already too late."

"She's awake?"

"She's in and out of consciousness. She's on oxygen for the time being, but the doctors say that's normal and expect her to make a full recovery."

I try to find relief in that, but that relief comes at a price.

"And they're positive Hayes Barlow is behind it?" I ask.

"His car has damage consistent with the damage to the SUV. And the royal police expect that once the forensics team completes their analysis, the paint transferred onto the SUV will match Hayes' vehicle, and vice versa. They also uncovered empty cans of white gas in the trunk of his car. And upon a search of his house, they found a pair of black pants, black long-sleeved shirt, and black hat in his garbage bins, all of them reeking of smoke and accelerant. There's a continent-wide search going on for him right now."

"He hasn't been found?" I ask, eyes wide.

"He will be. Trust me. I'll do everything I can to make sure he pays for what he's done, even if it's the last thing I do."

I nod, everything still surreal. I've never known a world without my brother in it. He was my first friend. My best friend, really, despite our differences.

After a protracted silence, I glance at my father. "And Rory? How's she handling things?"

"She's still in a state of shock. Hasn't cried yet. Or really spoken. Your mother's with her right now."

My chest squeezes at the thought of what Rory's going through. A week ago, they celebrated the life they were about to bring into this world. Now she'll have to go through it alone.

She'll have to go through *life* alone.

I'll do my best to make sure she doesn't. That she knows she still has family. I may not be able to make things right between Adam and me, but I can make sure Rory's taken care of. Make sure Adam's son is provided for, like I promised when he first shared the news of Rory's pregnancy and begged me to take care of them if anything ever happened to him.

Never did I think I'd have to act on that promise.

I drag myself to my feet, still in a daze. I have a feeling I'll be in a daze for a while.

"I'll throw on some clothes and head to the hospital."

"The hospital?" My father crosses his arms in front of his stomach.

"To check on Esme and see how Anders is—"

"*Her Highness* is being treated by top medical professionals," he snips out. "And *His Highness* isn't your family. *Adam* is." He relaxes his arms, but his expression remains severe as he steps toward me. "And right now, you need to put your family first. Put *Rory* first."

I don't bother telling him he's never put his family first. Not that I can remember.

Regardless, he has a point.

I broke the rules, and when my brother tried to talk some sense into me, tried to *protect* me, I lashed out at him. Accused him of putting his job before his family. In reality, *I* was the one who failed to put our family first. I chose a couple of months of amazing sex over my brother. And now he's gone.

I can't bring him back. But I can do everything to set things right going forward. To put my family first.

And like Adam constantly tried to tell me… Anderson and Esme aren't my family.

"I'll go check on Rory," I say.

My father nods his approval. "Good answer."

CHAPTER FORTY-FIVE

Esme

"Excuse me, Your Highness."

I look away from the window, the streets outside the hospital lined with concerned citizens holding signs wishing me a speedy recovery.

"Lieutenant Hawkins," I greet my private secretary in a scratchy voice.

Even though I'm currently under treatment here at the hospital, he's set up a temporary office in the room beside mine. That way, he can still fulfill his obligations to me, get me whatever I may need as I heal from my injuries.

"I understand your doctor mentioned you may still be suffering from exhaustion, but Her Majesty has requested a few minutes of your time."

She's the last person I want to see right now, but my grandmother isn't one to take no for an answer.

"Of course." I adjust myself in the bed, wincing through

the pain from my bandaged hands. At least I'm alive. That's more than I can say for Adam. "Send her in."

"Very well." Lieutenant Hawkins spins on his heels, but only makes it a few feet before I call out to him. "Thomas?"

He glances over his shoulder. "Yes, ma'am?"

"Has anyone else stopped by to see me today? Perhaps while I was sleeping?"

His expression drops. I don't have to mention who I hoped to receive a visit from. He knows.

I sense he knew all along.

"I'm sorry, ma'am. Not yet. But visiting hours have just begun."

I nod, pinching my lips together as I swallow through the lump in my throat.

It doesn't mean anything. Creed just lost his brother. Visiting me probably isn't high on his list of priorities, especially after the things I said to him the last time we saw each other.

"Thank you, Thomas."

"Of course, ma'am."

He opens the door, stepping to the side to allow my grandmother to enter before closing it behind him.

"Esme," she greets, striding purposefully toward the hospital bed, a look of disgust on her expression as she takes in my appearance.

My hair's disheveled from spending the past four days in the hospital. My face is devoid of makeup, not to mention sports a few bruises and burns I sustained in the crash. And I'm donning the latest fashion I like to refer to as hospital chic — a blue dotted gown.

Upon seeing a loved one in the hospital, most people would show signs of compassion, worry. Not my grandmother. Hell, I've been here four days now and neither she nor my father have come to visit.

"Your Majesty," I say, briefly lowering my eyes.

"How are you feeling?"

"Getting better every day."

"I see." She looks around the room, the walls crisp white, the only décor a framed print of an ocean scene. "Then I believe it's time to discuss what happened Saturday night so we can make sure your story is correct."

I lift my brows. "My story is correct? Why? Were you there?"

"We simply need to ensure your version is in line with—"

"Let me guess. In line with the version of events the palace PR team already released in a statement."

"Yes. Mainly that when Captain Lawson left your apartment and turned in the opposite direction of the palace, it was because you asked to visit your mother's final resting place. Since King's Day is a holiday in which we celebrate our monarchy, you wanted to pay your respects to the former wife of our current monarch. As well as the mother of our future monarch."

"So you want me to lie?"

"The path Captain Lawson took *is* on the way to your mother's final resting place. In fact, the attack occurred a short distance away from her gravesite. It's not a lie."

"It's not the truth, either."

"All things considered, this is the best course of action. You *are* supposed to be in a relationship with Jameson Gates."

"What if I don't want to be anymore?"

"Don't be ridiculous, Esme. Did you honestly think anything could come of your dalliance with that man?"

"That *man* is my brother's best friend. And the brother of my chief protection officer."

Her eyes light on fire. "*Was* the brother of your chief protection officer. The chief protection officer who's now dead because of *your* selfishness. Did you ever stop to think about that? That if you'd just done as you were supposed to, you never would have exposed yourselves to such a gruesome attack? But all you care about is yourself. Because of you, Captain Lawson is dead. And his killer is on the loose."

"*I know that!*" I shout, but my voice won't cooperate, struggling to even get the words out.

I clutch my throat, a sharp pinch of pain hitting me before subsiding. Grabbing my water from the bedside table, I take a sip, then refocus my attention on my grandmother.

"Of course I know that," I say, quieter this time. "That's all I've thought about since I woke up here. That still doesn't change things. I don't want to get married right now. Not to Jameson anyway."

"Because you think you're in love with Adam's brother?"

"And if I am?" I square my shoulders, indignant.

"You can't be with him, Esme."

"He may not come from the kind of background you'd prefer, but he's a good man. From a good family. His father has been the chief protection officer to King Gabriel for over ten years now. It's not like he's some bum off the street. He's a decent person. He—"

"He's been sworn into the royal guard."

Her words ring out around me, stealing my breath. I blink, not wanting to believe I heard her correctly.

"As a member of the elite protection squad. He took his oath this morning in a special ceremony."

"But his induction wasn't supposed to be until the end of the month."

"That's true." My grandmother straightens her spine. "But since Captain Lawson died in the line of duty, only members of the honor guard can have the privilege of carrying his casket during the funeral. And in order to be selected for the honor guard…"

"He has to be a member of the royal guard."

She nods. "After suffering such a tragic loss, the privy council felt this was the least we could do for him and his family. After all, they've made the ultimate sacrifice."

She gives me a pointed stare, and I know exactly what she's thinking. That I'm the reason his family was forced to make that sacrifice. That if I'd just done as expected, I wouldn't be here. Adam would still be alive.

"So you see, dear," she begins in a patronizing tone. "There's no reason for anyone to find out the truth. If anything, it's better they didn't. Do you really want this man you claim to love to learn that *you're* the reason his brother is now dead?"

I don't believe for a second Creed would blame me.

If anything, he'd blame himself. That's the type of man he is.

I can't stomach the idea of him shouldering the fault for this, regardless of how misplaced it is.

"Do we have an understanding, Esme?"

I stare at her, wanting to tell her we don't. But what's the point anymore?

Adam's gone. Creed's now officially a member of the royal guard.

It's what I knew would happen.

But now that it has, it hurts worse than I imagined.

Because his induction has taken away the one thing I've been able to cling onto all summer, even before I realized it.

It's taken away my hope.

CHAPTER FORTY-SIX

Esme

I look out the window at the brilliant sun, only a few clouds visible in the sky. It's criminal for the weather to be so nice, especially today. It might be easier if the weather fit my mood, melancholy and full of sorrow.

I've been dreading this day since I woke up in the hospital ten days ago and was reminded why I was there. That someone had forced Adam off the road, then lit the car on fire, leaving both of us to die. I try to find comfort in the knowledge that I survived. That *Adam* would find comfort in the knowledge that I survived.

But nothing brings me comfort these days, not when I'm plagued with guilt for the role I played in Adam's death.

If I hadn't been so selfish and listened to my head instead of my heart, he'd still be here.

From now on, that's what I plan to do. No more following my heart.

My grandmother told me years ago there's no place for love in a monarchy.

She's right.

I just wish it didn't take Adam's death to make me realize that.

When I hear a knock, I look away from the window. "Come in," I call out.

My voice is raspy, my throat still sore, but I'm getting better every day.

My doctor released me a few days ago under strict instructions to get plenty of rest and keep any stressful activity to a minimum, including work. That's been the silver lining in all of this, giving me a reprieve from answering where I stand with Jameson.

He's visited me daily, first in the hospital, then at my apartment. But we've kept our conversations light, neither of us discussing the giant elephant in the room.

"Are you ready?" Anderson asks as he steps into my living room, looking dashing in his military dress uniform.

I nod, lowering the small, black web veil in front of eyes. He strides toward me, placing a hand on the middle of my back as he helps me across the room. He's been like this since the accident, not allowing me to overexert myself too much while my lungs continue to heal.

It goes without saying he was quite shaken up by what happened. I am, too. Every time I close my eyes, I'm transported back to that night. To the burning in my lungs. The flames licking my face. The struggle to open the door. Then the horror when I looked at the front seat to see there was no way to save Adam.

All because of me.

"How are you holding up?" Anderson asks once we're

situated in the back seat of a dark SUV, his chief protection officer behind the wheel.

I force a smile, pushing down the nerves bubbling to the surface over the prospect of seeing Creed again. I'm not sure what to expect. All I know is today will be difficult. Not only because it'll mean saying goodbye to Adam. It'll also mean saying goodbye to Creed.

To the idea of us.

If there ever was an us.

"Okay. You?"

He returns my sad smile. "I'm okay."

I reach across the seat, squeezing his hand to the best of my ability through my bandages. At least they're not as thick as they were a week ago, my burns healing nicely.

Neither one of us says anything during the short drive to the National Cathedral. I can't even look out the window. If I do and see the hundreds of mourners lining the sidewalks to pay tribute to Adam, I'll lose it. I'm grateful they're out there, but it serves as a reminder he's gone.

And despite the fact it's been ten days without seeing him, without sitting in the back seat of the SUV listening to him excitedly remark about feeling the baby kick in Rory's belly, I still haven't fully accepted his death.

Just like I haven't fully accepted that Creed's now in the royal guard.

Two inevitabilities I'll have no choice but to come to terms with today.

When the SUV pulls to a stop, I look toward the cathedral steps. As expected, there's a huge security presence keeping the media sharks at bay. Men dressed in black surround the car, our protection team not taking any chances after recent events.

"Are you ready for this?" Anderson raises a concerned brow.

"As ready as I'll ever be."

He nods, giving me a reassuring smile before tapping on the window, signaling we're ready. A guard opens the door, and Anderson slides out before helping me to my feet, not letting go as we climb the steps up to the cathedral, guards flanking us on all sides.

Cameras flash, causing my irises to burn as reporters shout my name, asking how I feel. How I'm recovering from my injuries. If I'm concerned that Hayes Barlow is still at large. If Jameson's been taking care of me during my convalescence.

I don't answer any of them, biting my tongue when I'd love nothing more than to scream at them for asking such insensitive questions, considering this is a funeral for my chief protection officer who died in the line of duty.

Who died because of my selfishness.

Once we're escorted through the elaborate cathedral lobby and into the nave, silence surrounds us. Along with something bigger. Mercy. Compassion. Grace.

One of my clearest childhood memories is stepping into this cathedral for my father's coronation. How on display I felt walking down this aisle as everyone judged me.

Today, there's no one here to judge me, at least not yet, the space empty so the royal family can pay our respects in private before being put on display.

As I approach the altar, awareness prickles my skin, my stomach heavy, chest tight. I try not to look at Creed as he stands beside Rory and his parents, all of them waiting to receive us and accept our condolences. No matter how much I try to resist, I still feel a pull toward him.

Even if it's now just one-sided.

Anderson and I stop in front of the flag-covered casket and bow our heads, taking a moment to mourn the man lying beneath the pristine mahogany. Then Anderson squeezes my hand, leading me toward Adam's family. They bow or curtsey, addressing us with a round of "Your Highnesses."

We go down the line, offering our condolences to Adam's parents and Rory. I do my best to maintain the same composure as my brother, despite the fact I know he's torn up about this. Adam may have been my chief protection officer, but he always felt more like family.

When I reach Creed, I slowly lift my eyes to his. His hair is cut short, the unshaven jawline now smooth and free of even a hint of stubble. He wears the official dress uniform of the royal guard, the pins on his chest now denoting the rank of captain. Just like Adam.

But what's worse than how different and stoic he appears is the lack of heat in his gaze as he stares at me.

Now he peers at me with indifference.

And sorrow.

Despite knowing this goes against all protocol, I don't care. I fling my arms around his shoulders and hug him.

"I'm so sorry," I say, squeezing him with every ounce of strength I possess.

But he never hugs me back.

Instead, he remains as unmoving as a statue, his tone clipped as he says, "Thank you, Your Highness."

CHAPTER FORTY-SEVEN

Esme

Voices talk around me, but I barely hear a word they say. I simply stare ahead at the same familiar portrait I've stared at all summer whenever summoned to the conference room in my father's office to attend yet another meeting to discuss my relationship with Jameson Gates.

I've been lucky enough to avoid having to endure these meetings for the past three weeks.

Then again, I shouldn't say that, either, considering the reason for my absence.

Despite the passing of weeks, it's as if nothing's changed. I'm still in the same place, in the same chair, listening to the same people plan my future.

When I feel a squeeze on my hand, I look to my right, meeting Jameson's eyes.

"Are you okay?" Concern furrows his brow as he leans close. "Say the word, and I'll whisk us away to the land of pajama pants and serial killer documentaries."

A smile pulls on my lips at the reminder of how we've spent nearly every day since my release from the hospital.

Over the past few weeks, I've gotten to know him better than I have all summer. I can now say with absolute certainty that I like him.

But I don't love him.

And he doesn't love me.

"It's okay," I assure him. "I'm fine."

His face is heavy with disbelief. "Are you sure? Even with what they're discussing?"

I haven't exactly been paying attention. I don't need to in order to know they're planning our future without giving us a say.

"We did a recent poll," Gianna announces, pointing her clicker at the screen on the far wall. A graph appears. "We asked a representative sample how long after the death of a loved one they believe you should wait before announcing an engagement when you'd planned to do so before you learned of the death. As you can see, we're well within acceptable parameters. In fact, some of the written comments indicate the sooner the better, as it would give people a reason to celebrate instead of mourn.

"Based on all of this data, not to mention the fact that Her Highness and Mr. Gates haven't been seen together since the funeral, I'd like to schedule a press conference for tomorrow so His Majesty can officially announce the engagement."

She clicks the button again, a sample press release appearing.

"This will go out immediately afterwards, and we'll rework it to be the official announcement posted at the palace gates, as per tradition. The gist is that Captain Adam Lawson's death made the couple realize how short life is, and they decided to get engaged in order to start their lives together."

Fire bubbles in my veins as I listen to Gianna's plan.

Since I broke things off with Creed, I've remained indifferent. Like Jameson, I already had my strike of lightning. I wasn't holding out for a second one, so why fight this?

But using Adam's death to justify our engagement leaves a sour taste in my mind.

I can't help but think Adam would hate being used like that.

I also can't help but wonder what he would think of this situation in general, especially after the risk he took for me. He was fully aware he'd be fired when I didn't turn up at the King's Day gala. Yet, he didn't care.

He was willing to make that sacrifice. For me.

Is this really how I'm going to repay him? By returning to the status quo? Allowing the establishment to dictate the rules? Decide my future?

I can practically hear him screaming at me from the great beyond, telling me he didn't die so I could spend the rest of my life trapped in the same prison he tried to free me from.

I'd allowed my grandmother and the rest of the royal household to manipulate me into believing I was at fault. That I should stick to the original plan, despite my indiscretions, especially once Creed was no longer an option.

But this was never about choosing between Jameson and Creed.

It was about learning to choose myself.

Now that the smoke's cleared, I finally see that.

"No," I say firmly, interrupting Gianna as she discusses plans for a lavish engagement party next week.

Everyone looks my way, a hush falling over the room.

"What did you say, Esme?" my grandmother asks.

Placing my hands on the edge of the table, I slowly stand. "I said, no." I glower at her, almost willing her to fight me on this.

"What exactly do you object to, ma'am?" Gianna interjects. "Is it the *Fire and Ice* theme? I assure you, it's quite popular. I—"

"It's not the theme," I throw Gianna's way before looking back at my grandmother, doing my best to control my pounding heart.

I refuse to show her so much as a hint of weakness. Not when I'm just a lowly pawn on a quest to capture the queen herself.

"It's this entire scenario. I'm… Well, I'm done with it."

"I don't think so." My grandmother waves me off. "Need I remind you of your duty to the crown?"

"No need at all. You've reminded me of my so-called 'duty to the crown' at every turn. Let me ask you something, though. What would the public think of this duty to the crown if they learned you fabricated our entire relationship? That you *lied* to the public?" I glance at Jameson, remembering the story he shared about Callie. "And that Henry Gates threatened to defund the charities Jameson supports. You may not care about any backlash on Mr. Gates, but could you imagine what people would say if they thought you contributed to the idea of making hungry children starve? Throwing pregnant women out onto the street? Forcing refugees to return to war-torn countries where they awaited certain death?"

Pacing the length of the room, I tap my chin, my resolve and confidence increasing with every second. "Now, I don't have any fancy graphs or polls, but I'd venture to guess the responses would trend pretty far into the negative category." I fix my attention on Gianna. "What do you think?"

She pinches her lips into a tight line. "I believe you're correct."

"Right. Then what would the public think if they learned a certain missing woman, who Jameson admitted to have been in a relationship with, disappeared around the same time Silas Archer paid Henry Gates a visit to discuss a possible arrangement between Jameson and me?"

"What are you insinuating, ma'am?" Silas asks from his normal spot on the opposite end of the table, his eyes as cold as ever.

"Oh, I'm not insinuating anything. Merely stating the facts. I'll allow the public to draw their own conclusions from that little coincidence." A slow smirk crawls on my mouth. "But it's not exactly a great scenario, especially in this age of social media and clickbait. All it takes is one article to go viral and who knows? The next referendum to turn the monarch into more of a ceremonial role may just pass. And everyone in this room would lose their power and influence. I'm certain no one wants that."

Feeling quite proud of myself, I place my hands on my hips as everyone exchanges nervous glances, unsure how to respond.

Even Jameson appears surprised by this turn of events, his furrowed brow focused on Gianna. It strikes me as odd. I can't remember them ever talking much, other than in these meetings. As I watch them, I can't shake the feeling they're in the midst of a silent conversation.

"What do you want?" Silas asks finally, forcing my attention away from them.

"In the press release, you'll announce that, after much discussion, Her Royal Highness Princess Esme and Master

Jameson Gates have decided to part ways. The breakup is amicable and the two remain friends, but realized they want different things out of life."

I look at Jameson, a single brow arched. After he steals another glance Gianna's way, which only increases my confusion, he eventually nods his agreement. I study him for a beat, a nagging feeling settling in my stomach.

"Fine," Silas snips out. "Anything else?"

I dart my eyes back to him, brushing off my concern. "I'll be taking a leave from my duties as a senior royal to attend culinary school in Paris."

"You have to be accepted to attend culinary school," my grandmother states with superiority.

"And I have been. To one of the most prestigious schools in the world. I developed a passion for it during my time at university and have been invited to pursue it. So that's what I plan to do. Classes begin in a few weeks."

"You're a royal. Cooking isn't a skill you'll ever be required to use."

"This isn't merely cooking. It's creating art with food. If I recall correctly, you've always encouraged me to become knowledgeable about the arts. That's what I'm doing."

"But your charity work," she argues in one last attempt to make me reconsider. "Will that just fall to the wayside?"

"I didn't abandon it during my time in university. And I won't abandon it now, either."

While my grandmother seems lukewarm about the idea of announcing an end to my relationship with Jameson, she's vehemently opposed to the idea of me attending culinary school.

"I'm going no matter what. It just depends on whether my departure accompanies some unfavorable news about the royal household. Your call."

"You'd do that to your father? And your brother?"

"Anderson will understand. And my father can deal with it. I gave him a chance to put a stop to this. He chose not to. He can suffer the consequences, like I've had to do all summer."

I glare at him, expecting him to remain silent and ambivalent, as he has since the beginning. To my surprise, he doesn't.

"Agreed," he states firmly, remorse filling his expression.

"You can't honestly think this is a good idea," my grandmother chides, aghast.

"If Esme wants to take some time to pursue her passion, it's the least we can offer after she nearly lost her life. Like Gianna's press release stated. A near death experience makes you re-evaluate your priorities. Isn't that right?"

Gianna parts her lips, at a loss for words over the fact that the statement she wrote in order to shackle me to this life is now being used to free me from it.

When nobody responds, my father looks my way. "Agreed," he repeats, a finality in his tone.

I don't wait for any further argument, spinning on my heels and hurrying out of the conference room.

As I walk through the hallways, I feel lighter than I have in months.

Freer than I have in months.

Until my father calls out to me.

Pausing in my tracks, I debate whether to ignore him and continue out of here as quickly as my feet can carry. But I'm determined to be the bigger person.

To be the first ripple that causes a wave of change.

Facing him, I cross my arms in front of my chest. "Yes?"

Regret covers the lines of his face, a stark contrast from the assured and determined man he's always been. Who he's had to be in order to carry the weight of the country on his shoulders for over a decade. But in this moment, I can tell it wears on him.

Or maybe it's having to balance the politics of the monarchy against the politics of leading a country that wears on him. This summer taught me they're not mutually exclusive.

"I just wanted to tell you how proud I am of you. What you did in there…" He shakes his head, a twinkle in his eye. "For a minute, I thought it was your mother giving them a piece of her mind."

I smile at the comparison.

Before she passed away, I always looked up to and admired the woman who gave me life. It was her legacy that made me do so much volunteer work when I was younger. And now that volunteer work has transitioned to a passion for giving a voice to the voiceless.

Now I've finally given myself a voice, too.

"It never should have come to that. I shouldn't have been forced to make those kinds of threats. If you would have stood up for me when I begged you to—"

He holds up his hands. "I know. I understand that now. I thought you were happy. You and Jameson seemed to get along quite well."

"It doesn't matter if we get along. I used that same argument to convince myself it wasn't a big deal, too. Convinced myself it wasn't worth the fight. But it was never about whether we got along. Whether he made me smile. It was about the fact that you and everyone else in that room took away my freedom to choose."

"I see that now. And I apologize."

I tilt my head back, looking at the ornate ceiling before refocusing my stare on him. "It's too late for apologies. While

I appreciate that you finally stood up for me, it's too little too late. You had *so* many chances to put an end to this. But you refused every single one. Allowed me to be used as a pawn in whatever game Silas Archer is playing."

"Archer's harmless."

I raise a brow. "He was your father's private secretary. Now your mother's most trusted advisor, as well as a senior member of the privy council. I wouldn't call that harmless."

"Tell me what I can do to make it up to you," he says, ignoring my remarks. "Is there some cookware or something you'd like, perhaps?"

"I'm not a child anymore. You can't buy me ice cream or a new toy in the hopes all will be forgotten."

He sighs, pinching the bridge of his nose. "I know. I just…" He meets my eyes. "I'm not very good at being a father."

This is probably one of the most honest things I've ever heard him admit.

"Your mother was so good at it." He looks into the distance, a nostalgic gleam in his gaze. "Whenever either of you were upset about something, she knew what to say or do to make it better. Granted back then, sometimes all you needed was a hug or a new stuffed animal. Since she died…" He heaves a sigh, his lower lip quivering. "Well, suffice it to say I've fallen down on the job of being a parent. Since I was never any good at it, I focused on something I *am* good at… Leading this country."

I take a few slow steps toward him, placing my hand on his arm. "You don't have to be any good at being a parent. It's not a competition. You want to earn back my respect? Be there for me when I need you. Put me and Anderson first instead of the bloody royal household."

He nods, closing his eyes before returning them to me.

"I promise to do better."

"I need more than a promise. I need you to prove you've changed with your actions." I allow my words to linger for a beat before stepping back and curtseying toward him. "Your Majesty."

Then I spin around and walk through the halls of Lamberside Palace for what I hope will be the last time for a while.

CHAPTER FORTY-EIGHT

Esme

"You'd better be safe," I tell Anderson as I squeeze him tightly, not wanting to let go.

I'd originally planned to wait until he left on deployment to return to Paris, but that wouldn't have given me any time to get settled before starting classes. I didn't want to get kicked out of culinary school on the first day.

Instead of spending an extra week here, I opted to head to Paris so I'm prepared to fully immerse myself in the culinary arts, as well as brush up on my French since I've been out of practice all summer.

"I will be," Anderson assures me.

"I mean it." I poke him in the chest, giving him a stern look. "Don't do anything stupid because you think you're invincible. Bullets don't care if you're a royal or not."

"So you've told me. About a hundred times in the last twenty-four hours."

"Because I know how thick-headed you are." I playfully swat the side of his head.

"Then *you'd* better be safe, too. Don't do anything stupid because you think *you're* invincible. Hot ovens don't care if you're a royal or not." He winks.

"I will endeavor to steer clear of as many hot ovens as possible." I laugh, grateful I can always count on my brother to make light of a tense situation. "Or, at the very least, take appropriate precautions."

"And I will endeavor to steer clear of as many bullets as possible." His expression falls as he swallows hard.

While he may have volunteered for one last deployment, the reality he's as likely to be injured or killed as anyone else is starting to sink in.

"Or, at the very least, take all appropriate precautions." He grits a smile as he pulls me in for another hug. "I promise I'll come home in one piece," he says in a strained voice that causes my emotions to spill forward.

"You'd better," I choke out, tears staining his t-shirt. "Or I'll be so bloody mad at you."

He barks out a laugh. "And the last thing I want is to suffer your wrath."

"Good." I hug him tighter, knowing it'll be several months until I'm able to again. I refuse to consider the alternative.

"Pardon the interruption."

I tear away from Anderson, convinced my mind's playing tricks on me.

It's not the first time this has happened.

Since Adam's death, I hear his voice everywhere.

But this time, it's not just a memory. This is real. Sort of.

It may not be Adam, but Creed's voice has always sounded a lot like his brother's.

And when my eyes fall on Creed as he stands in the doorway of Anderson's apartment, posture straight, expression stoic, clad in the same dark suit all members of the elite protection squad wear, it's like I'm staring at Adam's ghost.

"I'd like to speak with you, if you can spare a minute," he states evenly.

I nod, then glance at Anderson. "I'll give you two some privacy." I start across his living room.

"Actually, I'd hoped to talk to you," Creed interjects before I can take another step.

Anderson and I share a look, both of us surprised. He arches a brow, silently asking if I'll be okay.

I give him a reassuring nod. "I'll be out in a minute."

"Okay." He makes his way toward the door, briefly shaking Creed's hand before leaving us alone for the first time since I broke his heart.

Since Adam died.

Since so many things died.

He looks good. Well, he always looks good. But seeing him in the dark suit makes him even sexier.

Until now, I thought the pinnacle of his sexiness was Creed Lawson in his military dress uniform. Or even his military fatigues, biceps stretching the arms of his t-shirt.

But the way he fills out his suit should be a crime.

"I wanted to wish you well in culinary school," he says formally.

I hate everything about this. Hate how stiff he is around me. How awkward I feel around him.

Mere weeks ago, I didn't struggle with what to say to him. Being with Creed was as natural as breathing. Now I feel like I'm being pulled under a riptide, every breath hard-fought and painful.

"I should offer you my congratulations, as well," I

respond brightly. "I understand it's no longer Lieutenant Lawson but Captain Lawson."

He nods. "I was promoted on my induction date."

"Of course." My smile falters slightly as another strained silence settles between us.

While I'm grateful Creed took the initiative to stop by, I hate this uneasiness. Wish I could wave a magic wand and make it disappear, return us to the people we were before. Better yet, rewind the clocks to that fateful night so I can tell Adam not to take the route he did. Or take a less conspicuous vehicle.

But we can't go back in time. We can only move forward.

"I heard what happened."

"About?" I give him a quizzical look.

He steps toward me, stopping a respectful distance away. But he's still close enough for me to pick up on the familiar scent of his body wash.

"Your last meeting with the royal household. How you stood up for yourself."

He takes another step closer, then another, erasing the space between us until he's mere inches away. But those inches may as well be miles with the distance in his gaze.

"I'm proud of you."

"What can I say? A wise man smacked some sense into me. Told me I'd spent all of my life choosing other people and it was finally time to choose myself."

His mouth lifts in the corners, and I've never been so grateful to see a smile. "Not sure I'd call your brother wise, but he does have his moments."

"He certainly does."

He licks his lips, eyes sweeping over my face in the way he always did right before kissing me. I can practically taste the need radiating off him.

Or maybe I'm still so addicted to him that I'm imagining it, the symptoms of withdrawal playing tricks on my mind.

When he inches toward me, I hold my breath, pulse kicking up, desperate to feel his mouth on me more than anything.

Suddenly, he abruptly pulls back, the spell broken.

"I wanted to offer my best wishes and say goodbye."

I take a moment to collect myself, fixing an unaffected smile on my mouth.

"I assume this means you weren't put on my protection team for Paris?" I feign indifference. Truthfully, a part of me hoped I'd arrive in Paris to learn Creed was assigned to my team.

After our not-so-secret tryst, I have a feeling he'll never be assigned to me, though.

"I've been placed on your father's advance team. I'd asked to stick around here as much as possible," he responds. "That way, I can help Rory out when the baby arrives. Thankfully, they honored my request."

My heart squeezes at the reminder that Rory's mere weeks away from bringing Adam's son into the world. But that's comforted by the image of Creed Lawson holding a little baby.

"That's really sweet of you."

His smile wavers. "It's the least I can do to honor Adam's legacy. Make sure his son knows what a good man his father was."

"And he was."

"The best."

"The best," I quiver, my guilt for the role I played creeping back in. But I remind myself I didn't light the match, not like the royal household wanted me to believe.

"Well then…" Creed clears his throat. "I'll be off." He bows. "Your Highness."

"Captain."

He turns, and I watch as he crosses the room.

I feel like I should say something more. I don't want to believe this is how it ends between us. That this is how we say goodbye. Not after everything.

But as much as I want to shout that I love him, that I was on my way to tell him that when we were attacked, I can't. Not when I see the weight of Adam's death already crushing him.

This needs to remain my cross to bear.

It won't change anything. Creed's royal guard now. Telling him the truth will make this even more difficult than it needs to be.

"You were never just the hired help," I call out as he's about to step into the hallway.

He pauses, but doesn't look back at me. He doesn't continue moving, either.

"I thought you should know that," I finish, secretly hoping he'll whirl around, rush toward me, pull me into his arms, and kiss me breathless.

But that's not what happens.

Instead, he shakes his head and walks away without a single glance back.

CHAPTER FORTY-NINE

Jameson

"I told you it would all work out in the end, did I not?"

When I hear Gianna's voice, I look away from the lake abutting my cabin in the mountains, watching as she strolls along the dock toward where I sit in an Adirondack chair.

Her heels and pencil skirt are out of place here in nature. An affront to the simplicity of this place. It's why I've always loved coming out here. No phones. No internet. No technology. It's a miracle I have running water and electricity. It's one of the few places anyone can come to and truly...disappear.

"I'm not sure I'd say things worked out," I reply, a hint of venom in my tone. "You were supposed to deal with the Callie problem. The problem *you* started when you had her killed before I was able to figure out if she was in possession of those recordings. If anyone has them, she was the most likely. You fucked that up."

"If anything, I *helped* you. Last I checked, those recordings wouldn't be shoved up her cunt. Or down her throat.

Yet, you seemed to forget what was important since you were getting laid."

"I told you I was handling things, but you and my father didn't believe me. Instead, the two of you conspired against me. Look where that led. To all of this nearly falling apart once Barlow started making waves."

"And I helped with that, too," Gianna insists as she smooths a hand down her straight blonde hair. "I told you manufacturing a relationship with the princess would make you two the top news story across the continent, if not the world. Any mention of Callie's disappearance was buried so deep, it was barely even a blip on the radar."

"You assured me it would stay that way. Instead, Hayes managed to weasel his way into the crowd and accuse me of murder in front of the entire goddamn world. Was *that* part of your plan?" I growl, still unnerved by how close things came to unraveling.

Hell, it feels like they're *still* unraveling, too many loose ends floating around, most notably the location of those damn recordings my father's been trying to locate for years now.

Recordings that could destroy everything for him.

And, in turn, destroy everything for me.

Everything we've built is a carefully constructed house of cards. If those recordings were to be discovered and released, it would cause everything to topple to the ground. And bring a lot of influential and powerful people down with it.

"Of course not. But I dealt with it."

"Dealt with it?" I bark out as I stand, placing my fishing rod in the holder beside me, still not so much as a nibble on the line. "By planning an engagement? I warned you it wasn't enough. Not with the princess' bloody bodyguard poking around the story I gave him. That *you* assured me would hold up. But it didn't. He somehow uncovered Callie's *true* connection to me. If he kept digging—"

"But he can't. Not anymore. I made sure of it. Took out two birds with one stone, so to speak. Disposed of Adam Lawson, as well as made sure Barlow no longer posed a threat. It was a fluke that Esme even survived the fire. She wasn't supposed to. Regardless, Callie's death will never be tied back to you. Or us. I've done everything I promised I would."

"No, you haven't. If anything, you made matters worse at every turn, starting with having Callie killed before I figured out her involvement!"

"Your father thought it best. As did Archer. You were too…distracted. She became too much of a liability."

"Distracted? I was earning her trust." My jaw ticks, veins burning the more I think about how out of control everything's become. "And now Hayes has been missing for weeks, Gianna! Fucking weeks! For all we know, Callie may have given him the recordings!"

"They weren't found anywhere on his property, even after our guys tore it apart. Plus, we both know if Callie did have them and gave them to Hayes, he would have already released them. He wouldn't have sat on that information. No way."

"If you're trying to placate me, you're doing a shitty job," I snip out.

"I'm just pointing out the positives here. Was this how any of us saw this going? Of course not. But sometimes it's necessary to change course."

"This wasn't just a change of course!" I throw up my hands, spittle forming in the corner of my mouth as I lean into her. "Do I need to remind you what's at stake here?"

She narrows her icy stare on me. "I'm perfectly aware what's at stake."

"Then you know how dangerous it can be to have any loose ends. And Hayes Barlow's unknown whereabouts is a giant loose end."

"Everyone in the world is looking for him. They think he's responsible for killing a so-called hero and almost killing their beloved princess. His face is plastered everywhere you turn. He won't be able to escape capture for long. When he *is* apprehended, law enforcement knows what needs to be done."

She allows her words to linger in the air for several long seconds, the only sound that of birds flying overhead and the occasional croaking from a frog.

"In the meantime, I've come up with a few ways to keep you in the headlines in case any negative publicity trickles in regarding Hayes Barlow's accusations," she continues in a bright voice. "A preemptive strike, if you will. While we'd originally hoped to paint you as the grieving boyfriend of a dead princess, that's not a possibility anymore. We can still use your relationship to our advantage. Perhaps even arrange a few chance encounters between the two of you, since the official press release did say you parted as friends. Maybe a trip to Paris within the next few weeks while I track down Barlow. I—"

"I don't think so," I interject gruffly, my tone harsh and threatening.

Gianna immediately snaps her mouth shut, eyes darting around nervously.

While I'm typically curt and decisive, making it a true testament to my acting abilities to play the part of the doting boyfriend all summer, I'm usually not this severe with Gianna.

"I suppose we could go in a different direction," she suggests with a tremble in her voice. "But considering so many people are hoping you'll get back together—"

"I'm not talking about your proposal." I take several slow steps toward her. "I'm talking about you in general. I don't think this…arrangement is going to work out any longer."

"What are you saying?"

"I'm saying that your services are no longer required."

She stares, mouth agape, disbelief heavy on her face. "You're…firing me?"

I shrug, feigning indifference.

"You… You can't fire me."

"I can. And I did. Regardless of any loyalties my father may feel toward you, I don't share those sentiments. You're supposed to *fix* things. Not make them worse. Killing Callie made them worse. Since then, nothing you've done has fixed your giant fuck up."

"That *you* started by falling under the spell of her pussy."

"Therefore, I have no use for you anymore," I finish, ignoring her statement.

"You…" She shakes her head, eyes turning fiery as she leans toward me. "If I were you, I'd reconsider. I know things about you and your father that could ruin you. Know precisely what's on those recordings. Worse, I *also* know about your father's involvement in the death of Prince Nicholas and his entire family during that 'skiing accident'," she threatens, using air quotes. "You don't want that kind of information to get out. Anything Callie or Hayes may know pales compared to what *I* know."

"I can't deny that," I admit with a long sigh. "You could certainly cause quite a bit of trouble for my father and me. Which is probably why he's kept you on as long as he has."

"Precisely." She straightens her spine. "So if I were you—"

Before she can utter another syllable, I reach into the back pocket of my jeans and grab my knife, plunging it into her stomach. She gasps, surprise evident in her expression as she looks from my eyes to the knife protruding from her and back again.

"Y-you st-stabbed me."

"Like I said…," I begin as a devilish smile curves the corners of my mouth. "Your services are no longer required."

I twist the blade, her pained scream echoing in the stillness of the air around me, causing birds along the bank to take flight. When I feel her go limp, the life slowly draining from her eyes, I yank the knife out of her, allowing her body to fall in a heap on the ground.

"You see, Gianna," I begin as I lift the blade, admiring the deep red hue against the silver blade. "*That's* how you tie up loose ends."

Thank you for reading *Royal Creed*! I hope you enjoyed the first part of Creed and Esme's story. Will they find their way back to each other, regardless of their past? Find out today!

https://www.tkleighauthor.com/fallen-knight

I appreciate your help in spreading the word about my books. Please leave a review on your favorite book site.

FALLEN KNIGHT

Princess Esme of Belmont finally freed herself from the chains shackling her to royal life and has been living in Paris for the past several years. It's what she wanted. What she fought for.

But there's still something missing.

She refuses to admit what that something is, though, doing everything she can to put the past behind her.

Until she receives a phone call that forces her to return home. And to her old life.

Creed Lawson has spent the last several years doing exactly what's expected of him. No more breaking the rules.

Until Esme walks back into his life, bringing all those feelings he fought to bury back to the surface.

They're caught between duty and freedom. Responsibility and redemption. Legacy and love.

But this time, their love isn't just forbidden…
It's deadly.

Scan below or type the address into your web browser.

https://www.tkleighauthor.com/fallen-knight

PLAYLIST

Let It All Go - Birdy, RHODES
My Bed - Leah Kate
Grey - Why Don't We
Head on Fire - Griff featuring Sigrid
Something to Someone - Demot Kennedy
How The Story Ends - Lily Williams
Chasing Stars - Alesso, Marshmello featuring James Bay
Incomplete - James Bay
Secret Love Song - Little Mix
Addicted - Morgan St. Jean
When It Ends - Avery Lynch, JORDY
I Would - Connie Talbot
Who We Are - Tristan Prettyman
Scared of Falling - Abigail Osborn
Illicit affairs - Taylor Swift
Dangerous - Madison Beer
Hurtless - Dean Lewis
Instead - Ryan Amador
Where Do We Go from Here? - Caleb Hearn

Using - RITUAL featuring Emily Warren
Lift Me Up - Rihanna
Goodbye - Mimi Webb
Hold Me Closer - Cornelia Jakobs
How the Story Ends - Lily Williams

ACKNOWLEDGMENTS

Thank you so much for picking up *Royal Creed*. I hope you enjoyed reading the start of Creed and Esme's story as much as I enjoyed writing it.

Truth be told, I wrote the first draft about three different times. If you've been reading my books for the past few years, you may recognize Creed and Esme from *Royal Games* and *Tangled Games*, where I first introduced them and hinted at their past.

Of course, so many people were itching to know what their story was. So I knew I had to write it.

But I wasn't sure where to begin. Do I pick up where I left off at the end of *Tangled Games*? Or do I go back to the very beginning?

After several failed attempts at a first draft, I knew I had to go back to the beginning. If hadn't, you never would have read any of the preceding 49 chapters. And to fully understand them, you needed more than a quick summary of their background.

Plus, I really wanted to write a virgin romance, something I've never done. LOL.

There are so many people who help me behind the scenes and I wanted to take a minute to thank them all!

First and foremost, a huge thanks to my little family — my husband, Stan, and my daughter, Harper Leigh. I couldn't do this without their support. And without Harper's adorable questions, like why I'm cleaning up the manuscript to the book I supposedly finished weeks ago, then telling me maybe I should have written it correctly the first time. Kids, y'all... No filter.

To my wonderful PA, Melissa Crump — I can't tell you how much I appreciate everything you do for me.

To my fantastic beta readers — Lin, Melissa, Sylvia, Stacy, and Vicky — thank you so much for offering your feedback. And not coming after me with pitchforks with that ending. You know how much I love my mindfucks.

To my admin team — Melissa, Vicky, and Lea. Thanks for keeping my reader group and page running. Love you ladies!

To my review team — Thank you for always not only reading my books but also taking the time to write reviews. Your support means the world to me.

To my reader group. Thanks for being my super-fans and giving me a place to go when I need a break from writing. Or a name for a character. You always come through.

And last but not least, a big thank you to YOU! My amazing readers. Whether this is your first T.K. book or you've read all of them, I'm so grateful you took a chance on my stories.

Love & Peace,

~ T.K.

ABOUT THE AUTHOR

T.K. Leigh is a *USA Today* Bestselling author of romance ranging from fun and flirty to sexy and suspenseful.

Originally from New England, she now resides just outside of Raleigh with her husband, beautiful daughter, rescued special needs dog, and three cats. When she's not writing, she can be found training for her next marathon or chasing her daughter around the house.

Made in the USA
Middletown, DE
18 February 2023